A KILLER'S WARNING

When Amy arrived at her apartment, she fitted her key into the lock. At her touch, the door swung inward and a putrid odor assaulted her nostrils.

Death. The familiar smell jammed her heart against her ribs. Not here. Not here too.

She forced herself to assume the observer mode she'd learned when she'd assisted with autopsies. She scanned the kitchen and living room and saw no one. Her muscles clinched tight, she ventured a few steps farther.

On the floor, a few paces away, her great-grandmother's cobalt blue wine carafe lay shattered into bits. Some of the pieces had been ground into fine glass splinters.

He always destroyed the things she cherished most. Apprehension rippled along her skin. How did he know?

Clamping her jaws together to control the waves of nausea, she headed for the half-open bathroom doorway.

The mirror came into view and she gaped at it. In red marker someone had scrawled across the glass surface.

SNOOPERS GET DEAD. VERY VERY DEAD.

Below it was listed her name with a red slash mark through it.

WITH DEADLY INTENT
A Dr. Amy Prescott Mystery

LOUISE HENDRICKSEN

ZEBRA BOOKS
KENSINGTON PUBLISHING CORP.

ZEBRA BOOKS are published by

Kensington Publishing Corp.
475 Park Avenue South
New York, NY 10016

First Printing: December, 1993

Printed in the United States of America

For my husband, Gene, a man who possesses the traits required of all those who choose to live with a writer—patience and a sense of humor.

One

Death. She dealt with it every day at the crime laboratory. Husbands, wives, lovers . . . friends . . . killing each other. Dr. Amy Prescott paced the length of the beach cottage. All of them strangers until now.

Footsteps clumped on the porch. She swung around, saw her father, and caught her breath. He wouldn't be here at two in the morning unless—

"Amy . . ." Dr. B.J. Prescott shoved open the door and plunged inside. "Thank God, you're here." Rain stippled his graying fringe of hair; dripped from his mustache and Van Dyke beard.

She clutched her elbows to warm herself. "What's happened?"

"Something bad, I'm afraid."

Her teeth began to chatter. "It's Oren. Isn't it?"

He stared at her. "How did you know?"

"He phoned while I was still at the crime lab—"

"When?" Rivulets of water ran off his yellow slicker and made dark spots on the braided wool rug.

"Five-thirty, just as I was leaving for my apartment." Her father gripped her arm and she felt the cold damp-

7

ness of his fingers through the sleeve of her flannel shirt.

"What did he say?"

Goosebumps prickled her skin. "What's Oren done?"

He regarded her with level blue eyes. "He's in trouble. Big trouble. I've got to know what's going on with him—and fast."

Fears that had scuttled around inside her brain on the eighty-mile trip from Seattle to Lomitas Island settled into a lump in her stomach. "Oren said he and . . . and . . . what's his fiancee's name?"

"Elise. Elise Dorset."

Amy felt a stab of guilt. She and her cousin had once been best friends. If she'd kept in touch, she would have known about his fiancee, about his problems. "They're coming to the island for the weekend. He begged me to come too so I could meet her. He sounded . . . strange."

" 'Strange.' What's that supposed to mean?"

"Wild talk." She shoved her fingers through short brown hair. "You know, like he used to when he was a kid . . . after Uncle Mike ran off and left him and Aunt Helen. . . . Remember?" She moistened her lips. "Evidently, he and Elise have been having some sort of . . . difficulties."

Her father ran a hand over his face. "Damn! I was hoping—" He let out a noisy breath. "—Sheriff Calder is over at Oren's apartment. The place is wrecked and Oren and Elise are gone."

"Oren said he hadn't been to Lomitas Island for weeks. Vandals could have broken in."

"Could be, but Tom's convinced Oren and Elise were there earlier in the evening."

"Hah! You know what I think about Calder and his screwball ideas." She thought fast, searching for expla-

8

nations to reassure her father—and herself. "Chances are, after the storm hit, Oren and Elise decided not to make the long drive after all. They're probably still at their condo in Seattle. Shoot, Dad, you know what a calamity howler Calder can be."

"Not this time. A Mrs. Michaels claims Elise called her around midnight. Crying. Hysterical. Terrified. Screamed Oren had—" His words thinned to a whisper and he stopped to clear his throat. "—had gone crazy. Said he was going to kill her."

Amy stood as if frozen, his words stinging her like pelting hailstones. "Oh, God! No!" She pressed her hand against her mouth. "He couldn't. *He couldn't!*"

Her father put his arm around her. "Sounds bad, Amy. Real bad. This Mrs. Michaels manages the endocrinology clinic where Elise works as a nurse. The woman claims Oren has beaten Elise before."

Amy lifted her chin. "I don't believe it. Oren wouldn't do such a thing." An instant later, her certainty vanished. "Would he?" she asked in a small voice.

"Who knows, kitten? He's spent less time on the island since you kids grew up and went off to college. Boys change when they turn into men."

"Not that much."

He fixed her with a solemn look. "Both of us have worked enough crime scenes to know better than that." He let out a long sigh and massaged a wind-reddened cheek. "I'd better get in gear. Don't want to leave Tom on his own too long." He turned toward the door.

"I'll meet you there," she whispered.

He forced a smile. "I was hoping you would." He paused in the doorway. "This storm has blown trees down all over the island, so be careful."

"You too." She grabbed her glasses, donned a slicker, and jammed a yellow sou'wester hat on her head.

As she rushed out into the darkness, she remembered Oren's final cry. *One of us is going mad. I have to know if it's Elise, or me.*

Two

Amy parked beside a white picket fence and dashed for the veranda of the converted Victorian house. She forced open the heavy oak door and found herself in a dimly lighted entrance hall. An odor of age-brittled wallpaper and thick dark varnish reminiscent of old-time funeral parlors filled her nostrils.

When he called, Oren had told her he and Elise lived on the second floor. Making wet tracks on ash-rose carpet treads, she tip-toed up the stairway. As Lomitas Island's medical examiner, her father had a right to be here—she didn't.

A grating creak drew her attention to the floor below. She peered down and caught sight of a sharp-eyed face beneath tousled white hair before the gap between door and frame dwindled to a peephole. Oren and Elise's life wouldn't stay private for long with a nosy landlady.

She continued her climb, dread increasing with each step. At the crime laboratory in Seattle, where she worked as a forensic scientist, she often went out with the mobile unit. Even so, it had taken her months to learn to distance herself from the carnage and get on with the job to be done. Tonight, she felt as weak-kneed as she had on her first run.

She grasped the flowered porcelain door knob with a sweaty hand and eased it open. A pallid glow from etched-glass wall sconces gave the room a murky underwater appearance.

Sheriff Tom Calder sprawled on a Chippendale corner chair in the miniature foyer, watching her father match up extension cords for his portable tripod lights.

When the door clicked shut, the sheriff wheeled around. "You can't come in here. Don't ya know this is a crime scene?"

Her father straightened, groaned and rubbed his back. "Amy and I are going to do this particular job together." He eyed Tom narrowly. "Whether you like it or not."

Tom's steely gaze fastened on her. "Humph! Just cause she's workin' with a bunch of highfalutin' Seattle cops don't give her no call to come pokin' her nose in our business."

Stiff-necked turkey. Her glare would have incinerated him if he hadn't had a rhinoceros hide. She opened her mouth to defend herself but her father spoke first.

"Back off Tom. If you're smart, you'll keep your eyes open and your mouth shut. You just might learn a few things about processing a crime scene."

"We'll see about that. You spill everything to her?"

"Sure did."

Tom slumped back onto his chair. "Probably doesn't matter. Be all over town by morning."

Amy dumped her rain gear out in the hall and came back to stand in front of Tom. "Sheriff, don't you think you're jumping the gun a little? You don't even know if a crime has been committed."

"The hell I don't." He sprang to his feet and glowered down at her. His long nose gave him the appearance of a crane honing in on a fish. "The landlady heard them two fighting. And just look at this room." His arm flapped

12

out to take in broken lamps and turned-over chairs. "That cousin of yours wasn't just waltzing his fi-an-cee around in here."

A yellow-toothed grin split his long-jawed face at what he apparently considered a witty remark. He swelled out his chest. "Besides, while I was waiting for B.J. here, I found some blood in the kitchen."

"I don't believe it." Her anxious gaze sought her father's.

"I'm afraid it's true, honey."

She shook her head in stubborn refusal. "Not Oren. He couldn't hurt anybody."

"Not much he couldn't." Tom smiled as if he relished the thought. "Thinks he's real clever too. Tried to mop up the evidence, but I was too smart for him. Found wet rags in their garbage can, I did."

The wattle of grizzled hair on his forehead bobbled as he nodded his head emphatically. "Looked innocent enough and mighta' fooled your average law officer. Not me. I gave those rags a good squeeze. There was blood in 'em all right." With that, he flopped himself down and stroked his droopy mustache as if he'd performed a praiseworthy feat.

Amy stared at him in disbelief. Of all the dumb stunts—even rookie cops knew enough not to contaminate physical evidence.

A noise shifted her attention to her father. His eyes blazed and he was clenching and unclenching his fists. She moved to his side and whispered, "Forget it, Dad. Some people can learn, others never will." She knelt and plugged in one of the extension cords. "Let's get these lights set up so we can take our pictures."

The two of them made a good team and the work went faster than usual. With Sheriff Calder dogging their footsteps, she and her father went through the apartment.

They dusted all surfaces for fingerprints, used an evidence vacuum with filter disks to go over floors and furniture. After finishing each area, they stopped, sealed the disk in a labeled, numbered bag and listed it in the evidence log.

By the time they were through, they knew two things for certain. One—the traps beneath the kitchen and the bathroom sinks held clots of blood. Two—the apartment didn't contain a single fingerprint—not even a smudged one.

Amy righted a gray damask wing chair and sank onto it. Drainage from meat or poultry might explain the blood in the kitchen, but not the large quantity in the bathroom.

Tom stalked over to her. "B.J. tells me you and young Prescott been running around together since you were kids. That the two of you know every trail, every hill, and every cove on this here island." He stabbed the air with a bony finger. "You got any idea where your buddy might hole-up?"

She massaged the tired muscles in her neck. "Did you check with the ferry office?"

He curled his lip. "I called them first thing. No one on any of last night's return runs saw either the Dorset woman, Prescott, or his van."

Amy took off her glasses and rubbed her eyes. "How could they be sure? The workers might not have noticed them."

A muscle bunched along Tom's jaw. "Since Prescott started working for Senator Halliday, his picture makes the papers real regular. Damn few people who wouldn't recognize that pretty boy face of his." He thrust out his chin. "You and his fi-an-cee pals too?"

Amy shriveled up inside. "We . . . we haven't met. Oren and I drifted apart after I got married." Mitch Jamison, her ex-husband, and Oren hadn't liked each other.

"Well," Tom said, drawing out the word as a prelude to another of his mind-shattering announcements. "She's a real knock-out. Eyes like sapphires. Silver blonde hair. And talk about shape. She coulda' given Marilyn Monroe a run for her money." He bobbed his head to give emphasis to his statement. "No way a man's going to miss a woman like that."

She got to her feet. "I'll check a few places."

Tom planted himself in her path. "Don't you go helping him get away. We got plenty of evidence to bring charges. All we need now is the Dorset woman's body. And I'm betting we'll have that before the day's out."

Amy met his stare straight on. "If something has happened to her, Oren didn't do it." She started for the door. "And when I find him, he'll tell you so himself."

"You keep your hands off that silver van of his, if you find it. This murder is Island business—not yours."

Her father rose from where he was packing equipment into an aluminum case. He drew himself up to his full five-foot ten and hunched muscular shoulders. "I've just made Amy my assistant. What do you say to that?"

Calder grabbed his hat and slapped it on his head. "This maniac is your nephew. By rights neither one of you should be allowed on the case." He glared at her father. "You see she doesn't foul things up, or I'll have your job. Other people may think you're a super sleuth—I don't." He shoved past them and stomped out of the apartment.

Her father lowered himself into a chair. "Might not do your budding career any good to get mixed up in this."

"That's the least of my worries right now. Did you ever meet Elise?"

"Yeah, about a month ago. She and Oren came by the house and asked if they could use the ketch. Oren wanted to show Elise some of the other islands."

"What did you think of her?"

"Sweet, soft-spoken young woman. Seemed to think the world of Oren. Didn't take her eyes, or her hands off him during the whole visit. Sure looked like a couple of love birds to me."

"Then why aren't they getting along?" She and Mitch had argued over his drinking, his gambling debts and—she pressed her arms tight to her sides—his habit of straying into other women's beds.

"Any relationship can go off track. You know that as well as I do."

She winced. A year had passed since her divorce and still the wounds hadn't healed. She gave a long sigh. "I'd better go before I fall asleep on my feet."

"Take my car. If you find Oren and Elise you can call Tom on the cellular phone."

"Good idea. Meanwhile you try and get some rest."

"No can do. I have an autopsy to do over on Orcas Island. I should be back by one. Maybe then you'll have located the two of them and we can forget this whole mess."

They were ready to leave when Amy let out a low cry. "Dad, I forgot all about Aunty Helen. She mustn't hear about this from anyone but us."

Her father put his arm around her. "You go search. I'll stop by Helen's house on my way to the ferry."

Amy turned and kissed his cheek. "Tell her I'll try to come see her sometime this weekend."

Amy transferred her camera, forensic satchel, and other necessary paraphernalia from her station wagon to her father's four-wheeler and drove back to the cottage. After a quick shower and a change of clothes, she put on her hiking boots. Oren's favorite haunts were varied. She

16

might have to explore several of them before she found him.

She fed Cleo, her black cocker and called Marcus Aurelius, her marmalade-colored Manx cat. He didn't answer. Marcus didn't forgive her long absences as readily as Cleo. She set out a dish of his favorite food and called again. From past experience she knew he was probably observing her from a limb of the big maple beside the cottage. Few people entered or left her house without him knowing it. The full-blooded Manx stood nearly as tall as Cleo. Unwary intruders who tangled with him never returned.

One glance at the overcast sky warned her she'd better prepare for anything. She tossed her slicker and down jacket onto the back seat.

The long driveway circled past her father's house. Weathered gray shingles covered roof and sides of the rambling two-story house and gave it the appearance of a fat, many petticoated dowager sprawled inelegantly on the wooded hillside. Perhaps not the most beautiful house in the world, but she'd been born and raised there and she loved every ancient inch of it.

She turned right on Westridge Avenue and headed toward Faircliff, the only town on the fifty-mile-square island. The avenue snaked up a wooded hill. On the other side, the route broke clear of the trees and curved along the shore. Mountainous green swells capped with bone-white spindrift thundered against craggy basalt rocks.

She blinked eyes that felt like they'd been sand blasted. During her medical internship, she'd lost many a night's sleep. Time well spent, but this could be just wasted effort. The sheriff, with his need to feel important, had probably made a mystery where none existed.

Wishful thinking and she knew it, but she had to believe Elise was alive and Oren innocent of the accusations

17

piled on him. Otherwise, she didn't know him—didn't know him at all.

After passing the ferry dock, she turned onto East Shore Road. When she reached Murres Bay, she didn't see Oren's van, but she got out and skidded down the steep, winding trail anyway.

She and Oren had always liked this place. Wind and waves had carved deep cavelike depressions in the rocks where the two of them could sit.

Maybe Oren had brought Elise here in hopes the calming atmosphere would help them communicate. It had worked for Amy and Oren in the past.

Oren's father had deserted him in much the same manner as her own mother had. When she and Oren were teenagers, they came here many times filled to the teeth with anger and bitterness. Usually, the blend of sand, sea, and surf worked its soothing magic.

Her search proved fruitless so she headed into the hills. Long ago Spanish explorers had named Lomitas Island after the many small promontories that formed a wooded spine down the center of the island. Tallest of these was Mt. Sosiego. The ancient seafarers had named the mountain after the peaceful vista.

Like many of the islanders, Sosiego was Oren's favorite haunt. She could easily imagine him bringing Elise here in the midst of last night's storm. The forested area had an uplifting effect, regardless of the weather.

Maybe, he was hiding out. She squelched the traitorous thought. For all she knew, this Mrs. Michaels could be working some kind of a hoax. As PR man for Senator Halliday, Oren made a prime target for a smear campaign.

Perked up with renewed hope, Amy got out of the car. Even though it was a rugged mile hike to the campgrounds, she had to find out if Oren and Elise were there.

They could have parked elsewhere and climbed up by one of the other trails.

The rain had stopped so she changed from her slicker to a down jacket and set out through the Douglas firs. Wind shushed through the needled canopy showering her with icy droplets of hoarded rain water. She swore and wiped her glasses.

Ahead of her, nuthatches flitted back and forth in the underbrush, twittering nervously. Inside her brain, a question imitated the small black and gray birds. What if she didn't find them? She lengthened stride.

In her haste, she tripped over a root and fell onto all fours. She gritted her teeth against smarting bruises, hoisted herself up and limped on.

Half an hour later, the smell of wood smoke took away all thought of aching leg muscles. The heavy timber growth thinned and she entered a clearing. On the far side, his back to her, a man in a green-hooded parka hunkered beside a fire.

"Oren . . . ?" He didn't move. Then, she realized she'd only whispered his name. What if it wasn't him? She picked up a club and took a couple of steps. "Oren . . . ?"

The man jerked upright and turned to stare at her. "Good Christ, Amy. What the hell are you doing up here?"

She dropped her weapon. "Thank God, it's you." She rushed forward to give him a joyous hug, but stopped before she reached him. Their friendship had been more boy to boy than boy to girl, and a sudden show of emotion would have embarrassed both of them. Besides, this unshaven, sullen-faced man bore little resemblance to the playmate of her youth.

She peered around, hoping to see a tent hidden among the trees. "Where's Elise?"

He shrugged, poured water on the fire and tossed dirt

over charred wood with a small shovel he took from his packsack.

Amy braced herself against a tree. "Oren, I'm not here by accident. I came looking for you." He raised an eyebrow, but didn't comment. She continued with her explanation. Upon hearing of Mrs. Michaels' call to the sheriff, his sullen expression grew even more so. But when Amy told him his apartment had been wrecked and Elise and his van were missing, he shouldered his packsack and started down the trail at a near run.

Neither of them spoke. Amy couldn't have if she'd wanted to. It took all of her breath just to keep up with him. When they reached her father's car, Oren waited impatiently while she called the sheriff's office. "I'm on Mt. Sosiego," she said, when Calder came on the line. "Oren's with me."

"Stay put. I'll be there in fifteen minutes."

Oren grabbed the phone. "Meet us at my apartment."

"Like hell," Calder shot back. "You set one foot off that mountain and I'll slap you in jail so fast you won't know what hit you. Is that clear?"

Oren crammed the phone into its receiver. "Officious hard-headed bastard," he muttered.

She rephrased her words several times before she gave up and blurted out, "What happened last night?"

He swung around. "Nothing."

She wet her lips. "Mrs. Michaels said you hit Elise, and that it wasn't the first time. Is . . . is that true?"

His gray eyes darkened. "What do you think?"

"I . . . I'm not sure."

He ran spread fingers through his tousled hair and glowered at her. "You're not sure?" His mouth twisted. "I thought you were my friend."

"I didn't mean . . ."

"Forget it." He hunched his shoulders and prowled back and forth across the parking lot.

The sheriff and one of his deputies arrived a short time later. While the deputy climbed to the campground to look around, Calder interrogated Amy. After he finished, he dismissed her and began on Oren.

As she drove down the mountain, Amy beat the steering wheel in impotent frustration. Tom hadn't let her hear Oren's story, so she knew no more than she had before.

She reached the main road and turned left. Nothing she'd done so far had helped Oren's cause. Perhaps if she located the van she'd also find Elise.

She circled the northern tip of the island. At Devil's Point, she asked fishermen gathered in the store if they'd seen a silver van, and none had. Undaunted, she went on, taking care to investigate all the side roads.

She stopped at the Fish Shack in Lomitas Harbor and ordered a ham sandwich. While she ate, she questioned the waitress and the men working at the marina. Finally, she admitted defeat and started for home.

Along this stretch of Westridge Avenue, evergreens grew so thickly she caught only fleeting glimpses of the surging white-tipped waves in Rosario Strait. All this land, from Lomitas Harbor to a mile beyond Otter Inlet, had belonged to the Prescotts for generations.

Like many others on the island, her great, great-grandfather had had to build the house and beach cottage on a long sloping hillside. The location had one disadvantage. A steep embankment at the foot of the slope prevented him from getting supplies to his anchored ship. To remedy the problem, he'd gone a quarter of a mile north of the house and carved another access through terrain broken by rocky hummocks and yawning ravines.

As Amy passed the road now known as Prescott's Byway, she noticed tire tracks. She stopped the car and walked back to explore the tree-enclosed lane. Although tire marks didn't show up well on gravel, bits of mud and disturbed pebbles indicated a vehicle of some kind had come this way.

Keeping to the shoulder so as not to obscure tracks, she scrambled through patches of bracken fern growing between alder and vine maple. She forced herself to go slow and choose her path with care. The lane straddled a narrow strip of land between two deep ravines, and a misstep would send her tumbling down into a rugged, bramble-festooned gully.

Gradually the road's downward pitch grew more abrupt. She rounded a bend and stopped short. Parked on the side of the road—a road Oren knew better than almost anyone else on the island—sat the silver van.

She swallowed hard and moved forward cautiously. The vehicle had skidded off the graveled surface and sunk to the axle in mud. Dreading what she might find, she peered in the windows. Empty. She took a relieved breath and returned to her car.

After she reported to the sheriff, she called her father's house and caught him as he walked in the front door. She quickly repeated her story.

"I'll be there in a few minutes," he said.

"I think I'll go on down to the beach," she said. "The van was on its way out when it got stuck."

"Take care, Amy. We haven't the vaguest notion who, or what we may be dealing with."

"Don't worry. I'll find me an equalizer." She put down the phone, took a crescent wrench from his tool box behind the front seat, and slipped it into her pocket. Her nerves drawn taut, she draped the strap of her camera kit over one shoulder, grabbed the handle of her forensic satchel, and, returned to the byway.

Where the road ended in a turnaround, she studied the

surrounding landscape. Anyone heading for the beach or the cliffs would have had to cross the sand dunes. And if he were carrying someone—a shudder went through her—his feet would have sunk into soft sand.

She stood rooted to the spot, picturing Oren lugging . . . no, she wouldn't consider it, not even for an instant. She cleared her mind and got down to business. With the infinite care drummed into her by her father and her instructors, she scanned the area, sector by sector. After a ten minute search, she discovered a man's footprint embedded in a mixture of damp clay and sand.

She recorded the time, the weather conditions, and made a sketch of the terrain. Basic requirements out of the way, she lay a ruler alongside the track and snapped several pictures. Wind had hastened evaporation, causing sand particles to sift lazily back and forth within the confines of the footprint.

A metal restraining frame she thrust into damp soil walled in the print. Dental stone mixed with bottled water produced a thick soup that she poured gently into the indentations. Before the cast set rock hard, she scratched the date, her initials and a number in the buff-colored medium.

She flagged the area with bright orange plastic ribbon and trudged over the dunes with an escort of shrieking gulls. On her left, the ravine gradually diminished to a shallow basin overgrown with salal and tall Rose Bay bushes.

Beyond them, she could see a bit of the beach cottage through a stand of Sitka spruce. Ebony-hued, with bark resembling alligator skin, the stunted, wind-twisted conifers straggled downhill. Like hairy-fingered hands, they spread out in wavery lines until they reached a thirty-foot embankment.

Her route led her to the embankment's base. She bypassed their supply shack and moved onto the beach of Otter Inlet. Anchored far out to avoid going aground, Sea King, their two-masted, forty-two foot ketch, rode the swells.

Farther along the beach, in hard-packed sand, she found several faint footprints to cast. As she worked, she tried not to dwell on Oren's reasons for coming to the inlet. Yet, all the while, she knew the direction the prints headed and what lay around a rocky projection blocking her view. The dingy had to be at the usual tie-up—it just had to be. But it wasn't.

The small, wooden craft she had dubbed Rosinante, after Don Quixote's horse, had been tied up at that particular spot for a number of years—a fact Oren knew well.

She slumped down on a piece of driftwood, kneaded a stiff muscle in her back and began to theorize. If a person had intended to use the ketch and couldn't because of the storm, would he be foolish enough to brave the sea in a rowboat? She shivered—a desperate man would.

With her satchel in hand, she ascended wooden steps leading up the embankment and headed north along sandstone cliffs fringed with Scotch broom and gnarled pine. She knew the ocean currents surrounding the island, and where a body would likely wash ashore. Each time she peered over the edge, she dreaded what she might see below.

The area to the north proved unrewarding. Wisps of fog tagging her weary feet, she retraced her steps and started south. The roar of surf grew quieter at Orca Narrows. Here, the sea swept into a broad channel created by a series of colossal sea stacks called Satan's Boot. When the tide poured through, the water became a mass of eddies and choppy, froth-tipped waves.

Along the rim of the bluff, she stooped to examine

broken Rose Bay twigs and crushed patches of bush lupine. In some sandy areas, fleshy-leafed succulents had been mashed to a pulpy greenish-gray mass. She studied them thoughtfully for a moment, then chose a more circuitous route.

Brush-clad hillocks made traveling difficult and the weight of the satchel made her shoulder feel as if her arm might pull from the socket.

She checked her watch and groaned. In another hour, daylight would be gone, and only a fool ventured along the cliffs at night. Damn! This whole day had been one frustration after another—this senseless search included. The dinghy might not have any connection with Elise's disappearance. Besides, it had probably come loose all on its own and been swept out to sea. She braced herself on a jagged boulder and took a half-hearted look over the edge.

The boat! She dashed along the verge until she found a slope. Slipping, sliding, snatching shrubbery to slow her descent, she made her way to the bottom and scrambled atop a pile of driftwood. At her noisy approach, a pair of tattlers gave a flute-like call and skittered away on yellow, matchstick legs.

Forty feet away, waves lashed the shingle, grinding black rock against black rock in a gigantic tumbler. Down the beach a couple dozen yards, good old Rosinante perched high and dry.

Her pulse beating loudly in her ears, she unslung her camera and took several distance shots. Nothing must be overlooked. By tomorrow the sand could be swept clean.

Choosing a half-buried cedar log that extended past the rowboat's resting place, she walked along its broad top. Dry mouthed, she jerked her head from side to side, peering into all the places where a body might—She grimaced and booted a chunk of wood out of her way. Murder took on a whole new meaning when it got close to home.

She studied odd striations between the log where she stood and the dinghy. Frowning, she knelt and snapped a number of views, then scooped sand samples into labeled vials. In the shelter of a rock, she discovered a saucer-sized patch of fine lines undisturbed by the wind. She poured a cast and inched closer to her main objective.

By some fortunate happenstance, when the sea had disgorged Rosinante she'd snagged her bow on a hunk of tree root. Bottom side up, she tilted at a precarious forty-five degree angle, but aside from an ugly two-foot gouge in the hull, she appeared sea worthy. Amy set down her satchel, lay her camera on top, and got down on all fours to peer into the boat's shadowy interior.

"It can't be," she whispered. She closed her eyes for an instant to adjust her pupils to the darkness and opened them quickly to take a better look. No, she hadn't been mistaken. Brown spots trailed across the rowing thwart and spattered the bleached hull.

She swore, adjusted her camera for a time shot, and fetched a spray bottle of Luminol from her bag. If the stains were blood, they'd glow in the dark. Taking the camera control in one hand, she worked the spray pump with the other, aiming a tiny squirt at an isolated brown splotch.

As the chemical reacted with the stain and became luminescent, she let out a groan and triggered the camera. Damn the luck. While she stowed her supplies, her mind grasped at her last fragment of hope. The stains may be blood, but the boards would have to be sawed out and taken to the lab for more sophisticated tests before they'd know if the blood came from a human. Until then, she'd pray that Elise showed up alive.

The plaintive moan of the fog horn at Devil's Point

startled her. She swiveled her head. Thick, vaporous clouds billowed toward her from each end of the narrows. She snatched up her things and labored up the slope.

By the time she reached the pathway, leading to her cottage, her arm ached from the load she carried. Quickly she removed a flashlight from a zippered compartment, stashed the bag under low hanging spruce branches, and hurried on. Her father always covered a crime scene with exacting thoroughness so she figured he and the sheriff would still be at work in the lane.

Instead of taking the roundabout route via Otter Inlet, she chose a short cut and scrambled down through foot-snagging roots to the bottom of the ravine. A bulwark of thorny blackberry vines stopped her from clambering up the opposite incline to the lane above as she had intended. Since she didn't want to backtrack, no other choice remained but to travel the boulder-strewn ravine floor.

In the fog-shrouded darkness, her flashlight scarcely penetrated the gloom. Damp strings of moss hanging from ghostly alder branches clung to her face making her heart lurch. A few steps farther on, she vaulted a shallow stream and sank into mud over her shoe tops. Would this horrible day never end?

Lunging to solid ground, she plodded on. As she pushed through a willow thicket, her bobbing light picked out something white in the brambles on the steep slope.

She halted, her heart beating in hard, painful thumps. She took a step, then another before pausing to stare at the sight before her. An ash rose area rug had been tossed from the byway above. As the rug unrolled and flattened out over the briar patch, a blood-stained sheet had tumbled out.

Trembling so violently she could scarcely hold the flashlight, she lowered the beam bit by bit until it shone on the ground. Her body went cold and her breath snagged in her aching chest. "Oh, my God. Oh, my God." Unable to stop herself, she kept murmuring the words over and over.

On a patch of dead leaves, a few feet in front of her lay a knife: Not just any knife. This one had a shaped stag-horn handle, a polished nickel silver bolster, and a five-inch, blood-smeared blade.

Oren's hunting knife.

Three

Monday, October 24

Amy flexed tense shoulder muscles and frowned at the flock of white-coated forensic scientists milling around the crime lab. As a rule, they worked in an atmosphere of quiet, purposeful concentration—except on Monday. Then the hubbub brought back memories of her high school science class. Actually, except for this department's more sophisticated equipment, the two places even resembled each other.

However, the similarity ended with appearance. At this facility, each individual, who stood beside one of the analytical machines fringing the room's perimeter, or who bent over the microscopes crowding the long table where she sat, qualified as an expert in his or her field. Chemical, drug, evidence, and body-fluid analysts—all worked in this room or one of the other eight rooms that made up the Western Washington State Crime Laboratory on the second floor of Seattle's Public Safety Building.

Since starting work here, she'd learned to dread the beginning of the week. The mass of material gathered over the weekend by the lab's mobile unit and the fire department's arson squad wrecked everyone's schedule.

She bowed her head over the stereomicroscope once more and peered through the lens. As she tried to center her attention on the wool fragment under the objective, the three dimensional image blurred. In its place, she saw the knife she'd found in the ravine on Saturday. A knife she'd given Oren on his seventeenth birthday. Now the gift had become damning, irrefutable evidence.

She sighed wearily. So much had gone on during the weekend she hadn't even gotten a chance to visit her Aunt Helen. Saturday night she'd scarcely slept. On Sunday, a gang of men had fanned out in a long line and searched the headlands for Elise's body. Meanwhile, Amy and her father had rowed out to the Sea King in a borrowed skiff to see if anyone had been aboard—no one had.

At mid-morning, the sheriff took them to Orca Narrows in his motor launch. No one discovered any new evidence so they loaded battered old Rosinante aboard and the sheriff headed for Faircliff. The dinghy would have to be cut into bits so the boards could be analyzed.

She pressed her fingers against the ache in her forehead. What rotten, rotten luck. With all her expertise, she had only helped to further incriminate Oren.

Taking a tissue from the pocket of her lab coat, she cleaned her glasses, and focused on the scrap of yarn under the microscope. If she expected to live up to the lab's credo of maximum production and maximum accuracy, she'd have to keep her mind on her work.

"Psst." Her friend and fellow employee, Gail Wong, swiveled her lab stool farther to the right and cupped a hand around her mouth. Her eyes glinted with humor and a dimple appeared in one cheek as she grinned. "Who's the enticing VEEP?"

Amy glanced over her shoulder. At a far door, their white jacketed director stood talking to a man who looked to be in his early thirties. Amy shrugged. "Must have pull to wangle his way past our tight security." She went back to her microscope.

"Geez, Amy. Have you gone blind?"

Amy turned slowly. "Not that I'm aware of. Why?"

Gail flipped her short, wavy bob and frowned. "When are you going to wake up and rejoin the living? That is one beautiful hunk of man and you didn't even give him a second glance."

Amy smiled, swung around on her stool, and started going through the basics of a police description. "The subject is approximately six-feet tall with medium build. Ruddy complexion, thick, auburn-colored hair, with eyebrows to match. Nose—straight, but a trifle large. Wide mouth with a genial upturn at the corners."

She paused to seriously scrutinize the man for the first time, and something fluttered in her chest. *Such a gentle looking mouth.* She filed the errant thought under "N" for nonsense and faced Gail. "I suppose he'll do."

The young woman shook her head. "You're hopeless."

"Yep, I guess I am." *But not completely.* She'd felt a flicker of interest, hadn't she? For her, that in itself signified progress. Dismissing the man from her thoughts, she concentrated on the material she'd been trying to study before Gail's interruption.

After noting her findings, she mounted two strands of hair on a slide and moved to a comparison microscope. Soon she became totally absorbed and started when she heard the director's voice.

"Here's the young lady you should interview," he said. "She's determined to become proficient in all of the forensic sciences and she's almost achieved her goal." He touched her shoulder. "Amy . . ."

Irritated at the interruption, she pivoted on her stool. "Yes . . . ?" The director's stern countenance cut off the protest she wanted to make.

"I'd like you to meet Simon Kittredge, investigative reporter for *Global News Magazine*. Simon, this is Dr. Amy Prescott."

She gave a curt nod. "Mr. Kittredge."

The man's deep-set hazel eyes met hers in a steady, thoughtful gaze. "Read the article about your cousin. Damn shame. Oren's a good man."

She tensed. The morning *Times* had printed the news of Oren's arrest in two-inch headlines. She'd expected reporters to track her down, but not this soon.

Kittredge proffered his hand. She hesitated until she heard the director cough. Not wanting a lecture on the importance of maintaining good public relations, she reluctantly let him envelope her slender fingers with his.

He smiled warmly. "It's a pleasure to meet you, Dr. Prescott."

"Oh? Why is that?" At her suspicious stare, he released her and moved back several steps. She shoved her hands into the pockets of her lab coat and balled them into fists. A nosy reporter was something she could do without right now.

The director cleared his throat. "Amy's been processing material found on the body and clothing of a male homicide victim. Have you learned anything helpful?"

She nodded. "His assailant, or someone he knew may be Asian, blood type A, group M, Rh positive. The person works at a metals trade specializing in aluminum and he, or she, may own wearing apparel containing dark green wool."

Kittredge turned a page of his note book and came closer. "Could I ask how you arrived at your conclusions?"

"I had three strands of hair two inches long. The short, sharply clipped length indicates they probably came from a man. The hair shaft's circumference measured more than that of the average Caucasian, which makes me suspect the person may be Asian. The hair roots enabled me to determine the blood group and Rh." She shrugged. "That's about all I know at the moment."

"You mentioned clothing."

"Oh, yes. A scrap of wool one-thirty-second of an inch in length had gotten caught on the victim's jacket zipper. It may, or may not have come from the assailant."

He gave a low whistle. "One thirty-second! Good Lord, how'd you find it?"

She lifted an eyebrow. "With a magnifying glass." A faint smile touched her lips. "Just like Sherlock Holmes."

He flushed. "What about the man's trade?"

"No magic there either. All three hair strands showed traces of aluminum dust." She fiddled with a button dangling by one thread and glanced at her watch. "If that's all, I'd better get on with my analysis."

"Yes, of course." He chewed his lower lip. "Perhaps another time. How about . . . ?"

"No." She slid off her stool and left the room without looking back.

When she returned, the reporter had gone, but just before noon one of the secretaries brought her a message. Simon Kittredge wanted to meet her in the coffee shop for lunch. She wadded up the note and flung it into the waste basket.

He had some gall, thinking she'd help him pick Oren's life apart so he could have a story. Anger churning inside her, she went to the women's lounge and wolfed down her tuna sandwich and apple. The food landed in a lump in her stomach and she spent the afternoon chewing Rolaids.

That evening, she came out of the elevator and started along the crowded double-wide corridor. Before she reached the two guards stationed by the front door, the man who had ruined her day materialized at her side.

"Amy . . . uh—Dr. Prescott," he said quickly. "I wanted to talk to you about Oren."

"Leave me alone," she said, and kept on going.

In two strides, he was in front of her. "But, you don't understand . . . Please, let's have dinner. I need to . . ."

She dodged past him, and made it to the door. Rain struck her in the face as she rushed outside. Neons touting bail bond companies and Spin's Friendly Tavern tinted the swirling fog a blush pink.

Snatching off her glasses, she shoved them into her tote bag and headed up Third Avenue. At the Arctic Building, she turned the corner and started up the hill. For once she didn't pause to study the sculpted walrus heads circling the white stone structure's midriff. First she would lose the reporter in the crowd of homeward bound commuters. Then it would be safe to grab a bus to her apartment.

Breathless from the climb, she threaded her way through the crush on Fourth Avenue. Halfway up the block, she got a catch in her side and had to stop. She peered through a steamy window at diners seated at tables inside McCormick's Fish House & Bar. Someone tapped her on the shoulder. She started, and spun around to find Kittredge standing behind her.

"Please, I must speak to you," he said.

She scowled at him. "I'm not talking to you or any other reporter. Now, shove off, or I'll call a cop." He made no move toward her, so she unfurled the umbrella she should have used much sooner and set off again.

"I . . . knew . . . Elise . . ."

His words, spoken as if he'd ripped them from his throat one-by-one, turned her around. "When?" she began, then stopped. The man had his arms wrapped across

34

his chest as though holding himself together. One glimpse of his misery-etched face erased the rest of her questions.

Water from her drenched hair dripped down her neck as she studied him. Could he be putting on an act to get her attention?

He stared back at her with pleading eyes. "You'll catch cold standing out here."

She flung up her hands. "Oh, what the hell? Is Italian okay with you?" She handed him the umbrella so both of them could take advantage of its shelter.

"Any place you like. I've just returned to Seattle after a six month absence, so I'm practically a stranger."

"It's a five-block hike, but worth it." She took his arm so she could match her stride to his. "Where've you been?"

"Working out of the London office."

She indicated a left turn. "When did you get back?"

"Three days ago."

"Oh . . ." Letting go of his arm, she strode along in silence, her mind teeming with the possibilities his chance remark had opened up.

Obviously the man had been in love with Elise. Why else would he have reacted as he did to the mere mention of her name? He could have gone to Lomitas Island, learned Elise was living with Oren, killed her in a jealous rage, and made it look as if Oren had done it.

She walked faster and her mind kept pace. If she phrased her questions subtly enough, perhaps he'd give himself away. She shivered. Then, both of them would know he was a murderer. Another chill climbed her spine. How far did she dare go to free Oren?

Down the block, she glimpsed the red and white striped metal canopy that shielded the entrance to Maria's Pasta House. She pointed. "There it is." With Simon loping along at her side, she made a dash for it.

35

Inside, subdued lights and stubby candles in circular, red containers on white-clothed tables provided the only illumination.

A rotund man clad in black pants and a pink shirt with flowing sleeves bustled up to them. "Good evening, Amy. It's a pleasure to see you." His welcoming smile broadened as Simon emerged from the shadows. "Ah, how nice. You have a gentleman friend." He arched an eyebrow and sidled closer to Simon. "Often, I have told her that brown eyes as beautiful as hers were made for smiling, not sadness. Don't you agree?"

"Hm-m-m?" Simon stared blankly, as if the man had spoken in some foreign language, then he blinked and said, "Oh . . . yes. Yes, of course."

Amy gave her umbrella a threatening shake. "Cut the sales pitch, Errol, and find us a quiet table where we won't be disturbed."

His hearty chuckle jiggled his three chins. "Right this way. I have just the place for you"—he chuckled again—"and your friend." He hung up their coats and led them to the back where a lattice screened them from the rest of the patrons, handed them menus and left. A few minutes later, he put his head around the edge of the screen. "Victorio has arrived. I could have him serenade you with his violin."

Amy glared at him. "You do and I'll brain him with it."

After the man retreated, Simon said, "Isn't Errol an unusual name for an Italian."

Amy put on her glasses and opened the menu. "His mother never missed an Errol Flynn movie." When the waiter came, she chose Fettuccine Alle Vongole. The baby clams simmered in cream sauce and topped with grated cheese were the best in town. Simon selected the fettuccine also, and a bottle of Zinfandel.

When the waiter brought the wine and started to fill her goblet, she shook her head. After he left, Simon picked up the bottle. "You'd better have some of this."

"No, thanks, I seldom drink," she said primly. What a whopper. While married to Mitch, she had had to drink. If she didn't, he accused her of spoiling his good time with her holier-than-thou attitude.

Simon still held the bottle. "Try a few swallows, Amy. You're probably chilled clear through." He drew his brows together in a concerned frown. "If you don't get warm, you'll be sick."

For no accountable reason, her throat filled. She blinked fast to keep from disgracing herself in front of a stranger. "All right, but take it easy."

She took a swallow and regarded him over the rim of her glass. His damp hair had just enough wave to curl into wispy duck tails above the neck of a white, cable knit sweater that stretched tight over muscular shoulders and chest.

She clamped her teeth together, hard. A person like her would give Freud a nervous breakdown. First, she chose a man to play the villain. Then, knowing he was off limits, she felt "safe" and started getting romantic twinges.

Dumb. Real dumb. She tossed back another gulp of Zinfandel and immediately regretted it. If she kept on at this rate, she'd soon be chattering like a chipmunk—and that's just what he wanted. Well, two could play that game.

The arrival of the waiter with their salads delayed her next move. She waited until Simon began to eat before she leaned forward and asked, "Were you in love with Elise?"

His lettuce-laden fork halted on the way to his mouth and he set it back on his plate. "I thought I was. And for all the wrong reasons."

"Wrong reasons? I don't understand."

37

He picked up his fork and made roads through torn bits of romaine. Finally, he let out a long sigh. "I met my wife, Julie, just after I graduated from college. We were married five years." He frowned. "Five good, happy years."

He drained his wine glass, refilled it, and downed another swallow. "I was on assignment in Africa. Julie decided to join me for a visit. The plane crashed . . ." He swallowed and continued in a flat, emotionless tone. "She and our unborn son were killed."

Amy drew back. "How terrible."

He carefully aligned his knife and spoon with his plate. "My work kept me from going completely out of my mind." He ran his hand over his face. "But even so, I'd find myself listening for Julie's step outside the apartment door, or I'd run after some woman on the street, thinking it was her. I couldn't believe someone as vital and full of life as Julie could be dead."

Amy put out her hand to touch his arm, but drew it back before he noticed.

Simon lapsed into silence while the waiter removed their scarcely touched salad plates. "Ten months ago, while doing an article on the Empty Space Theater, I met Elise. She was helping with props, make-up, and wardrobe. She had Julie's silver blonde hair, the same sapphire blue eyes—she even resembled her."

He looked directly at Amy for the first time. "Three weeks after we met, I asked her to move in with me." He shifted in his seat. "It didn't work. I expected her to have the same sweetness, the same warmhearted nature as Julie." He shook his head. "Stupid of me."

Their fettuccine came and for a time they concentrated on their food. As she ate, Amy decided to take a roundabout route to gain the information she needed.

"My father is medical examiner for Lomitas Island," she began.

"Yes, I know." He dabbed his mouth with his napkin. "As a matter of fact, I met him when I visited Lomitas." He regarded her for a moment. "And I know quite a bit about you too."

She stared at him, unable to believe how easy he'd made it for her. "So you *were* on the island this weekend."

A puzzled expression came over his face. "No, this happened several years ago. I'd been assigned to do a profile on Senator Halliday. He referred me to Oren who invited me to stay on Lomitas Island with him and his mother while I worked on my story."

Amy felt like a child holding a popped balloon. "You came to the lab this morning to get a story on Oren, didn't you?"

"Not exactly. I knew you worked there and decided we should talk about the charges brought against Oren."

She listened with growing frustration. "Someone else could have killed her."

He frowned. "According to the paper all the evidence indicates . . ." He pointed his finger at her. "You think I did it, don't you? No way, lady. And I can prove it."

Eyeing her, he knocked back a healthy draft of wine. "But, I can understand how Oren could have been driven to it." His fingers gripping the wine glass whitened at the knuckles. "Elise did . . . things."

"Things . . . ? What kind of things?"

He wet his lips. "I'd rather not go into the specifics."

Amy crumbled a piece of bread stick. "A number of details in this case don't jibe."

"Like what?"

"We didn't find any fingerprints, not even on Elise's purse or billfold."

"Don't most criminals know enough to wipe everything they may have touched."

"Generally. But Oren and Elise had had that island apartment for several months and people leave their prints on surfaces they don't even think about." She picked up another bread stick and nibbled the end. "How would you describe Elise?"

His eyebrows shot up. "You've never met her? Oren gave me the impression you and he were very close."

She hesitated, not wanting to reveal her past to a stranger. After an instant, she gave an inward sigh. If she expected to get information, she'd have to make a fair exchange. "I got married five years ago." She creased her napkin into tiny pleats. "Afterwards, Oren and I didn't see much of each other."

Simon glanced at her bare ring finger. "Oh, I didn't realize you were married."

She lifted her chin. "Following my divorce a year ago, I took back my maiden name." The clink of their eating utensils sounded loud in the tight silence that followed. After an awkward interval, she gathered her thoughts and went on. "Dad says even Oren's mother didn't know Elise well. She had come visiting with Oren only a few times. Aunt Helen said Elise seemed to resent her for some reason."

Simon's lips thinned to a taut line across even teeth. "Elise resented all women." His gaze dropped and he seemed to have gone off into some other world of his own. After awhile, he added, "Living, or dead."

Amy waited for him to go on. When he didn't, she said, "Do you think she could have defended herself against an attacker?"

"Possibly. Elise was five-eight and well built, but her Dresden-china type of beauty"—he paused for a moment, his brows drawn together, then went on—"made you think she was fragile . . . and she wasn't." For a second, it seemed as if he was about to elaborate on his remark, but he turned his attention to his food instead.

Amy repressed an urge to shout at the man. One minute he told her more about his life than she wanted to know, the next he turned into the proverbial sphinx. "Her beauty must be natural. We found no make-up except a lipstick in the apartment." She twirled strands of fettuccine around her fork. "Evidently, she was different from the beautiful women I've known."

Simon glanced up. "Oh? In what way?"

"Seems to me most of them go in for expensive jewelry." She smoothed a wrinkle in the table cloth. "Elise had only cheap junk."

"Junk! Elise never wore anything that didn't have a three figure price tag. Good God, I gave her a square-cut emerald ring and bracelet that set me back six month's pay." His eyes narrowed. "She had cases crammed with necklaces, bracelets, and rings. Diamonds, rubies, sapphires." He cleared his throat. "She expected men to give her costly presents."

In her mind, Amy dug through the tiny cardboard box that held her stuff. She found two broken watches, a locket her father had given her, and a charm bracelet she'd had at age fourteen. Perhaps her expectations hadn't been high enough. "Did she make a good salary as Dr. Tambor's nurse?"

"She didn't say. I know she had a charge account at a couple of shops on Fifth Avenue."

"Hm-m-m." Amy speared a clam and chewed as she thought over his remark. "Maybe she got overextended and had to cut back. Most of her clothing came from K-Mart."

Simon choked on the swallow of water he'd taken and began to cough. When he regained his breath, he said,

"Something's haywire here. We're not talking about the same woman." He pushed his plate to the side and tossed his napkin on the table. "Look, maybe we can help each other."

"Oh . . ." she said on a rising note. "In what way?"

"You want to know more about Elise, right?"

"Learning a homicide victim's habits and lifestyle is always helpful in solving a case."

He blew out his breath. "I own a condo on Western Avenue. Elise and I lived there." He passed both hands over his face as if he were doing a dry wash. "I haven't been inside the place since I walked out six months ago and went to London."

He glanced at the check the waiter had laid on the table and pulled several twenties from his wallet. "Elise wasn't very organized, she's bound to have left some of her things behind."

His gaze lifted and caught hers in a silent plea. "To be honest, I need the moral support, and you might find something helpful. What do you say? Are you game?"

Amy contemplated his offer. Was the man on the up-and-up, or could this be a ruse to get her into his apartment? The absurdity of her question nearly produced a snicker. A man with Simon's sex appeal wouldn't need to concoct excuses. Most women would come running at a crook of his finger. Still, she'd better take a few precautions. "Mind if I call my father first?"

A smile spread across his face. "No, of course not. Tell him hello for me."

She used the pay phone at the back of the restaurant. "Got any encouraging news about Oren?" she asked, after they'd greeted each other.

"His attorney entered a 'not guilty' plea at the hearing," her father said. "Helen and I are trying to arrange bail."

"Have you had a chance to talk to him?"

He made a sound of disgust. "The sheriff's not letting anyone near him except his lawyer. What are you up to this evening?"

She told him about Simon and his suggestion. "What do you think? Should I go?"

"Sure. Why not? We need to find out all we can about Elise."

He paused for a double beat and she could almost hear his brain cells enumerating the possibilities. He longed to see her married and happy so he could look forward to a grandchild. This impromptu dinner was the nearest she'd been to a man in over a year.

"Simon's intelligent," her father said quickly. "And . . . and personable too as I recall. This may be a real lucky break, Amy."

"Don't count on it, Dad." She berated herself for being so abrupt with him. The mess she'd made of her life wasn't his fault.

"Oh? Well, a change of pace never hurt anyone. Right?"

"Look who's talking. You're the closest thing to perpetual motion I know." She wished him a good night and returned to the table to gather up her things. "Let's go."

The cab driver acted as if he'd taken his training at the Indianapolis Speedway. He jetted down Columbia spraying gutter water over a gray clump of street people huddled in a debris-strewn doorway. Sheeting rain filmed the windows and she recognized only a few of the weathered brick buildings they zipped past. Fifteen minutes later, the cab skidded to a stop in front of a tall building.

An uneasy silence prevailed as the elevator whisked them upward and deposited them on the sixth floor. Simon fumbled through his keys. After two attempts, he

43

managed to find the right key, trigger the lock, and wave her inside.

He slammed the door behind them, setting into motion dozens of crystal teardrops that hung from the cobwebby chandelier overhead. Each facet caught the light, spreading shimmering shafts over stark white walls.

Simon glanced around as if surprised. "Never saw it so clean. Elise must have had someone come in and do the cleaning," he said, his voice unnaturally gruff. Squaring his shoulders, he strode across jet black carpet, and threaded his way between a white satin sofa of olympic proportions fronted by a glass coffee table of equal size. On the table, dust filmed artificial fruit spilling artfully over the edges of a pedestalled lead crystal bowl—grapes carved of polished jade, amethyst plums, carnelian peaches.

"Elise redecorated the apartment when she moved in." He went to a window spanning the living room's end wall, and drew back variegated gunmetal drapes. Amy joined him, and caught a blurred glimmer of lights reflecting off Elliott Bay's inky waters.

"Puget Sound and the Olympic Mountains must look spectacular from here."

His inner stress cut furrows in his cheeks and pulled his features out of line. "Yes . . . yes, they are. Julie and I couldn't afford the place, but after we saw the view . . ." He spread his hands. "When she got pregnant, we used to sit here in the evenings and . . . and make plans for us and the baby." His Adam's apple jerked convulsively. He opened and closed his mouth several times before he said in a strained whisper, "We were going to call him Jason, after my father."

Amy touched his arm. "Maybe this wasn't such a good idea."

"No, I've spent a helluva a lot of money on psychia-

44

trists just to learn I'm badly in need of some therapeutic exorcism." He turned toward the hall. "Come along. I'll give you the ten cent tour."

He opened the door of a room containing an ancient oak desk, an equally battered file cabinet, and shelves loaded with books. "Once upon a time, I intended to write a novel. One that'd make the publishing world forget all about Hemingway." He laughed—a bitter, humorless sound. "That was back when I could honestly call myself a writer." His mouth twisted. "Foolish dream anyway."

He pointed to the next door. "That's the bedroom. You might find something of Elise's in the closet."

Amy looked up at him. "Aren't you coming?"

He shook his head. "I can't . . . not just yet. I'll wait in my study."

Amy pushed open the door and entered a white-walled room dominated by a king-sized bed. A photograph album lay open on the black satin spread. Ragged edged pages were strewn in every direction. Snapshot after snapshot of Simon and a slender woman lay scattered about. In each picture, someone had torn off the woman's head and tossed the scraps into a pile.

Although Amy didn't remember making a sound, she must have. The next thing she knew Simon stood beside her. He stared down at the desecrated photos of the woman who must have been his beloved Julie, and his face paled.

"Bloody bitch!" He ripped the spread off the bed, showering fragments of paper onto the white carpet. "Dirty, conniving, black-hearted bitch." He flung the wadded fabric into the farthest corner, and clenched his fists at his sides. "I should have killed her."

Four

Amy urged Simon out of the condo. He came, stumbling like a man gone suddenly blind. Through the thin fiber of his raincoat, she felt his muscles quiver and tense, quiver and tense. Once on the street, she found a diner, steered him inside, and ordered coffee.

He gripped the thick, brown mug tightly but his hands shook and hot liquid splashed his skin. "It's no use," he muttered, and lowered the mug to the table. "Why don't you go on home? I'll work my way through this." He grimaced. "I always do." His gaze met hers for an instant, and in the depths of his soft hazel eyes, she glimpsed a bleak, heart-rending sadness.

"Humph!" she said, memories of her own sleepless nights bringing a bitter taste to her mouth. "Don't try to kid someone who's been there." She got to her feet. "Besides, there are times when a person shouldn't be alone."

She ordered a cab, insisted he get in, and gave the driver her address. We're just off Broadway, Mitch had always told his friends, giving their four-story walk-up a New York panache the crumbling, red-brick building didn't rate.

When they reached her three-room apartment, she poured him a healthy shot of bourbon and clamped his fingers around the glass. "Drink up. You need something to warm your insides." She smiled faintly at the constant reversals in their roles. Poor Simon was a natural born caretaker, too—a trait that had wounded her so deeply, she wouldn't wish it on her worst enemy.

She took sheets and a blue print comforter from the hall closet. When Mitch had moved out, she'd insisted he take the Lucite chrome and marshmallow Naugahyde furniture he'd liked so much. She replaced them with a comfortable blue-gray corduroy hide-a-bed couch and matching overstuffed chair from the neighborhood thrift store.

After making Simon's bed, she turned to look at him. His shoulders were bent and his head hung loosely as if the effort of holding it upright were too much for him.

She moved to Simon's side and took his empty glass. "Would you like to tell me about Elise?"

He jerked erect. "No! I wished to God I'd never met her, that I never had to think of her again." His body went slack, and he sighed. "But it looks as if that's not possible." He stood and took off his raincoat. "Go to bed, Amy. It's late and you need your rest."

She started out, then came back. "Are you sure you'll be all right?"

A wry smile twisted his mouth. "I've been fairly self sufficient for most of my thirty-four years."

Amy grinned. "Yeah. Sure. That's two of us—and we're both damn liars. Get some sleep, you look like a beached jellyfish." She took a few steps and turned once more. "If you can't sleep, and want to talk, just knock on my door."

"I'll be fine."

She was halfway down the hall when he called her name. She rejoined him. "Thanks." He combed his fingers through his hair. "Just being here is a big help.

This"—he waved his arm—"reminds me of my parents' home." A wan smile lifted the corners of his mouth. "There were six of us kids."

"Must have been nice. I was an only child."

"You can still get lonely." A frown creased his forehead. "There's five years between me and my brother. When you're a kid that's too wide a gap to breach. By the time you're grown, it's too late."

"Maybe that's why you're a writer."

His eyes widened. "How'd you know about writers?"

She wrinkled her nose. "I grind out a poem now and then."

"Publish any?"

"A couple back in college. Haven't had time for such stuff lately."

"I see . . ." He stretched out his long legs, settled his head on the chair's backrest and closed his eyes.

She turned on a table lamp and switched off the ceiling fixture. "I'll put a toothbrush and a disposable razor in the bathroom."

He roused himself. "You must make a habit of picking up strays."

She swung around and gave him a frigid stare. "Sure I do. At least three or four men a night." She turned on her heel and left the room.

Tuesday, October 25

Early the next morning, the sound of water drumming on the shower walls brought her upright in bed. *Mitch?* She remembered Simon and lay back down. After her exit last night, she was surprised he was still there. An image of him drying his lean, muscular body on her tow-

48

els drifted unbidden into her mind and gave her a peculiar feeling in her midriff.

She sat up and hugged her knees to her chest. She didn't need a man. Hadn't Mitch taught her marriage wasn't the answer to loneliness?

She grabbed the phone receiver and punched in her father's number. "Morning, Dad," she said, when he came on the line. "Were you able to get Oren out of jail?"

"Yeah. He's staying at Helen's." He let out a noisy breath. "The prosecuting attorney says his apartment is off limits. My house is too since I have physical evidence pertaining to his case in the basement lab."

"How's he holding up emotionally?"

"Depressed. And I sure as hell can't blame him for that. He resigned from his job. Said he didn't want to hurt Senator Halliday's election chances."

"It's not fair." She fished an antacid from a bottle on the nightstand. "Simon says even if he's proven innocent, his career in public relations is over."

"He's probably right. Worse luck."

The muscles at the back of her neck drew tight. "Have you processed any of the physical evidence yet?"

"Not a lot. I have a case waiting on San Juan Island and another on Shaw." He grunted. "I have a hunch Tom's farming me out. He figures this case will make him a star. And he doesn't want me to find anything that'll prove he's all wet. Did you learn anything from Kittredge?"

As she was about to answer, her alarm went off. She punched the alarm button and got out of bed. "I have to get ready for work." She cradled the receiver between cheek and shoulder and began to pull the blankets into place. "Don't be surprised if you see my car go down the drive late tonight or early tomorrow. Personnel's been bugging me to use my vacation time. Think I'll take a couple weeks and come help you."

49

"Hallelujah!" B.J. shouted. "Honey, when Tom finds out he's going to turn six shades of purple. But everybody in this county knows damned well I need an assistant, and they sure as hell can't object if you're willing to work for free."

His delighted chuckle bubbled over the line and she smiled. He loved to topple pompous, self-important people. "See you when I get there," she said, and hung up.

By the time she'd showered and dressed, the odor of fresh-brewed coffee filtered into the bedroom. She dabbed on make-up and gave her hair a twitch or two with the curling iron. When she could think of nothing else to delay her, she squared her shoulders and marched down the hall. This was her apartment—hiding in the bedroom because of some man was pure nonsense.

"Good morning," Simon said, as she appeared. "Sit down. Breakfast's all ready." His eyes were clear, his face clean-shaven, his damp hair neatly combed.

"But I don't usually eat . . ."

"Please." He pulled out a chair for her. "Consider this a peace offering. After you've eaten maybe you'll feel mellow enough to forgive me for my big mouth."

She perched on the edge of the chair, her back ramrod stiff. He must want something, otherwise why had he stuck around?

He poured coffee for both of them, then opened the oven, took out a saucer-sized cinnamon roll with melted butter dripping down the sides and set it in front of her.

The spicy fragrance started her mouth to watering. Blast the man, by some strange coincidence he'd chosen her favorite confection. She took a quick gulp of coffee to stem sudden hunger. "Mrs. Magee's Bakery is a ten-block round trip. Were you up all night?"

"Nope. Slept good, for a change." He brought a roll for himself and sat down opposite her. "I took an early morning run. Haven't felt like it in quite awhile." He cut off a piece of the caramelized crust with his fork, took a bite, and a blissful expression settled over his face. "Just like my mother used to make." Laughter glinted in his eyes. "Trite, but true."

They ate in silence for several minutes. Occasionally, Amy glanced at him through lowered lashes and caught him doing the same. She almost giggled. Their stiff, standoffish manner reminded her of her cat, Marcus, when he met up with another tom.

Simon swallowed the last of his coffee and set down his cup. "I've decided to do a run-down on Elise."

Amy studied him over the rim of her cup. "You think that's a good idea?"

He leaned forward. "I have to, Amy. She . . . she's messed up my head." The skin of his face whitened over his cheek bones and around his mouth. "I can't remember Julie right anymore."

Amy's throat closed up. Mitch had never loved her like that. Never. Not even in the very beginning when he'd been so full of pretty words and promises. "Where are you going to start?" she asked, when she got her voice under control.

"With Dr. Coskun Tambor. I'm going to pretend I'm a patient—at first. If he knows I'm a reporter, he might not see me at all."

"What if Elise has told him about you?"

He smiled. "I'm going to use a friend's name and press card. People are strange. Some will babble away to a reporter when they wouldn't give anyone else the time of day."

Laugh lines fanned out from his eyes and an unexpected dimple appeared in one cheek. "I'll go early and try a little charm on the ladies in the staff."

Amy smiled faintly. "Is that ethical?"

He sobered. "I'm prepared to do whatever it takes."

"Does that include having your blood drawn?"

He looked startled. "My blood! What for?"

She concealed her amusement. "Endocrinologists treat glandular problems. Their tests are usually done on blood."

Simon shook his head. "No way. Not on me. I detest needles."

Amy shrugged, gathered up the last few cinnamon-coated crumbs and licked her fingertip. "Would you call me, if you learn anything helpful?" She found one of her business cards. "You can reach me here at the apartment or at the beach house on Lomitas." She wrote the number on the back of the card.

He got to his feet. "Thanks for everything, Amy. I'll keep you posted."

She followed him to the door and stuck out her hand. When he clasped it, she said, "Sorry I was so touchy last night."

He gripped her hand hard. "My fault. I'm an insensitive bastard these days. I didn't mean to insinuate that you pick up men all the time."

She withdrew her hand. "Did you think I brought you here to seduce you?"

"It happens a lot when you bum around the world."

She scarcely heard his comment. "Me? Seduce a man?" She made a harsh, bitter sound. "That's a laugh."

He cocked his head and peered down at her. "Why not for God's sake? You're an attractive woman."

Without any warning at all, her carefully glued edges came unstuck. A terrible quivering began inside of her, her face wobbled, her bottom lip trembled. "I have to go *very* soon," she rasped. She managed to get him outside and the key turned in the lock before the first sob tore loose from her aching chest.

Others followed as she slid down the door and put her head on her bent knees. She clutched her stomach as sobs convulsed her. They doubled her over in repeated spasms so excruciating she half expected some vital organ to burst and erupt through her mouth.

At last, drained dry as ashes, she blew her nose and struggled to her feet. As she started toward the bathroom to bathe her swollen eyes, someone tapped softly on the door. She steadied her voice. "Who is it?"

"Simon. I forgot my raincoat."

She opened the door a few inches and thrust out the coat. Simon stuck his foot in the gap and shoved. "I'm coming in."

"Go away." She pushed with all her strength, but proved no match for him.

He eased the door open and she turned her back to him. "Are you all right?" he asked, his tone soft.

"You heard?"

"Yes."

"All of it?"

"I'm afraid so."

"I guess you loosened a chink in the dam."

"Shrinks tell me it's good to let go."

"A lot they know. I feel like I've been run over by a truck."

He cleared his throat and patted her shoulder. "People need you, Amy—your father, your aunt, and especially Oren."

His awkward attempt to comfort her only made her more aware of her shortcomings. She wagged her throbbing head. "I don't know, Simon. I bolstered Mitch until he sapped all my strength. I'm not sure I can do it again."

He turned her around and gave her a stern look. "I may not know you well, but I'd bet money you'd never let a friend down."

"I already did. I should have gone to Elise and Oren's apartment Friday night, then all this might not have happened."

"And if I'd stayed in town six months ago and done what I should have, Elise might still be alive. We can't change all that, Amy. Still, if we can find the reasons behind what's happened, we might help ourselves . . . and Oren."

She managed a half-hearted smile. "I'll do my best, Professor Kittredge."

He laughed out loud. "I do tend to lecture, don't I?" He grazed her shoulder with a gentle cuff. "Socks up, partner." He snatched his raincoat from the floor where it'd landed and strode out. In a few minutes, his cheery whistle spiraled up the stairwell.

That evening as she and Gail Wong were leaving work and getting off the elevator, Simon dashed up to them. A green wool driving cap was cocked at a rakish angle atop his head and excitement glowed in his face. "Let's go grab a hamburger," he said. "I've got lots to tell you."

Gail glanced from Simon to Amy and her mouth rounded into an "O." Her thoughts showed so plainly that Amy smiled and introduced her to Simon. "We're working on a private project," she said, feeling she had to explain his presence. Too late, she realized her words would only pique Gail's interest more.

"Call me," Gail said. She shot Amy a threatening look and scooted out the door.

Amy and Simon located a hole-in-the-wall diner and huddled over a clean but age-yellowed table splotched with cigarette burns. "A Mrs. Michaels is filling in until the doctor finds a replacement for Elise," Simon said.

"Evidently she's been with the doctor for years and practically runs the office single-handedly."

Amy nodded. "She's the one Elise phoned the night she disappeared. According to her, Elise sounded terrified of Oren. And she claims Oren had beaten Elise in the past."

Simon's mouth twisted. *"Yesterday,* I might have believed her story. *Today,* I have my doubts. I asked her if Elise made a habit of associating with abusive men. She said, 'Oh, yes. One by the name of Simon Kittredge not only abused her, but cleaned out her bank account and left her with a pile of bills.'" His fingers curled into a fist. "I did not mistreat her, and I paid the bills—all of them—from the day she moved in."

"Perhaps Mrs. Michaels is one of those women who likes to create juicy gossip."

"Maybe." Simon narrowed his eyes. "Either way, I don't like it."

Amy shifted her position to allow a pony-tailed young man with a dishtowel tied around his waist to set bacon-cheese burgers and cups of coffee in front of them. Silence fell between them until she roused herself enough to ask his impression of the doctor.

"Nervous." Simon took a swallow of coffee and set down his cup. "I'd better start at the beginning. He's one of those dark-haired, melancholy-eyed men that women find so attractive. Has a trace of an accent. Pakistani, I think."

Simon took a bite of his hamburger and chewed it thoughtfully. "I try to sense people's moods, to watch for any inconsistencies that'll give me an edge. The man kept repeating questions. Never flickered an eyelash when I told him my condition had begun while in pursuit of a yeti in Tibet."

Amy giggled. "What condition is that?"

Simon's lips twitched. "Elephantiasis congenita cystica."

"He really must have been out of it. Any second year medical student knows that's a tropical disease."

"Right." Simon picked up a french fry and used it to accent his words. "Why, I asked myself, should he be so distracted? I decided a frontal attack might shake loose something of interest."

He dunked the french fry in a glob of ketchup and bit off a piece. "I plopped my friend's press card on the doctor's desk and asked him how well he knew Elise. The man's face turned the color of wet putty. He said she'd been his nurse for three years, otherwise he knew nothing."

A sudden hope electrified Amy. She leaned toward Simon in eager anticipation. "Do you believe him?"

He shrugged. "Something had him uptight. He kept fussing with the things on his desk and repeatedly touching a photograph of him, his wife, and six daughters."

Some of her enthusiasm dwindled away. This wasn't a movie where a new suspect came on scene just when the star's situation looked hopeless. "Doctors get nervous about publicity. If it shows him in a bad light, it could affect his practice."

"Hm-m-m, that could have been his problem. Still, he refused to let me copy Elise's personnel records, until I pointed out the court would probably subpoena them anyway. Finally we struck a bargain—the records for my word that he'll not be mentioned in the article he thinks I'm writing."

Amy scooted her chair closer. "Anything in the records we can use?"

"Not much. You might be interested in knowing her blood is type B, Rh positive. Seems one of the doctor's daughters had surgery and all of his employees donated blood. Elise was thirty-five, I didn't know that. She looked much younger."

Amy smiled to herself at his remark—applying the right make-up to look younger was a talent women learned when they saw thirty approaching. "Dad'll be happy to learn her blood type. He has a number of stains to analyze."

"Good, that's one small victory." Simon raked his fingers through hair that was already wind tousled. "Her file says she was born in White Bird, Montana and worked at the Marchmont Hospital there before moving to Seattle. Looked up the town, it's out in the middle of nowhere." He frowned. "How the hell did someone as sophisticated as Elise ever spring from a place like that?"

Amy smiled faintly. "Personality and circumstances have more affect than the size of the town."

"Yeah, I guess you're right." He gnawed his lip and glanced across at Amy. "I still want to check out Tambor. Make sure he's not hiding anything." He regarded her intently. "I've got a plan. Only thing is, I need someone to drive the getaway car."

She set down her coffee mug. "The getaway car? Good grief, what've you got cooked-up this time?"

He inched closer and lowered his voice. "The disposal truck empties the doctor's dumpster tomorrow." He cocked his head and grinned. "So I want to steal his trash tonight."

Five

Simon herded the rented van down the suburban street at a crawl that caused Amy to grind her teeth. She'd endured the repeated honking of the drivers behind them as Simon plugged along the freeway at a sedate pace while everyone else was going sixty plus. Her impatience finally got the better of her. "Speed up a little, or you'll get a ticket for impeding traffic."

"Don't bug me. Dammit, I haven't driven on the right hand side of the road for months."

"Oh . . . sorry. I guess that *would* muddle a person's mind." She tried to concentrate on the scenery.

Bruised-looking clouds pressed down on the roof tops of the village as if to blot it out. On either side of the broad thoroughfare, warehouse-type buildings were scattered in a hodge-podge fashion over wide sweeps of black asphalt—Payless, Pay'n Save, Pay'n Pak, liquidators, bargain marts, and thrift stores.

Sodium flood lights edged the street giving buildings, cars, and anemic shrubbery the sharp, hard-edged clarity of an operating room.

A brisk wind had sprung up, and as they passed a fast food drive-in, gusts swirled soft drink containers and hamburger cartons into the air.

Amy prayed the weather would keep people inside. Probably a law against garbage-napping hadn't yet been enacted, but if someone caught them, she'd be darned embarrassed.

"They've got medical buildings all over the place in this part of town." Simon signaled, took a right, drove half a block and made an abrupt left into a narrow alley that ran behind an oblong, four-story building.

He gestured to the right. "That's Dr. Tambor's. His office is on the top floor. It's a new building and the other offices are still vacant." He backed up to a large, blue, metal bin, stopped and shut off the motor.

Darkness settled around them. Only the whoosh of the wind and the tick-tick of the cooling motor broke the silence. A shiver coursed through her. As a member of the mobile crime lab team, she'd been to scenes of robberies, murders, and assaults. Yet each time she found herself quivering, her senses as touchy as an exposed nerve.

"Won't you have to crawl inside the dumpster?" she asked.

"Probably. I'll load the bags I can reach first." He zipped his jacket. "Slide behind the steering wheel soon as I get out."

"I will. Be careful."

"Don't worry. My friends on the P.I. and *Times* would love to run a story about me getting hauled in for malicious mischief or some other such charge." He pushed open the door, stepped out, and eased it closed until the catch snapped.

She heard the crunch of his footsteps, then he yanked open the rear doors and a blast of cold air struck her neck. Seconds later, white plastic bags began to thud onto the carpeting behind her. After a few minutes, all was silence. She pictured Simon hoisting himself over the rim of the bin.

A moment later, a tossed bag thudded on the pavement, something inside "popped" and glass clattered. She jumped out of the van and ran to the dumpster. "Hand them to me," she whispered, grabbing the bag he was about to drop over the side. "I'll do the loading."

She moved rapidly between him and the vehicle, until her breath wheezed and her perspiration-dampened clothing stuck to her skin. A searchlight brushed the trees bordering a side street and she crouched down. "Quick, Simon, a patrol car."

"Go start the motor."

She'd just hoisted herself into the front seat and started fumbling for the key when a thump and a muffled oath came from the dumpster.

She turned the key in the ignition. The motor ground, but didn't catch. The arching lights came closer. Damn. She rubbed sweat-slicked fingers on her jeans.

Behind her, the loaded sacks gave a rustling, scritchity sound as Simon gave them a shove, and slammed the rear door. An instant later, he tumbled into the seat beside her. "Hurt my ankle," he gasped. Down the alley a car turned in and came toward them, its headlights growing brighter by the second. "Get going, Amy. We gotta get out of here."

She gave the key another twist and held her breath. The motor roared to life. She fed in the clutch, shifted gears, jammed her foot on the accelerator and rocketed into the doctor's parking lot. Spying an outlet, she swerved around a concrete barrier, plunged between a row of bare limbed oaks, and hit the side street going fifty. She braked, fish-tailed and spun sideways. "Hang on." She steadied the van, double-clutched and peeled out leaving a patch of rubber half a block long.

"Jesus Maria," Simon breathed. "I've taken up with a female hot-rodder."

Amy glanced in the rearview mirror, saw no one in pursuit, switched on her headlights, and slowed to a legal speed. "Just a little something Oren taught me," she said, and turned to grin at Simon. "Did I scare you?"

"Oh, no, I always go around with my heart in my mouth." He rubbed his ankle. "We'll off load at my condo. He glanced sideways. "If we get there."

She delivered him, nervous but unscathed, and was glad to find the condo had underground parking. They'd attracted enough attention for one night.

Simon hobbled from van to elevator carrying four bags to her two until they had the six by eight foot space crammed full. Upstairs Simon flipped a switch to hold the elevator on his floor and led the way to his apartment.

After the traumatic discovery the night before, Amy dreaded going inside. When he swung the door inward, her mouth nearly dropped open. The room had been stripped clean. All the furniture, pictures, drapes, even the elaborate chandelier and white carpeting were gone. She felt sick and could scarcely bear to think what this new blow would do to him. "Oh, Simon, you do have the worst luck."

His chuckle surprised her. "Frankly, I think it's a vast improvement." She pivoted to stare at him, and he laughed out loud. "Soon as I left your place this morning, I commissioned some people to clear out the stuff Elise bought and sell it."

"You didn't get rid of the things in your study, did you?"

"No, but if I don't start doing some decent writing soon, that's going too." He started back to the waiting elevator and its bulging contents. "Let's put the sacks in the kitchen."

She followed him out and noticed his limp had grown worse. After they dumped the first load, she said, "You'd better let me take a look at your ankle."

"I'm okay."

As he started out after another batch, she planted herself in front of him. "Like hell. I'll get the rest of the sacks. You can start going through the ones we've brought in."

He scowled at her, his face closed and resentful. "I'll do as I damn please."

She didn't budge. "You had any first aid training, mister?"

"So what if I haven't?"

"I've been to medical school and *I* know what *I'm* doing." He didn't unbend an iota, so she went on, "A sprain's nothing to mess with. So stop being so blasted macho."

His eyes shifted and he shrugged. "All right, all right. Have it your own way."

"Sit down, please." She gave an inward sigh as he sank down on the white, gold-flecked linoleum. She removed his shoe and sock. His ankle had already begun to swell. She gently palpated the bones. "Don't feel a break," she said at last. "But soon as we're through here, we'd better get it x-rayed. You could have a hairline fracture."

He reached for his shoe. "Knock it off. We've got work to do."

"Sit still, I'm not through." Luckily, someone had filled the refrigerator's ice trays. Aware of his eyes following her, she tied several cubes in a plastic bag and dropped them into the toe of his navy blue sock. "Got a safety pin?"

He scrutinized her with a blank expression. "What would I be doing with a safety pin?"

She found one in her purse, fastened the makeshift cold

pack around his ankle and sat back on her heels. "That ought to do until we can get you to the emergency room."

He peered down at her handiwork. "That's it?" His lips twitched. "You went to medical school to learn how to do that?" He let out a howl of laughter.

She smiled, then began to chuckle. Each time they glanced at each other their laughter grew in volume until both of them lay limp and gasping on the floor.

Finally, Simon sat up and wiped his streaming eyes. "God, I needed that. I really, really needed to let go."

Amy struggled to her feet. "Me too." She tossed him a sack of trash to start on. "Do you have any plastic gloves? You never know what might end up in a doctor's waste can." He pointed to a drawer. She brought him a pair, stuck another in her jeans pocket, and went to bring in the rest of the bags.

Soon both of them were at opposite ends of the kitchen transferring wads of crumbled paper—gowns, drapes, sheets, table covers—from a full bag to an empty one.

They worked quickly, each scrabbling through the mounds of litter like dogs after a bone. Amy had labored through ten sacks when Simon let out a long, "Ah-h-h." She straightened and massaged her aching shoulders. "Find something?"

"Maybe. I'm not sure. Don't get your hopes up." He pushed himself upright and teetered on one foot. "I need some paste and a desk to work on." He grinned at her. "Carry on, doc," he said, and hopped off toward his study.

She toiled through two more sacks, pausing from time to time to glance toward the study and wonder what Simon had found. She untied the last bag. Inside were copies of *Medical Economics, Physician's Management,* and dog-eared issues of *The New England Journal of Medicine.*

After tossing the magazines aside, she sorted through

messages from doctors, patients, and pharmacies. Under these, she came upon some torn fragments of paper. She picked them out, lay them on the counter and went to borrow Simon's paste.

"Take a look at this," Simon said, as she came in. He wore amber-framed glasses that added new dimensions to his sturdy features.

She leaned over the desk. Scraps of a colored photograph lay scattered in all directions. On a sheet of paper, he'd put together enough of the bits to produce the upper portion of a woman's face.

"It's Elise." He pushed back strands of hair that had fallen over his forehead.

Amy's dampened optimism gave a gentle shake and began to unfurl. "Her and Oren's apartment didn't have any photos at all. Although Oren might have had some at his office." She mulled the thought over for a moment. "Did Elise give you a picture?"

"Nope. She didn't like having her picture taken."

Amy bent and studied a jagged fragment, then fitted it into an empty space below Elise's cheek bone. "So why would she give an eight by ten photograph to someone in Tambor's office?"

"That, as they say, is the sixty-four dollar question. Did you come up with anything?"

"Pieces of torn paper. Got any more paste?" She took the paper and glue stick he handed her and returned to the kitchen. The task proved difficult until she established the approximate size; after that the whole thing went together easily. When fully reassembled, she found it to be a master charge slip from Sibleys on Fifth Avenue. The slip had been imprinted October third and listed the purchase of a coat and some jewelry.

With reserved anticipations, she took her handiwork in to Simon. "What do you think?"

He looked at the listed prices and whistled. "The man's certainly not cheap." He folded his arms and leaned back in his chair. "Tambor's wife and daughters are small and slender. If that coat turns out to be a size ten, we've got a real lead."

Amy chewed the inside of her lip and frowned. "Elise and Oren were to be married in December. Surely she wouldn't have accepted an expensive gift from another man two months before her wedding?"

Simon raised his shoulders in an elaborate shrug and shook his head. "Sibleys' accounting department would have the coat's size. Rotten part is, they won't give out the information to just anybody."

Amy glanced at her watch. "I know a detective or two who might be able to find out for me. Your phone hooked up?" At his nod, she made a couple of calls and found a man who promised to see what he could do. When she finished, she turned back to Simon. "How's your project coming?"

"Nearly finished." He swabbed the remaining three pieces with glue, stuck them in place and wiped his fingertips on a rag. "Well, there she is."

"Can I pick it up?"

"Sure, go ahead." He folded his hands behind his head and tilted back his chair.

She held the picture at arm's length and ran through her usual routine. Blonde hair, high forehead, thick eyebrows, round blue eyes, straight nose, and full sensual lips that drooped at the corners. "Did she have periods of depression?"

The back of Simon's swivel chair gave a metallic thunk as he jerked upright. "How'd you know that?"

She lay the photo on the desk. "See the white portion under the iris of her eye? Gives her a sexy look, right? Actually, it's more often an indication of melancholia."

65

"That's Elise, all right. She had the weirdest moods. Laughing one minute, bitchy as hell the next." He scowled and rubbed a hand over his face. "And for no reason I could ever make out."

"Hm-m-m, that's not exactly . . ." she murmured as she absorbed his statement. She touched the corner of Elise's mouth. "This petulant droop at the corners of the mouth usually accompanies melancholia. But take note of the firm chin. This is a woman who intends to get what she wants."

Simon grunted in disgust. "Oh, brother. Why couldn't I see it?" He managed a forced smile. "Hereafter I'll insist on a photo for you to screen before I jump in with both feet."

She stared at the floor, then lifted her gaze to meet his. "Would you have listened, if anyone had told you? I didn't."

He spread his hands. "Who knows?" He lifted the picture. "I used transparent paper in case the studio imprinted their name on the back." He flipped the picture over. "I'll be damned."

She leaned over his shoulder and read the words scribbled in small, cramped letters across one corner. *To my Cosky whose talents are endless.*

She let out a squeal and grabbed Simon's arm. "The doctor did it. He knew she was living with Oren, knew they intended to marry soon. He gave her an ultimatum and when she turned him down, he killed her."

Simon considered her announcement with an attitude of amusement. "Is this the forensic specialist speaking?"

Her shoulders sagged. "Okay, it's wishful thinking. But when I get to Lomitas tomorrow, I intend to tell Sheriff Calder."

Simon frowned. "You're going home?"

"Yes. Calder has Dad so bogged down with work,

he can't get to Oren's case. I took two weeks off to help."

"Could I go with you? I'd like to talk to Oren. I think the two of us should uh . . . compare notes."

"What about the trash in your kitchen and your job?"

"I'll have the janitors get rid of the trash. And Global has me on R and R. They're probably hoping a change of scene will improve my writing."

"In that case you're welcome to come along, but there's one condition."

"And that is?"

"We stop at the emergency room first."

Simon let out an exasperated breath. "Anybody ever tell you you're a pain in the ass?"

His comment caught her off guard. She hunched her shoulders, wrapped her arms across the sudden cramp in her stomach, and forced words between tightly drawn lips. "Yes, repeatedly."

"Oh, hell." Simon reached out to touch her, but she backed away. "Please don't look like that, Amy." He smacked his forehead with the heel of his hand. "Me and my big mouth."

What made him think it mattered in the least what he said? She flung him a sharp look. "Where's your suitcase?"

"In the hall closet with my laptop computer. I take both wherever I go." He stood, and bracing himself on the wall, he hopped to the elevator.

At the emergency room, the doctors diagnosed a fractured fibula. After the ankle was cast, they took a taxi to her apartment to get her luggage. Then, with her at the wheel of her station wagon, they traveled north through the waning darkness to Anacortes and boarded the ferry.

They arrived at Lomitas Island at 7 A.M. and by mutual agreement went directly to her aunt's house. To her surprise, her father answered her knock. "Amy!" he shouted. He put out an arm and brought her into his embrace. At the same time, he grasped Simon's hand. "Good to see you, Simon. Come on inside."

"Sorry to intrude on you like this, Dr. Prescott." Simon swore as he tried to maneuver his crutches through the door B.J. held open.

B.J. chuckled. "If you'd ever lived on an island, you'd know any break in the monotony is a downright pleasure." He rubbed his bearded cheek against Amy's forehead as he propelled her down the hallway. "Sure glad you're here, kitten."

At the arched living room entryway, she glanced quickly at Simon to catch his reaction to the Spartan decor. Years ago, after Uncle Mike Prescott took off with his secretary, Aunt Helen had gone to work as B.J.'s office manager. When B.J. sold his practice, Helen had stayed on with the new doctor. In order to work the long hours and still care for her home and young son, she'd cleared out all but the bare essentials. The starkness of the room often startled people, but Simon didn't even blink.

A large upright tapestry loom rested against a clean expanse of sea green wall that ended at a floor to ceiling window with a view of the water. On the bare oak floor, beside the loom sat a woven grass basket overflowing with twisted skeins of brown, beige, and avocado green yarn.

B.J. motioned them to the one piece of furniture, a pale coral couch that took up half a wall and one corner. "Have a seat," he said. "Helen's gone to work, so I'll play host and get you folks some coffee."

"Is Oren here?" Amy asked.

"He's down on the bluff. Spends a lot of time there." He disappeared into the kitchen.

She leaned back against soft cushions and instantly her eyelids began to droop. She straightened and pushed herself to her feet. "I'll go find Oren."

A weathered cedar deck wrapped around two sides of the Cape Cod-style house. From the deck, wide shallow steps led down to a red cinder walkway bordered by gold and russet chrysanthemums. At the end of the path lay Oren's wood shop.

She peeked in to see if he might be working. Amid piles of shavings stood a partially finished dresser of rich grained cherry. She stared at it, black despair drenching her mind. No fiancee, no wedding, no home—and no longer any need for a beautiful woman's dressing table.

She rushed out and around the building to a path that meandered down a slope. Curled brown leaves and scraps of bark discarded by constantly shedding madrona trees crunched underfoot. Chest-high salal showered her with lingering sea mist when she brushed the branches.

Where an ancient cataclysm had upthrust great basaltic hummocks and ridges, she found Oren sitting in a semicircle of rocks overlooking Rosario Strait. She slid in beside him and sat without speaking.

After a few minutes, he sighed, reached down and took her hand. "Good to see you."

She put her other hand over his. "You may wish you hadn't, when you hear what I have to say."

"Nothing can make things any worse than they are. It's been a nightmare." He faced her squarely, his features gray and drawn with despair. "I didn't do it, Amy. You believe that, don't you?"

She longed to reply without any reservations. Still, how well did anyone ever know another? She squeezed his hand and said, "Of course, I believe you," and hoped she sounded more convincing than she felt.

He didn't comment when she told him Simon had once been in love with Elise. "Both Simon and I feel we have to learn more about Elise. Somewhere in her life there must be someone who had reason to kill her." She stood up and went to gaze at a slate-colored sea that bulged and flexed like a weight lifter's biceps before it dashed against the cliff's base. Oren looked close to the breaking point. Would her words be more than he could take?

He came to stand beside her. "Say it. Nothing can faze me now."

"Elise may have been having an affair with Dr. Tambor."

His eyes opened wide, wildness flaring in their depths. "She loved me." He smacked his chest with his palm. "She . . . she . . ." He went rigid and terribly still as if listening to some inner voice. Then he seemed to cave in all at once. He braced a shaking hand on a boulder beside him. "Would a woman do a thing like that?"

She put her arm around his waist. "That's what Simon and I hope to find out." She half-led him toward the path. "Let's go up to the house. Simon wants to talk to you."

When they reached the garden, Oren stopped. "Send Simon out. I'd rather talk to him alone."

She nodded. "I'll go tell him." Inside, she found her father and Simon in deep conversation.

B.J. smiled at her. "You certainly brought me a nice surprise. Simon and I have been having a rare old chat." He drew her down beside him in the corner of the couch.

She returned his smile. "I'll bet. Did Simon get a word in edgewise?"

He chuckled and put his arm around her. "Oh, I ran down once or twice and he leaped into the breach. He wants to do an article on me for his magazine. Can you tie that?"

She met Simon's gaze with a hostile one of her own. "When did you get that idea?"

Simon grinned. "After the twelfth story. Dr.—" He glanced at her father. "Uh . . . B.J. could make a fortune on the lecture circuit."

"No way, Simon. It's my work that's interesting, not me. Without it, I'd have nothing to say."

Amy narrowed her eyes and continued her scrutiny of Simon. He didn't care about Oren—or her father—all he wanted was a story. "Oren's waiting in the garden," she snapped, and ignored the puzzled looks the two men gave her.

Simon struggled upward, adjusted his crutches, and left the room. B.J. regarded her with raised eyebrows. "Something eating you?"

She sat a little taller. "Not a damned thing." He continued to study her with a worried expression. To avoid the questions she knew he'd start asking any minute, she went to the kitchen, poured herself a cup of coffee, and observed Oren and Simon's meeting from the window.

The men shook hands and settled themselves on a wrought iron bench. Five minutes later, Oren got up and started to pace. Simon made calming gestures, but as the conversation continued both men began to scowl and use their arms. Once, Simon shouted and pounded his fist into the palm of his hand.

Afraid they'd see her, she took her coffee into the living room and told her father what they'd found in Dr. Tambor's trash.

"Good Lord, don't tell Calder until you've got something more concrete," B.J. said. "Tom'll see you don't come within a mile of this case if you start rocking his boat."

"I won't rush things." She set her cup on the oak serving cart her father had brought in for Simon. "According to Simon, Elise used to have some very expensive jewelry. If Oren says she still has it, we'll have to let Tom know. This wouldn't be the first time robbery has led to murder."

"Right. I'll check it out with—" B.J.'s words were drowned out as the kitchen door slammed, rattling the windows.

Simon's crutches hit the floor in hard, vicious thuds as he crossed the kitchen. He came into the room where they sat and turned to face them. The change in his appearance made her shrink back. His eyes were blazing, his face pinched and hard-set. "I'm going to Montana," he said, and started for the front door.

Six

B.J. got to his feet. "Whoa there, boy. No sense rushing. The next ferry doesn't leave until evening."

Simon stopped so suddenly he nearly fell. "Damn, I forgot about that."

B.J. put a hand on his shoulder. "It takes a little getting used to. After awhile you learn it's something us gun jumpers need. Makes us think before we leap."

Amy heard a slight sound and turned to see Oren sagged against the door jam. A grayish pallor covered his features, and he looked as if he might collapse any minute.

She hurried to his side. "Dad, see if you can find some brandy, will you?" She took Oren's arm. "Let's get you to the couch."

Her father arrived with the brandy and shoved the drink into Oren's hand. "Here, son. Not what I'd call medicinal, but it appears to be what you need at the moment."

Oren downed the liquor in a few gulps and sat as if he'd turned to ice. No one spoke and when she could stand the uneasy silence no longer, she touched his shoulder. "Would it help to talk about it?"

He laughed and the harsh sound tore at her heart. "You'd never understand. Never. You couldn't." He hauled himself to his feet and stumbled down the hall toward his bedroom.

She stalked over to Simon who stood propped on his crutches. "What's he talking about? What did you say to him to make him like that?" When Simon didn't reply, her irritation grew. "Don't we have enough puzzles without you making more?" She folded her arms across her chest and glared. "Say something. I'm sick of not knowing what's going on."

He blew out his breath. "Oren's trying to say Elise may have played one too many games." He slumped against the wall as if suddenly very weary. "If she did her number here, she must have done it in Montana too . . . and that may be why she's dead."

"Oh . . ." Her anger dissolved leaving her drained and exhausted. She picked up her purse. "Shall we go?"

"Put Simon in the guest room," B.J. said.

"No, no, that's not necessary," Simon said. "I'll have Amy let me off at the motel by the ferry dock."

"Don't be ridiculous. I like your company and I have an empty guest room." B.J. followed them out and waited until Simon had gotten seated in the car. He leaned in the window. "I've got a mound of paper work to clear up at the morgue. When I get home, we'll talk some more. Meanwhile, catch up on your sleep."

Amy fed Cleo and Marcus, slept for a few hours, and set out for the big house up the hill. When she came in the front entrance, she heard voices in the kitchen and headed toward them. Simon and her father sat at Grandmother Prescott's trestle table in the kitchen eating lunch.

"Good morning." She slid her arm around her father's shoulders and kissed his bald, sun-tanned pate. She gave Simon a curt nod.

He observed her and B.J. with an engrossed expression. "Did you get some sleep?"

"Enough."

B.J. gave her a one-armed hug. "God, girl, you're sure getting skinny. Have a chicken sandwich. I aim to put some meat on your bones while you're home."

She pulled away from him. "You worry about your own weight. That extra flab around your middle isn't doing your health any good." She glanced sideways at Simon and saw him smiling at their nagging exchange. "I'm going downstairs and get to work."

"Great. I may join you in a bit." B.J. took a sip of his coffee. "Got your keys?"

She jingled the collection she carried, brushed by a tub-sized Boston fern that filled half the bay window where the men sat, and turned down a passageway.

In Grandfather Thaddeus's house, you ran into oddities everywhere, this wing happened to be one of them. He'd imported and exported goods and for many years had used his home as a warehouse. To meet his needs, the builders had constructed a full basement plus several multi-shelved store rooms along the hall.

At the end of the corridor, she turned off an alarm, unlocked a dead-bolted door, stepped through and re-locked it. She was now in a tiny anteroom. In front of her stood a sliding metal panel with a combination lock. The C.I.A. had nothing on her father when it came to security. His lab was a veritable fortress—barred windows, unbreakable glass, separate house and lab alarms. Only she and her father possessed keys and knew the lock combination.

His precautions had been forced on him by necessity. The penny-pinching county council frowned on up-dating the medical examiner's antiquated lab in Faircliff. Exasperated by their lack of foresight, her father had set up and furnished his own forensic laboratory. As a consequence, he stored much of the physical evidence he gathered here at home—a practice that galled Sheriff Calder.

She flipped a switch, triggering banks of ceiling fluorescents, and descended into the cool, white depths. Beside a microscope sat several dated, numbered, and sealed polyethylene bags. Each held material she and B.J. had vacuumed onto paper filters while examining Oren's apartment.

Processing the rug lint and microscopic particles proved time consuming and unrewarding. Two hour's labor produced only one item of interest—a number of gray, one millimeter long fibers. She'd have to use some of the instruments at the crime lab to determine the chemical composition.

She prepared several slides to take to Seattle when she returned, and browsed around in search of the blood-stained material. A table she passed contained the footprint casts she'd made. She paused to examine each with a magnifying glass, before continuing her hunt.

As she poked through head-high, metal shelf racks, a faint niggling began at the back of her mind. Something about the casts didn't quite . . . Two separately packaged shoes with Oren's case number rested on a lower shelf. Her father had probably already compared them to the print. Still, she wanted to be certain they hadn't overlooked some vital detail.

She set one of the shoes in the most distinct cast—a perfect match. Stone by stone, she continued to build a prison around Oren.

She sighed, went upstairs and found her father alone. "Thought I'd try to process the blood-stained stuff. Where is everything?"

"Locked in Tom's property room. He and the prosecuting attorney claim any decisions I make are bound to

76

be prejudiced. They've put in a request for an impartial medical examiner."

"Great. That's all Oren needs." She slumped onto a ladder backed chair. "Where's Simon?"

"He took a lot of notes and retired to the study to write his article." B.J. set a plate of cookies on the table, poured her a glass of milk and returned to his chair. "Interesting young man." He eyed her closely. "Don't you think so?"

She bit into a cookie. "M-m-m-m," she said, using her eating as an excuse to be noncommittal.

"Been everywhere." B.J. persisted, his manner still suspiciously watchful. "Seen a lot. Got several awards for outstanding journalism."

She studied him over the rim of her glass. *Don't start, Dad.* "If he spent the morning talking about himself, when did he have time to interview you?"

A pink tinge spread over B.J.'s cheeks. "Wasn't him, I did a bit of checking."

She shoved the plate of cookies aside. "Don't go getting ideas. Simon and I have only one interest in common, and that's Oren."

He moved the blue willowware sugar bowl an inch and lined the creamer up beside it. "A doctor or a nurse might get more information at that hospital in White Bird, Montana."

Still frowning, she mulled over his remark. Hospital personnel weren't necessarily loyal to each other, but let a lay person threaten any one of them and they formed a tight circle of silence. Only people in white penetrated the sanctum sanctorum. "You may be right."

His blue eyes glinted as he beamed at her. "Sure I am."

"Shouldn't the evidence we gathered come first?"

"No sense in doing much until the blood work is done. Besides, it won't take you more than a couple of days."

She scowled at him. "Are you sure you're not just trying to throw me and Simon together?"

"Ah . . . honey. I only want . . ." His fingers curled into a fist. "Dammit, it's time you forgot what that no-good bastard did to you and got on with your life."

She stood up so fast her chair tipped back against the wainscoted wall. "I'll decide." She took off for the study, her heels thudding the carpet at every step.

As she entered, Simon glanced up from where he sat at her father's desk. "Just the person I wanted to talk to."

She stopped short. Blast him, he always managed to put her off balance. "Oh . . . what about?"

He pushed his laptop computer to one side. "Mind if I mention your name in my article? B.J. says you two plan on going into the forensic consulting business. If my editor decides this is worth printing, it'll give you a lot of visibility."

Who was he *really* thinking about—her or himself? She scraped her shoe against her left ankle while she thought over his suggestion. "Wouldn't hurt I guess. Our profession needs informed, intelligent exposure—and it's difficult to come by."

"Fine." He pulled his computer in front of him, bent over the keys and seemed to forget she was present.

After shifting from one foot to the other several times, she screwed up her courage. "I'm going with you."

He straightened so quickly the computer case shot halfway across the desk. "You are not. I'm in no mood to cope with a woman—any woman."

She planted her hands on her hips. "With, or without you, I'm going." They glowered at each other.

"Jesus Christ, Amy, one woman's already been killed. I could be walking into all kinds of trouble."

She stood her ground. "Yeah, and you're in great shape to walk anywhere."

He opened his mouth as if to give her an argument. Closed it, and shrugged. "Take some warm clothes."

Two hours later, when she drove the station wagon up the hill to pick up Simon, her father handed her a large brown envelope. "Helen and I did some creative thinking," he said. "We figured you'd learn more if they think you're applying for a position as a nurse. So we fabricated a great resume and gave you a faultless recommendation on my old letterhead paper. We even invented a private hospital and administrator to applaud your superior qualifications and ran it off on a desktop printer."

She shook her head. "Dad, I do believe you have a criminal mind." She pulled out the resume and saw Amy Jamison printed at the top of the page. "Did you have to make it in my married name for heaven's sake?"

"We decided you shouldn't go in under Prescott. They may have seen my name and Oren's in the papers." He kissed her goodbye, and went around the car to grip Simon's hand. "Come back real soon." He smiled and waved as they drove away. "Take care."

When they arrived in Seattle, Simon had her drive past *Global News* so he could drop off the computer disk with his story, At 8 P.M., they caught Western Airlines flight out of SeaTac, changed planes twice and reached Lewistown, Montana at 7 A.M. As the fifteen seat Cessna circled for a landing, she noticed straight streets and many trees. The town was probably pretty as a picture postcard in summer. Now, it looked stark and cold.

When they disembarked she found the frigid, milky white air full of spinning ice crystals. The passengers hunched their shoulders and set off toward the waiting room. Simon followed, testing the icy pavement with his crutches before each swing forward. She straggled along behind lugging both their bags. The sound of the plane's engines still roared inside her head, setting up a painful throb.

Simon asked several of the passengers if they were going into town. A man who stood about six foot four, and looked as if he'd been born in his sweat-stained, low-crowned Stetson, Levi jacket, and jeans said, "Sure thing." He stuck out his hand. "I'm Clyde Freeman, owner of the Circle R ranch."

Simon shook his proffered hand, Simon introduced himself and Amy. "We'd appreciate it, if you'd give us a ride."

Mr. Freeman touched the brim of his hat, but his gaze didn't even acknowledge her presence. "Be glad to." He led the way to a mud-caked 1973 Buick, took the two bags she carried and jerked his head toward the back seat. After stowing the bags in the trunk, he smiled at Simon and opened the front door. "Sit up here, son."

Simon caught her eye, raised his brows and followed the rancher's directions. "You ever been to White Bird?" he asked after they were under way.

"Once or twice. You think this is cold? Don't hold a candle to White Bird."

Amy huddled in a corner of the backseat trying not to let her teeth chatter. She wore a flannel shirt, wool slacks, and a hooded coat, and still the cold sliced through as if she had nothing on.

Mr. Freeman lit a cigar and puffed a couple times until the fat tip glowed. "Wouldn't go near the place 'less I had friends there," he said.

"Oh? Why is that?" Amy asked. He made no reply until Simon repeated the question.

The big man grasped his cigar between two meaty fingers and swiveled his head toward Simon. "You still going?"

Simon frowned. "Of course we're going."

"Then I won't waste my breath." He jammed his cigar back in his mouth.

Seven

Thursday, October 27

Amy headed out of Lewistown on Highway 191. The car rental agency had had only a rather battered Toyota station wagon available. They hadn't quibbled. They'd already learned the bus traveled to White Bird only every other day. Besides, the Toyota had four-wheel drive and she might need it before they reached their destination.

"Were you able to find some warm clothing?" she asked.

Simon smiled and patted his leg. "Two piece thermals. Sure is an improvement. How about you?"

She shook her head. "I guess someone who's five foot five isn't supposed to wear a size four."

His heavy brows drew together. "Are you warm enough?"

"I brought a sweater and some extra socks. They help a little."

The road traveled past ranches and harrowed wheat fields. Frost laced every tree, every building, and every fence post. According to their map, White Bird lay in the Judith Mountains fifty or sixty miles to the northeast.

As she drove, she mulled over what she'd learned about

Elise: attractive, moody, evidently someone who manipulated men. She frowned. What had Simon meant by "games." Perhaps, Elise had bruised his and Oren's male ego—sufficient reason for both of them to want to keep it to themselves—but frustrating for someone trying to investigate a murder.

She looked over at Simon and smiled. He had the trouser leg of his suit stretched taut. His brows drawn together in a scowl, he gripped the razor blade he held, and concentrated on cutting stitches instead of blue worsted wool. "It's refreshing to meet a man who isn't helpless. Mitch couldn't cook, clean, or even make a bed."

Simon pushed his glasses farther up his nose. "Any man can. Maybe Mitch didn't want to."

"Probably. He was adept at side-stepping responsibility."

Simon studied her before returning to his task. "I'll be an expert seamstress by the time my ankle is healed."

She grinned. "Then you'll have another skill to fall back on in case your writing . . ." Oh, God, how stupid could she get? She glanced at him almost fearfully. He sat terribly still with tiny drops of blood oozing from a thin red line along his thumb. "I'm sorry, Simon. I didn't think." She stopped the car and pawed through her purse until she found a Band-Aid. He didn't resist when she took his hand and wrapped the Band-Aid across the cut.

After she finished, he released a long breath. "That's a nightmare every writer has to learn to live with." He gave a hollow laugh. "To quote my father, 'then I can get a real job.' "

She squeezed the hand she still held. "I'm sure you're much too critical of your work." She found herself becoming acutely conscious of the warmth of his hand. She quickly set it back in his lap and got the car under way.

At a sign post, she turned off the highway onto a two-lane road. Before many miles had passed, the cultivated land gave way to stretches of sage brush broken by deep gullies. The air had cleared, but a gray sky brushed the tops of shadowed mountains spanning the horizon.

They brought to mind the mountains at home, and from somewhere in her subconscious, an idea surfaced. "I wonder how Elise got from Seattle to the ferry dock last Friday?"

Simon gazed out the window at the harsh, shrub-dotted scenery. "She used to own a sports car."

"Suppose she still owned one. Where would it be?"

"Possibly at the ferry dock in either Anacortes or Faircliff." He chewed his lip. "I should think the sheriff would have checked that out first thing."

"Probably. I haven't talked to Tom Calder and he's not apt to tell me much when I do. But, if he hasn't found her car, we should try to. It could be important."

"I'll scout around when we get back." He fiddled with the heater control. "This thing is blowing cold air." Nothing he did seemed to bring forth heat, finally he turned it off. "We're going to get damned cold, Amy. Maybe we'd better turn around."

"Let's chance it. Shouldn't take us more than thirty minutes to get to White Bird."

"Okay . . . but just remember weather like this can be deadly."

She shivered. "I don't doubt it." The road straightened and her optimism rose as she increased her speed. The restful interval lasted for only a few miles before rough, pot-holed pavement slowed her to a crawl. Then it began to snow. The flakes weren't the big, fat, lazy kind—these whirled in a white mass. They upset her depth perception, disoriented her, and made her dizzy.

Her concentration became so intense, she jumped when Simon spoke. "Hm-m-m? . . . What did you say?"

"Can you feel your toes and fingers?"

She tried to think. "I don't know. They're just kind of a dead weight."

"Stop the car."

She stepped on the brake but had no sensation of doing so.

"Stamp your feet. Slap your hands together, blow on them."

She did as he instructed.

"Anything?"

"They feel as if I could break them off like dried sticks."

"Get out of the car."

She stared at him. "Into that? You must be nuts."

"Do it, dammit, and don't give me any argument." He got out on his side and teetered on one leg, so she reluctantly opened her door. "Run around the car. When you feel your feet you can stop." He balanced himself by holding onto the door and began to hop up and down.

She pulled up the hood of her coat and stuffed numb fingers in her pockets. Stiff legged as a female Frankenstein, she began to clump around the Toyota. She skidded and fell on the slippery blacktop.

"You all right?" Simon grabbed his crutches and started toward her.

"No, no . . . stay where you are." She pushed herself upright. "You don't need any more fractures." Ice-edged sleet stinging her face, she slogged round and round. Finally, she slumped against a fender beside him.

"Better?"

"Slightly." She plodded around to her side of the car. Each creaky movement of her joints took twice as much effort as usual and with the return of circulation came pain. She got inside and sat down before the cramps began in earnest.

"Damn, oh, damn." She gripped the steering wheel and clinched her teeth in an attempt to hide her agony, yet a whimper escaped her.

"Hurts like hell, doesn't it?"

She could only nod.

"As a rule, my internal heater keeps me warm, but one night in China, I thought I'd bought it for sure. An old man found me and thawed me out. Then I really wanted to die."

By the time she'd recovered enough to go on, the snow had changed to bigger, slower flakes. With improved visibility, she hoped the remaining miles would go faster.

The road wound through the mountains, growing steeper and rougher with every turn of the wheels and another hour passed before she began to see scattered hovels perched on the hillsides. Black smoke billowed from tin stove pipes protruding from tarpaper roofs. Hunks of cardboard patched broken windows and at least three half-dismantled cars littered each yard.

Simon looked at her and grinned impishly. "Want to go halves on one of these cozy little bungalows?"

She laughed. "Doubt if I could afford it. Real estate values must be out of sight."

The town was situated in a narrow cleft with cliffs rising on either side. Tufts of frost-blackened grass sprouted from cracked sidewalks, a row of half-dead trees pointed broken white snags at the sky. In the distant past, a stonemason had erected half a dozen ponderous rough granite structures. All were square with few windows and the man had made no attempt to soften or beautify the stern facades. Several of the buildings appeared vacant—doors stood ajar, windows had been smashed, and wild, untrimmed shrubbery surrounded them.

"Beautiful downtown White Bird." Simon rubbed a hole in the steam clouded windshield and peered out.

"There's a restaurant up ahead. Let's grab a bite, then use their rest room to change into our powerhouse duds."

She glanced at her watch. Simon had an appointment with Marchmont Hospital's administrator at two-thirty. She had one with the Director of Nurses at three. "Ought to work out just right."

Inside, wonderful warmth enveloped her. Sharp tingling in her fingers and toes blunted her enjoyment and she sought to ignore it by looking over the place. Spurs, bridles, horse shoes, and blackened cattle brands decorated weathered barn board walls. They found a booth upholstered in saddle tan vinyl and sat down.

Simon flashed a big smile when a waitress detached herself from a counter where she'd been leaning and came toward them. "Now watch the old Kittredge charm."

The young woman raised and lowered thickly mascaraed lashes and curved carmine lips into a smile. "Did you fall off your horse, Lancelot?"

Simon's smile broadened. "Nope, a dragon took a bite out of it."

An ample hip clad in lime green nylon brushed his arm. "That's a crying shame. Good men are hard to find." She pulled a pencil from her thatch of permed blonde hair, wet the tip, and leaned toward him displaying an astounding amount of cleavage. "See anything you'd like to have?"

Simon's amused gaze met Amy's over the edge of the menu and his right eyebrow lifted ever so slightly as if to say, 'Told you so.' She returned it with a 'We'll see' expression. As she sat back to watch, she realized their relationship had taken several steps forward. Although she'd known him only four days, they were already able to communicate with eye signals.

"What would you suggest?" Simon asked.

The waitress ran the tip of her tongue along her lip.

"You want something cold"—her glance slid to Amy and back to Simon—"or something hot."

Amy covered a smile and Simon's cheeks reddened. "Soup," he said hastily. "Any kind. I need something to warm the inner man."

She tossed her head. "You need some educatin' fella." She favored Amy with a bland, disinterested look and took her order.

"You lived here long?" Simon asked, after she put her order book in her pocket.

"All my life."

He bestowed a smile that brought forth a dimple in his cheek. "Maybe you could help me. I'm trying to locate a woman by the name of Elise Dorset. She was born in White Bird. Have you ever heard of her or her family?"

"You a reporter?" Her gaze darted around the room. "People in White Bird don't take to reporters."

"No, no, nothing like that. I'm doing a family genealogy. The Dorsets are distant relatives."

Her brow puckered and she scratched her head with her pencil. "A jean-ee-ology huh? Oh . . . that's different." She swayed toward him. "The name Dorset does sound kinda familiar."

"She worked at Marchmont Hospital," Amy said, hoping to jar the woman's memory before she got too engrossed with Simon.

The woman stiffened and started backing away. "I gotta get to work," she said, and scuttled away.

The restaurant's service was slow. By the time they'd eaten and changed clothes, not enough time remained before their appointment to have the car's heater checked. The minute she got outside cold penetrated Amy's dark blue pin-striped suit and nylon stockings instantly. Inside the car the temperature was only slightly warmer and goose pimples prickled her arms and legs.

The road leading to the hospital snaked through scabrous hills where snow had reached a depth of six or eight inches. The covering did little to improve the surroundings. Enormous rocks hemmed in the narrow track on one side, on the other the ground dropped off sharply. In the arroyo below, boulders stuck through the blanketing white like jagged black teeth.

At last, they came to a mesa where a high stone wall stretched out on both sides of massive iron gates. A guard checked their identification and she issued up a prayer of thanks that she hadn't thrown away the driver's license with her married name.

"Why the tight security?" Simon asked.

"Mr. Marchmont's orders," the guard said, and returned to the small building from which he had emerged.

She drove by a series of turreted six-story gothic structures and let Simon off in front of the largest one.

"If this is a hospital, I hope to God I don't get sick while I'm in White Bird," Simon said.

"Amen to that."

Since she had a half hour to squander, she decided to drive through the grounds. The track angled off to the right where it passed three four-story, red brick buildings that appeared to be apartments.

Around the curve, the terrain angled upward and on a knoll, silhouetted against the sky, sat a white Georgian-style house. On the far side, a head-high boxwood hedge blocked the sweep of rolling lawn surrounding the residence. Through a gap in the branches, she glimpsed a row of white crosses.

She got out, pushed open a wooden gate and moved hesitantly toward the first row of crosses.

"What the hell you doing, lady?" A burly man clad in blue coveralls rushed out of a wood frame hut. "You got no business in this place. Ya hear?" Wild eyes glistened under a tangle of black hair. His fingers fastened on her shoulder and bit into the flesh. "Only person's allowed in is Mr. Marchmont. You got that?" He spun her around. "Now you git."

She needed no urging. Ten minutes later when she entered the hospital, her hands were still shaking. At the reception desk, she asked for Mrs. Demetrius. The woman directed her down a broad hall.

She hadn't gone far when a metal door blocked the way. A sign said to ring the bell. She did, and again had to produce ID. before the guard let her past him. Inside, the odor of pine disinfectant filled her nostrils. Women attired in shapeless, pink-striped dresses shuffled by, their unkempt hair framing dull, uncaring eyes. A white-clad nurse or orderly accompanied each patient.

When she arrived at another metal door, the nerves in her back tightened. What kind of a hospital was this anyway? Again a guard let her through. In this section, the women wore blue and white-striped dresses and seemed a trifle more alert. The corridor took several bends before she came to an office labeled Director of Nurses.

The receptionist checked Amy's name off a clipboard list and handed her a job application form to fill out. When Amy finished, the bland-faced woman ushered her into the director's office. "Mrs. Demetrius will be with you shortly." She lay Amy's application in a wire basket and left.

A massive desk with a brass name plate proclaiming Jacenta Demetrius as owner, dominated the large room. Against a far wall ranged several file cabinets.

Amy heard a slight cough and realized a woman holding a sheaf of papers stood near one of the cabinets. She had pale blonde hair and was stick thin. Her pallid face and washed-out blue-striped dress blended with the walls. No wonder she hadn't seen her. For an instant the file clerk's faded blue eyes met hers and she thought she saw her head move from side to side.

Before she could be sure, a side door burst open and a woman who looked at least six feet tall strode in. At her right temple an inch wide swathe of white swept upward through coal black hair. On either side of her high cheek-boned face, intricately carved carnelian combs held back her straight hair, accentuating dark, deep-set eyes. The red silk blouse she wore with her black suit made her even more striking.

Jacenta Demetrius. Amy wet her dry throat, stood up and stretched out her hand. "I'm Mrs. Jamison."

The director clasped it in a perfunctory greeting. "So you got here in spite of the blizzard." As she spoke, her gaze swept over Amy in a swift inventory. "Sit down." She picked up Amy's application and seated herself in a deeply upholstered white leather chair behind the desk.

Amy perched on the edge of the only chair available—straight-backed, hard-seated, and placed directly in front of the imposing expanse of gleaming teak.

She tried to keep her hands still and her face serenely composed as the minutes dragged by. Nevertheless, as the woman went over the questionnaire and read the letters of recommendation, perspiration gathered beneath Amy's clothing. Would she get an opportunity to ask about Elise, or would all this anxiety be for nothing?

"Do you have people in White Bird?" Mrs. Demetrius asked.

"No. I'm staying with a cousin in Lewistown temporarily." Amy let her gaze fall to her hands, bit her lip and called upon all her acting ability. "I'm recently divorced. I . . . I have to find a place where my husband won't be able to . . ." When she raised her head her eyes were filmed with tears. "To find me," she finished in a small voice.

"Ah, I see." Mrs. Demetrius's piercing black eyes met Amy's and held until Amy gave way and lowered her gaze. The director tapped the letters of recommendation. "Evidently, from what these say, you have good nursing skills."

She lay the sheets of paper on the desk and scrutinized Amy. "Takes a certain kind of person to work in a place like this. We get all kinds you know, manic depressives, paranoid schizophrenics, and criminally insane."

Oh my God. Amy flattened her spine against the wooden chairback, using the hard pressure point to keep her mind centered and her face expressionless. "Yes, so I understand."

Mrs. Demetrius picked up an ivory-handled letter opener. Light glinted on the long steel blade as she ran it between thumb and forefinger. "Who told you about Marchmont?"

My move. Amy slowed her speeding pulse. "When one of my friends heard I was moving to Lewistown, she mentioned the hospital." She hesitated unsure how far to go, then continued in a smooth, unruffled tone. "She was born and raised in White Bird and used to work at Marchmont."

Mrs. Demetrius pursed thin lips. "How fortuitous. What's her name?"

Amy fixed her gaze on the director's face. "Elise Dorset."

The letter opener fell from Mrs. Demetrius's hand and clattered on the desk. She opened her mouth, closed it, then opened it again. "No one named Elise Dorset has ever been employed here."

A slight cough drew Amy's gaze to the cabinets behind Mrs. Demetrius. The clerk she'd thought so listless stood braced against the wall. Her eyes blazed and anger contorted her face. When she saw she had Amy's attention, she mouthed words Amy couldn't make out.

Mrs. Demetrius caught the momentary lapse in Amy's attention and swiveled her chair, but the blonde had already reverted to her former posture of lassitude. "What're you doing here? You know trustees aren't supposed to be in this room when I'm interviewing."

"I . . . I only had a few more things to file. I thought I'd . . ."

Demetrius pointed to the door. "Get out." When it closed behind the shuffle-gaited trustee, she turned back to Amy.

"That's strange . . . really strange." Amy said in a last ditch effort to make her trip pay off. "Why would Elise lie about a thing like that?"

"I can't imagine." Mrs. Demetrius swept Amy's application papers into a drawer and closed it with a bang. "We don't have any openings at present."

"No openings at all? I really need a job."

Demetrius leveled an icy glance. "This is a mental institution not a social service bureau." She stood up. "That'll be all, Ms. Jamison, I have work to do."

Battle-ax. Amy straightened her shoulders, raised her chin and marched from the room. But, when the outer office door closed behind her, all the starch went out of her legs and she leaned against the wall. After a few minutes, she regained her composure, gave her skirt a twitch and set out for the first check point.

"P-s-st . . . Miss."

The blonde beckoned from a bend in the corridor. Amy took a step toward her. A low watt light globe overhead caused darkness to pool in recessed doorways. This wasn't smart. Trustee or not, the woman must be mentally unstable otherwise she wouldn't be here—unless she'd been committed for a crime. A chill climbed her spine.

Nevertheless, she hesitated only an instant before moving forward. She'd come for information and she'd get it wherever she could.

A claw-like hand clutched her arm. "My name is Francine . . . Francine Anseth." She drew Amy deeper into the shadows. "She lied to you," she hissed. She darted a glance over her shoulder. "The stupid bitch has the hots for him. She'll learn just like all the rest of 'em have." She pulled Amy closer and her sour breath struck Amy in the face. "Elise was here. I knew her. She—" A door slammed and the woman's eyes went wild. "I got to go. If she catches me, she'll put me in the cage."

"Wait." Amy rummaged in her purse, found a business card and wrote her island phone number on the back. "If you get a chance, call me collect. I must talk to you." The woman jammed the card in her pocket and scurried away like a mouse searching for cover.

Feeling vaguely like Alice in Wonderland, Amy pumped up her courage again and started down the passageway. Marchmont was a mental institution—yet no one had mentioned it, not Elise's job application, nor the man who'd given them a lift in Lewistown, nor the waitress in White Bird. Why?

The back of her neck tingled as she made her way through straggling patients. Were eyes watching her? Or had the aura of paranoia tainted *her* mind too? Panic squeezing her chest, she rushed down the corridor, turned the corner, and collided with an obese man.

He wore a knit watch cap, blue coveralls, and a full beard fell over his chest in a tousled mass. She shifted to the right. With a gap-toothed grin, he slid in front of her. She stepped to the left and he followed suit.

"My, my, little lady," he wheezed. ''You in a hurry or sumpthin'?"

She held her ground and eyed him coldly. "Get the hell out of my way, or I'll call a guard."

"Who-o-e-e, and she's got spirit too." He moved nearer. "I like women with spirit."

She rammed her high heel into his instep, he let out a bellow and grabbed for her, but she dodged past him, dashed down the hall, and out the front door.

Eight

Her breath came in noisy gasps as she slid into the front seat of the car.

Simon regarded her with concern. "What happened?"

She gulped air. "Some slob made a pass at me."

"A pass? Good God, what a zoo. Did you find out anything?"

She related her encounter with Mrs. Demetrius and Francine Anseth. "When the dragon lady told me Marchmont was a mental institution, I nearly gave myself away."

"I lucked out, Wade Marchmont's secretary clued me in, otherwise I might have blown my whole story."

"What's he like?"

"Tall, well built, thick wavy hair. It's pure white, but he looks to be in his early fifties. He's one of those salesman types—stock smile, firm grip, hawk-eyed."

"Was he helpful?"

"No way. I told him I was doing a follow-up on a story and shoved a copy of the headline article on Elise in front of him. For a second, he looked as if he'd been hit in the stomach." Simon leaned toward her. "But get this. When I mentioned Elise had once worked for him, he said I'd been misinformed, that he'd never heard of the woman."

"Someone's lying."

"That's for sure. The question is who."

"Something else strange. I wandered into a cemetery and the caretaker ran me off. Said only Mr. Marchmont was allowed in."

"Weird." He scowled and nodded his head. "Damned weird as a matter of fact." He peered out the window at a couple of men who were hurrying down the hospital steps.

She followed his gaze. "That's him." She pointed. "The big guy with a beard. He's the one who made the pass."

"Let's get out of here, Amy. Now!"

She gunned the motor, shot the car in reverse, and took off, spraying slush behind her. Just as she leaned into the gravel road's first switchback, she heard the rumble of a full-throated engine and looked in the rearview mirror. A black high-jacked truck caromed around the corner and bore down on them.

She moved to the right to let him go by, but he rammed the Toyota from behind instead. "Sweet Jesus!" She jammed on the brakes as the station wagon lurched and veered toward a jagged wall of heaped stone thrusting skyward on the inside shoulder.

Simon grabbed the dashboard to brace himself. "What the hell's going on?"

She jerked the wheel, the Toyota missed a boulder, fishtailed and began to side slip toward another. Cold sweat springing out on her skin, she spun the wheel in the direction of the skid. The car headed for a jutting crag. "Overdid it. Damn, oh damn." She gunned the motor and they squeaked past with only inches to spare.

In the outside lane, the driver of the truck drew even with her. She glimpsed the two men who'd come out of the hospital. The bearded one grinned, yanked the wheel, and smacked her car with his front fender. The lighter vehicle jounced sideways. She steadied it, floored the accelerator, and took off, steering toward the center of the two-lane track.

Her move backfired. As soon as the man saw an opening, he edged his truck into the inside lane. His motor revved to an ear-splitting howl, he pulled alongside and crowded her toward the road's precipitous edge. Fear clutched her insides. The rock-choked arroyo lay far below.

The truck's wide-track tires pressed nearer and nearer until the vehicle's black presence filled her vision. Metal shrieked against metal. Perspiration stung her eyes and her arms ached from holding the steering wheel. Inch by inch she gave way. "Let up, damn you." She clenched her teeth and took a tighter grip on the wheel. "Get ready to jump, Simon, another foot or two and we'll go over." Suddenly, the truck shot by them, sped down the road, spun around, and roared straight for them.

"Look out, Amy. He's going to ram us." Simon braced his arms.

She crammed the gears into reverse. *Please God make it work.* Blue smoke billowing and gravel spurting like machine gun bullets, the Toyota plowed an uphill furrow. Foot by agonizing foot, she cork-screwed the car backward until only empty space stood between the speeding truck and the road's edge. The driver saw the danger, braked, and went into a tire squealing skid.

Amy shifted into low and waited. "Hang on, Simon, this may be close." Soon as she saw a clear path, she double-clutched, shifted into second and careened past the yawing vehicle.

Simon craned his neck to look back. "They're going over." He straightened around. "Both of them got out. More than the sons-a-bitches deserve."

She stopped the car and put her head on her folded

arms. Her body quivered. She felt sick to her stomach. Tears filled her throat and she fought to keep them from flooding her eyes.

Simon rested his hand on her shoulder. "You did a great job of driving, doc. Andretti couldn't have done any better."

She blinked and gave a shaky laugh. "I used to live such a sedate, ordered life." She ran a hand over her face. "That jerk tried to run us off the road just because I refused to play games with him. Can you believe it?"

"I wonder . . ." Simon scowled and shook his head. "We've sure stepped into a cesspool up to our arm pits."

"You said it. Let's get the heater fixed and get out of this burg."

"I'm for that."

She drove to Demski's Auto Repair, the only garage in town. When they pulled in, a man came out to the car. His narrow, distended chest and gaunt face hinted at emphysema, but a cigarette hung from thin, colorless lips. She rolled down the window.

He plucked the cigarette from his mouth with grease-stained fingers. "I'm Boris Demski. You folks want something?"

Simon explained about the heater. The man sniffed and wiped a drip from his thin nose with the sleeve of his faded flannel shirt. "I'll get to it soon as I can, but you'll have to leave it overnight."

She and Simon exchanged startled glances, then she shrugged. "I guess it's either that, or head back to Lewistown as is."

"No way," Simon said. "The temperature in these hills can plummet at night." He dipped his head to get the garage man's attention. "Are there any motels?"

"Only one is the Mountain View." He pointed down

the street. "Four blocks that way." He eyed their clothes. "Ain't what you folks are used to, that's for sure."

"Thanks," Amy said, and started the motor.

Simon caught sight of the motel first. "God, what a dump."

She pulled into the Mountain View's rutted driveway and parked in front of a door marked office. Rust streaks from a broken gutter stained peeling white paint. She exhaled deeply. "I guess this is what you call roughing it."

They went inside, found no one there and rang the bell on the desk. Five minutes went by before a frail, white-haired man tottered in. "Can I help you?" Pale watery blue eyes peered at them through thick-lensed glasses.

"We need a couple of rooms," Simon told him.

"Yes, sir." The man frowned, opened a drawer, and hunted inside. "Now what did I do with those cards? My son usually tends the place, but he's away right now." After two more attempts, he finally came up with what he needed.

They registered and got their keys. "If you'll open your door, I'll bring in your luggage," she said. A few minutes later, when she came into his room, she was struck by the incongruent picture he made. Cracked and yellowed plaster walls, cigarette burned linoleum, and Simon standing in the middle of the tawdry surroundings wearing a Lord & Taylor suit.

"It's all my fault," he said. "I got you into this mess. First, I get you damned near killed and now this." He waved his hand.

"Don't be silly. I insisted on coming."

"Well, I've lived in this kinda country. I should have known how it'd be."

"Stop it, Simon, we're here and we'll make do."

"Yeah, take a look at that. You weren't kidding about roughing it." He pointed to a lumpy bed covered with grayed sheets and a raveled wool blanket. "And wait until you see the bathroom. Damn thing looks as if it was put in before I was born."

She set his suitcase in a corner. "Let's change clothes and go get something to eat. When we're warm and have a full stomach, maybe we can find a funny side to all this."

He pinched his lips together. "That'll take some doing."

She turned up the thermostat. "The place will look less bleak when it's warm." In her room next door, she changed into slacks, rejoined him and drove the car to the garage. After arrangements had been made with Mr. Demski, they walked across the street to the restaurant.

She grinned at him as she held the door open. "One thing nice about White Bird, you needn't make a lot of choices."

He managed a smile. "Cause there aren't any."

They settled in a booth of the nearly empty cafe and she looked around for the blonde waitress. A thickset lady with permed gray hair appeared instead. She beamed at them with lively brown eyes and took their order. Later, after they'd eaten a surprisingly good steak, she returned to ask if they wanted desert.

Both of them chose the apple pie with hot cinnamon sauce. "It's good," the woman said. "I made it myself."

Amy smiled at her. "Jack of all trades, huh?"

"Kind of. What're you kids doing in this end of creation? You lose your way?"

"We're looking for a relative," Simon said. "You ever heard of the Dorsets?"

"Sorry. I've only been here a couple a months. My brother's ailing and I came to look after him." She pursed her lips. "Why don't you try old Doc Yates? He seems to know everybody"—she winked—"and what they've done that they shouldn't." She jerked her head toward the street. "He's just up the block."

When she returned with their pie, she leaned toward them and said in a low pitched voice, "You best go when you're done here. Doc tends to hoist a few, soon as his patients are gone."

By the time they got outside, night had fallen. In the center of the street, a light with a metal reflector twisted and clanked with each gust of icy wind.

Amy turned up her coat collar to shield her face. "Spooky, isn't it?" Each word made a frosty puff in the night air.

"You said it. Add a few bats and ghosts and we'd be all set for Halloween." Simon set off in the direction the waitress had indicated.

Amy matched her stride to that of his crutches, each step making a squeaky crunch in blue-white ankle-deep snow. Near the end of the block, they came to a neatly trimmed hedge. When she glimpsed the beautifully preserved Queen Anne Victorian house it surrounded, she stopped in amazement. White gables topped off blue, fish-scale shingled walls.

She clasped Simon's arm. "Isn't it beautiful?" She took a few more steps. "Look at the arched bays and all that stained glass."

"It's something all right. Seems out of place in a decaying town like this."

The hedge ended a little farther on at an elaborate wrought iron gate. From an overhead bracket hung a sign with Harold Yates, M.D. painted in crisp black script.

"Get a load of the grounds." Simon opened the gate and started up the walk. "He must work at Marchmont too. Takes money to keep up a mini-park."

They climbed wide porch steps. "Maybe," she said. "But, salaries are seldom high at state-run institutions."

102

She lifted the brass knocker and gave the metal plate several sharp raps.

Footsteps sounded, the door swung wide and a balding, stoop-shouldered man stood swaying before them. "Well, what can I do for you, young lady?" Simon stepped into the circle of light, and the man spied his crutches. "Come in. Come in." He made a broad gesture that nearly unbalanced him. "Doc Yates never turns away a wounded pilgrim."

Simon shrugged and led the way inside. The drawing room they entered had a decorative pressed tin ceiling, parquet floor and a carved marble mantelpiece that Amy would have given her eyeteeth to own.

"Sir, we don't want to take up your time, we . . ." Simon began.

The doctor shambled up behind them. "No problem. No problem. Jes go on in there." He pointed to a door. "I'll be with ya soon as I find my white coat." He grinned at Amy, laid a finger along side his bulbous, blue-veined nose and snickered. "Gotta look pro-fesh-in-ul doncha know."

Simon let out a noisy breath. "Dr. Yates," he said. "This is a personal, not a professional call."

The doctor rocked forward onto his toes, then back onto his heels as he absorbed this bit of news. "At's great. Don't get to talk to anyone new in this God-forsaken hole. Sit down. Sit down."

He waved them to a tufted, gold velvet sofa and lowered his bulky body onto a throne-like chair. An instant later, he levered himself upward. "I'll getcha a drink. Can't go out in this cold unless you're fortified."

Simon put out his hand. "No. No. Please don't bother. I'm wobbly enough on these aluminum pins as it is."

The doctor directed a longing glance toward the cherry

103

wood cabinet and sank back in his chair. "So who are you and what's your problem?"

Simon introduced Amy and himself, then leaned forward. "I was told you could help me locate a relative of mine."

Dr. Yates's deep chuckle caused his ample belly to jiggle. "Don't doubt it. I been birthin' babies and helpin' the old ones take their last breath for close onto forty years. What's this person's name?"

Simon's eyes centered on the doctor's face. "Elise, Doctor Yates. Elise Dorset."

The man's face turned chalk-white, his eyes bulged, and his mouth worked like a fish gulping air. "Who sent you here with their filthy lies?"

Simon's hand closed over hers and gripped it hard. "Marchmont said—"

Dr. Yates plunged to his feet. "I knew it." He staggered across the room, turned, flattened himself against the wall and glowered at them. "Wade won't get away with this. I know things." A furtive, calculating expression spread over his face. "Lots of things." He pointed a shaky finger at them. "You tell him that. Now get out of my house."

Neither of them spoke until the doctor's gate closed behind them, then Simon grabbed her in a one-armed hug. "Talk about a hunch paying off."

She hugged him back. "And how. Off hand I'd say you lit a fuse."

He let her go. "Right. But if those two start comparing notes, it won't be too healthy for us around here."

She hurried along at his side. "Why should the mention of Elise's name scare people?"

"It's weird. If she was a threat to Marchmont, you'd think he'd have been relieved by her death. But that wasn't the impression I got." He blew on his hands to warm

104

them. "Move closer to the buildings. The wind's less sharp there."

Ponderous gray stone hunkered like great prehistoric beasts on both sides of them greedily sucking up the street light's faint beam. Wind whined through vacant rooms, banging doors, rattling broken windows. Frigid air seared her lungs with each breath. She lengthened her stride. "Never thought I'd look forward to reaching that motel."

Something rustled in the doorway beside her. She swung to the right and saw a dark form detach itself from the gloom. *A man!* She got out a scream before he grabbed her and muffled the sound with his hand.

"What the hell—?" Simon began. An instant later, she heard the metal clangor of his crutches, a grunt, and the thud as someone fell.

"Got him," a voice wheezed in the darkness. "Damned city-bred punk didn't know what hit him."

Oh, God. The bearded man!

"Good goin', Con." The man who held her tightened his grip around her waist and dragged her inside. She twisted, kicked, got an arm free and hit out at him, but his heavy coveralls cushioned her blows.

When he reached the middle of the barnlike room, he dumped her on the floor. The minute his hand unclamped from her mouth, she let out a piercing scream.

"Dammit, Cecil, shut her up. Can't you do anything right?"

Cecil sprang toward her. "Smart-ass bitch. You'd better pipe down, if you know what's good for you."

She scooted backwards, hoping to elude him in the dark.

"Don't try it, damn you." He flung himself on top of her.

They rolled on the floor, kicking bottles, cans, and

cardboard cartons. Finally, he wrapped his thin wiry legs around her, held her down, and tore off her coat.

Boards splintered somewhere and in the faint glimmer of the swinging street light she saw Simon ram his head into Con's belly. Hope renewed her strength and another resounding shriek burst from her. Cecil punched her in the jaw and for a second everything went gray at the edges.

"Save your breath, lady. Nobody in this town's gonna do nuthin'." He chuckled over his private joke. "They know who butters their bread." He ripped her blouse from neck to hem, then snatched off her bra and tossed it aside. "Man, would you look at that," he breathed. "For a skinny broad, you sure got a great pair of knockers."

"Get off me, you filthy bastard." She heaved her body upward in an effort to unseat him.

He laughed, bent down and licked her breast. "Let's have some fun. What do ya say, baby?"

Simon stopped pummeling Con and turned his head. "You try it and I'll kill you." Con's fist caught Simon off balance and he crumpled to the floor.

Con stood over him, and the sound of his rasping wheeze filled the room. "That'll hold you, you nosy sonuvabitch."

Cecil ran his hand down her bare belly until he found the band of her slacks. He gave a couple of yanks, the zipper parted, the seams ripped. He tossed them aside. Breathing fast, he clawed at her stockings until he got them off and gazed down at her bikini panties. "Whoo—ee lady, you really turn a guy on." He unzipped his coveralls. "I'm gonna take her in the back room, Con."

"Bull said to strip her, knock her out, and let the weather do the rest," Con bellowed. "Now, you get with it 'fore I club you one."

"Ah, geez Con, I'm really hurtin'. I ain't had a woman

since Bull sent those last two kooks to the cage." He got to his feet. "Who's to know, if you don't tell him?"

She bent her leg, straightened it, and rammed her foot into his crotch. He let out a strangled scream and collapsed in a moaning heap. She scrabbled through the litter, found a rock, and brought it down on his head.

"What's going on over there?" Con started toward her, his big arms outspread.

Naked except for her shredded blouse and panties, she leaped up and scuttled into the shadows. If she could keep out of his reach until she got to the door maybe . . . Something sharp stabbed into the sole of her left foot. A twist of pain caught her and she cried out.

Con reached her in one stride. "Think you're going to get away, do ya?" He backhanded her, she went flying, struck the wall, and slid down.

In a red haze, she saw the glint of light on metal as Simon swung his crutch. She fought off faintness until darkness closed over her.

Nine

A noise brought Amy to. She jerked upright and looked wildly around the lighted room. What had happened? Where was she? Simon appeared in a doorway. "Oh, thank God, it's you." She flopped back on the pillow. This was his motel room and his jacket covered her half naked body.

Simon sat on the edge of the bed and gently bathed her bruised face. The cold cloth took away her weakness, but didn't quiet the quivering in her stomach. If Simon hadn't recovered, both of them would be . . . She grabbed Simon's hand. "What happened? Are they dead?"

A muscle knotted in his jaw. "No. Bent my crutch on the big one, but his head's hard. That scrawny bastard didn't rape you, did he?" She shook her head and he released his breath.

A terrifying thought made her struggle upward. "Will they come here?"

"They might." He eased her back on the pillow. "You lie still, I want to take a look at your foot." He wiped blood from the sole of her left foot with the washcloth. "This is a good sized wound, Amy. You'd better see a doctor when we get to Lewistown."

She sat up. "I have to take a shower."

"There's no hot water." He went over and moved the thermostat back and forth. "And it's colder than hell in here."

"I don't care. That slime ball had his hands on me. He . . . he . . ." She shuddered. "I have to get clean."

He pulled the blanket around her. "Stay put. I'll go talk to the manager." He frowned, then crossed to a wooden kitchen chair that leaned against the wall. He worked the wobbly leg loose and handed it to her. "If anybody tries to gets in, hit 'em."

As he started out, she noticed he didn't have his crutches. "You aren't supposed to put your weight on your foot for a week."

He bowed his shoulders, but didn't turn around. "Just add it to the list of other things I shouldn't have done."

In a short while, she heard banging noises coming from her room next door. A few minutes later, Simon appeared carrying a blanket and her suitcase. His face was tight with anger.

"The manager's gone. A note on his door says he won't be back until morning." He flung the blanket on a chair, and set her suitcase beside the bathroom door. "And there isn't any hot water or heat in your room either." He pushed the heavy bureau in front of the window. "I'm going to barricade us in. Okay?"

"Yes, oh yes." When he started shoving the bed toward the door, she eased her weight onto her foot and insisted on helping. He protested but she wouldn't be put off.

After they got the bed into place and had moved the dresser in front of the one window, Simon gazed around the room. "That's about all we can do." He picked up the blanket he'd brought. "I'll spread this on the bed while you put on your night things."

"But . . ."

"I'm going to stand watch."

She folded her arms. "But, Simon." Her shivering made her determined stance look ludicrous. "Your eye is bruised and God knows what else. That man hurt you. I know he did. You need to rest."

Simon tucked in a blanket corner and squinted up at her. "Your legs are turning blue and you're getting blood on the linoleum."

She sighed noisily, took her suitcase, and went into the bathroom. The shower dribbled, the faucets dripped, the toilet flowed steadily. Frost coated the window and a thick layer of ice covered the sill.

Reluctantly, she unzipped Simon's coat, stepped into the rust stained bathtub, took a speedy shower, and tried to dry herself on a threadbare towel. Goose flesh pimpled her skin as she pawed through the clothes she'd packed. After she got her flannel pajamas on, she'd feel fine, she told herself. She dressed quickly, wrapped a handkerchief around her foot, put on a pair of socks and rejoined Simon.

He lay the coat she handed him on a chair and turned back the covers of the bed. "Get in before you get any more chilled than you are."

Her chattering teeth prevented her from arguing. She did as he directed, curled up in a ball, and waited for her body to thaw out. Cold air came in from the walls and up from the floor. She couldn't stop shaking.

She heard footsteps, peeked from the covers, and found Simon draping the towels and bath mat over her.

"We have to get you warm." He unzipped his jacket and put that over her too.

She reared up in bed. "You can't do that, you'll freeze. Maybe we could find a way to get into the other rooms. They must have blankets in them."

He shook his head. "My key fit all the doors so I checked. All the rooms were bare. Not even a mattress."

He clumped back and forth. "I'm sorry, Amy. I've done some screw-loose things in my time, but this tops them all."

"You're not God, Simon." She flipped back the blankets. "Get in here."

"No, I'll manage."

Her shivering grew more violent. She stiffened her muscles in an attempt at control. "Don't be a damned fool."

"All right. All right." He moved a night stand to his side of the bed, set the lamp and the wooden chair leg on it, then switched off the light. After considerable rustling around, he slid into bed. "Careful you don't hit my cast with your sore foot. My socks and long johns won't stretch over it." He wrapped his arms around her and pulled her into the curve of his body.

His wonderful warmth enveloped her, and her muscles unclenched for the first time since she'd landed in Lewistown. She patted his jersey-clad arm. "Thanks," she said sleepily, and sank into a delightfully warm oblivion.

Sometime during the night, she dreamed she was making love in a sun-drenched meadow. At first, she thought the man to be Mitch and she struggled to get free. Then he laughed and called her, Doc, and she realized it was Simon.

Her body came alive and that Simon should be the one who sparked it seemed not at all out of reason. As he bent over her, the sun's rays caught on his chestnut hair and turned it into a glowing crown. "You're the woman for me," he said, and nuzzled her neck.

She awoke to find what she'd dreamed had been triggered by more than her subconscious. Simon's hand had worked its way under her pajama top and cupped her bare breast. His lips caressed her neck.

"Julie," he whispered. "Julie, love." His hand left her breast and moved across her abdomen.

She whimpered—a thin childlike sound. Not her. Never her. A golf-ball-sized lump jammed her throat. She slipped out of bed, crept into the bathroom and stayed there until the frigid cold drove her back.

The bed squeaked as she got in, waking Simon. He turned on the light. "You okay?"

"I'm just f-fine." She forced her shivering body to be still.

He stared down at her with dream-clouded eyes. "Amy"—he moved closer, bent his head—"I need . . ." He brushed his fingers across her cheek and touched her bottom lip with his forefinger. "Amy, would it be all right if I kiss you?"

She felt his erection against her thigh and knew what he really wanted. "Yes," she murmured, closing her eyes and tilting her chin. She cringed at her weakness—a strong woman wouldn't barter her body for a word, a touch, some show of tenderness to fill the void where her heart had once been.

His lips met hers, gentle, soft, questioning.

Blood that had been moving like slush through her veins warmed and her lips parted under his. Then, they were kissing hungrily as if neither of them would ever get enough. Yet, even then she could hear Mitch's jeering voice, "Why shouldn't I bed other women? You got about as much sex appeal as a dead fish."

Simon unbuttoned her pajama jacket and covered her breast with his hand. "Um-m-m, you feel so nice." Suddenly his entire body went rigid. "Oh, Christ!" He broke away from her, sat up and swung his legs over the edge of the bed. "It was you I touched in my dream, wasn't it? Holy Jesus, I'm as bad as that baboon who was pawing you." He rose, picked up his clothes and marched into the bathroom.

She turned on her side, drew her knees up to her chest and let silent tears slide down her face. She ached, didn't know why she ached, and hurt too much to try and figure it out.

The bathroom door hinges creaked, footsteps crossed the floor and stopped by the bed. She didn't move and hoped he'd think she was asleep. He'd said women often came on to him, and she'd been like all the others. She cringed with shame. Now, he'd think she was starved for sex. She released a soft sob.

Simon uncovered her head, knelt on the floor and took her face in his hands. "Look at me, Amy," he said in a soft voice.

She opened wet lashes and a tear escaped. He wiped it away with his fingers. "You're a very desirable woman, and don't you let my actions, or those of your ex-husband, make you think otherwise."

His earnest hazel eyes stared into hers. "You're attractive, feminine, and caring. Everything a man would want in a woman."

But she wasn't Julie. And at that moment she wanted very much to be her. She wanted to be loved and cared for in the way she knew he had Julie. Another tear spilled over.

His lower lip trembled and his eyes got wet looking. "Amy . . . I needed the release you could give me." His gaze sharpened. "But you knew that, didn't you?"

She sniffed and nodded.

"You deserve better than that." He took out his handkerchief, wiped her face, and blew his nose. "A helluva lot better."

She covered his hand with hers. "So do you, Simon."

113

His mouth twisted. "One of these days you'll meet a guy who can love you as you should be loved."

But he wasn't the one. He couldn't have made it any plainer. His gaze held hers until she said, "I know" to put his mind at ease.

He let out his breath. "Good." He swept aside her tangled bangs and planted a kiss on her forehead. "You get some sleep. I'm going to walk around awhile. Don't be frightened 'cause I'll stay close by."

She managed a weak smile. "Thanks, Professor. I feel better now."

His smile wobbled as much as hers. "So do I. For a change, I did something right." He turned off the light, pushed the dresser away from the window, climbed through, and closed the window from the outside.

She slept thinly, aware of her unfulfilled needs, of the empty space beside her and Simon's lingering scent. The struggle to sleep strained her already frayed nerves, causing her mind to teem with scraps of unfinished business. The man who'd attacked her had flung her jacket aside. She had to find it. Her money, credit cards, and plane tickets were in an inside pocket.

Friday, October 28

When the sky began to lighten, she got out of bed. Her foot hurt and she felt as if every bone and muscle ached. Hobbling back and forth from suitcase to the bed, she pulled a pair of jeans over her pajama pants, donned a T-shirt and put a coral-colored sweater over the top. Today, she'd be warm.

She glanced at her reflection in the mirror and heard Simon's words *You're a desirable, attractive woman.* She

114

touched a bruise that extended from cheekbone to chin. What did he see that she couldn't?

Her glasses had gotten lost during the skirmish, so she put in her contacts. She seldom wore them. They were time consuming, a vanity item. Who needed to boost their self esteem? A laugh burst from her. She did, that's who.

She studied her eyes. Maybe a little vanity wasn't such a bad thing. After applying make-up, she softened the appearance of her unruly brown hair with a curling iron.

Perhaps if she . . . Leaving the thought unfinished, she tried to move the bed from in front of the door. She couldn't budge it so she snatched the chair leg Simon had left behind, climbed out the window and headed up the street toward the vacant stone building.

As she neared it, her heart rate increased. She swallowed and no saliva moistened her cottony mouth. Straighten up, she told herself. Keep a cool head. She made a face. What an asinine suggestion. This time she was the victim, not the investigator, and the difference yawned wide as a canyon.

At the front entrance, she gripped her billy club and gave the door a shove. As she eased inside, a small animal squeaked and skittered through the litter. Her eyes adjusted to the gloom and she attempted to get her bearings. She took a step, waited and took another. Suddenly, a light flashed full in her eyes and she screamed.

"Sorry," Simon said. "Didn't know it was you."

She gulped air and waited for her pulse to slow. "Where'd you get the flashlight?"

"Borrowed it from the restaurant. Wanted to find your glasses."

"Don't worry about them, it's my coat I need."

They found it not too far from his crutches. Evidently, Cecil's mind had been on his pain instead of thievery because nothing had been taken.

Simon examined the badly bent crutch. "Maybe those jokers learned city dudes aren't so easy after all." He slipped both under one arm. "Let's get something to eat."

During breakfast Amy frowned and broke the rather uncomfortable silence that lay between them. "I hate to see those creeps get off scot-free, but if we file a report we'll have to come back when their case comes up."

Simon set down his cup. "It's more complicated than that. The cook says the guards at the hospital are the only law White Bird has. The nearest sheriff is in Lewistown."

She studied the purple bruises on his face. "Are you feeling okay?"

"Stiff and sore, but nothing serious. How about you?"

"The same." She shrugged. "We can discuss what to do on the way."

By the time they finished, the lights were on in Demski's Auto Repair. They went across the street and entered the glassed-in office. It was empty, but noises came from the garage portion. They followed the sounds.

Their Toyota and several other half-dismantled cars formed a straggly line leading up to a long tool bench. Nearby a tall, lean-bodied young man raised a cloud of dust as he pushed a broom across the floor. When he saw them approaching, he dropped his broom and loped toward them. He stopped several feet away and began to pick at the frayed cuff of his jacket.

"Good morning," Simon said.

The young man raised his gaze to meet Simon's. "Hi, mister. I'm Donny Quinlan."

Simon grasped his hand, shook it, and introduced himself and Amy.

The young man took in Simon's crutch and their bruised faces. "Gol—ly, you been in a wreck?"

Simon glanced at Amy and raised an eyebrow. "Yeah, you might say that." He handed the young man the slip

116

Boris Demski had given them the previous day. "Can we pick up our car?"

Donny stared at the piece of paper and handed it back. "I can't read." He frowned. "My mother says I'm slow. I . . . I guess I am, but . . ." His eyes lighted up. "But I can add better than she can." He straightened bony shoulders. "And you know what?" His face beamed and he seemed about to explode.

"What?" Amy asked.

"I can pitch a baseball better than anybody in White Bird."

Simon shifted his feet. "And all of them want you on their team."

"Sure do." He swelled his chest. " 'Cause I can pitch a no hit game."

"I wasn't much of a baseball player," Amy said. "How about you, Simon?"

"They called me, 'No hope' Kittredge. Couldn't hit, couldn't throw, couldn't catch." He smiled at Donny. "I'll bet you know everybody in town, don't you?"

"Sure do." He inched forward.

"You know a man named Bull?"

Donny grinned. "Everybody in White Bird does. That's Mr. Marchmont." He snickered and looked at them with the clear and guileless eyes of a child. "I heard the guys say it's a fittin' name. Him bein' penned up like he is with a bunch of heifers."

"Shut your trap, Donny."

Amy turned to see the garage owner standing in the office doorway.

A fit of coughing bent the man over. When he recovered, he glowered at the young man who stood with hunched shoulders and bowed head. "I pay you to sweep, not work your jaws, so get to it. Ya hear?"

Donny shuffled over to the work bench and picked up

117

his broom, then his head came up. "I can add better'n you too."

"Don't pay the boy no mind," Demski said, raising his voice so Donny couldn't help hearing him. "He's missing two-thirds of his cogs." He held the door open. "Come in, and we'll get your paper work done so you can be on your way."

Simon held back. "Be right with you." He guided Amy to the other side of the Toyota and took a twenty dollar bill from his wallet. "If you can get Donny aside, give him this. Tell him to buy a new mitt, or something. The only honest person in this town deserves some kind of reward."

She smiled. "I like you, Simon Kittredge. You're a nice man."

He met her gaze somewhat shyly. "Not all the time." He drew his eyebrows together. "Sounds as if reporting those two guys would be useless."

She nodded. "That creep said this town knows who butters its bread." Simon rejoined Demski and she walked over to Donny.

He gazed at her with a sad expression. "Makes me feel bad, when Mr. Demski says things like that about me."

She patted his shoulder. "Just believe in yourself. What others think doesn't matter."

"Really?" He began to pick at his coat sleeve again. "People tease me a lot you know."

"Ignore them. You're the best pitcher in town, aren't you?"

"Yeah . . ."

"That's something no one else can say, right?"

He grinned. "Sure can't. I'm the best, that's what Miss Dorset always said. Once she took my picture and they put it in the Lewistown paper."

Amy's heart gave a bound. "When was that?"

118

He frowned and scraped his toe on the cement. "I can't remember." He brightened. "She was a real, nice lady. Helped my mom, when she got sick and . . . and lots of other people too."

"Why did she leave White Bird?"

Donny squirmed and his gaze dropped to the floor. "Uh . . . I gotta get to work now."

In Lewistown, a doctor sutured the wound in her foot and gave her a tetanus and penicillin injection. Afterwards they had two hours to squander until the plane departed so she and Simon split up. Lewistown was the county seat, so Simon decided to speak to the Town Clerk, while Amy went to the newspaper office. If some sort of scandal had taken place in White Bird three years ago perhaps it'd be documented in one place or the other.

Later, when they met at the airport, she told him of finding the article about Donny and that it had had Elise Dorset's byline. In her search, she'd found other human interest stories written by Elise, but nothing about White Bird that'd cause the reactions they'd observed.

"Strange," Simon said. "I wonder why she never mentioned her writing to me."

"Perhaps she didn't feel hers was in the same class with yours."

"I could have helped her. It would have given us a common bond. That's more than—" He abandoned the thought and told her that he'd located records of Elise's birth and the death of her parents and that was all.

He sat silent for several minutes before he stirred restlessly and said, "Some day, I'm going to launch a full scale investigation of Wade Marchmont's operation. People who have total power bring out the Don Quixote in me."

119

Amy grinned. "From the looks of you, your windmill got in some good licks, Quixote."

He returned the grin. "Judge not by appearances my skeptical friend. My flesh may be weak"—he thumped his chest—"but inside this battered body beats a heart as fierce as a lion's."

On the way back to Seattle, she and Simon slept most of the way. Their plane arrived at 7 P.M. She took Simon to his condo and carried his luggage inside.

"Amy . . ." Simon lifted his hands as if to put them on her shoulders. An uncertain expression crossed his face and he shoved his hands into the pockets of his jeans instead. "I couldn't have made this trip without you." He raised his gaze to meet hers. "That's not an easy admission to make. I've always prided myself on my independence."

Amy smiled and shook his hand. "Welcome Brother Kittredge. I'm a lifetime member of the 'I'd rather do it myself club.' "

He chuckled. "I'd never have guessed."

Her cheeks warmed as he continued to hold onto her hand.

He cleared his throat. "The traffic's terrible. You're not planning on going to the island tonight are you?"

She ran her tongue along her upper lip, saw the color deepen in his eyes and the heat in her cheeks grew more intense. "No, I thought I . . ." Her mind went blank and she searched wildly through her tangled thoughts for the ones she'd lost. "I think I'll wait until morning."

"Great. Go home and take a hot bath." He smiled and she answered it, knowing they were both picturing that awful motel. "And get a good rest. Call me if anything new comes up." He took out a three by five card and wrote down several numbers.

He moved with her to the door. "Thanks, Amy."

She looked up at him. "What for?"

He frowned and gazed at some point above her head. "I don't quite know. But I think it's for just being you."

When she reached her apartment, she checked her answering machine and found she'd forgotten to turn it on. She swore and called her father. He didn't answer and his message phone wasn't on either. Prescott absent-mindedness must be hereditary. She filled the bath tub, poured in her most expensive bath salts and soaked for half an hour.

Afterwards, she donned pajamas and a robe and dialed her father again. Still no answer. She looked at the clock—9 P.M.—he was almost always home by this time. She made a cup of tea and dialed the number again. No answer. He could be out on a case. She roamed the apartment fluffing pillows, dusting shelves, straightening books.

At ten, she dialed the island again. When her father didn't answer, she tried her aunt's number. Perhaps, she would know where he'd gone. Oren answered on the first ring.

"I'm glad you called," he said, as soon as she greeted him. "I've been sitting here wondering how to reach you."

A chill crept along her skin. "What's wrong?"

"B.J.'s been hurt."

A quivering began inside her. "Hurt? How?"

"Someone found him on the road between your place and Lomitas Harbor about two hours ago. He's badly injured and unconscious. The sheriff thinks a car hit him."

"Where . . . where is he?"

"He was airlifted to Harborview Medical Center in Seattle. Mom caught the eight o'clock ferry, she should be there by now."

Numb with shock, Amy thanked him, hung up, and got dressed. As she grabbed her coat from the closet, the phone rang and her heart gave a fearful thump. Her hand shook as she picked up the receiver and answered.

"Amy," Simon said. "I've just heard the most wonderful news."

"I'll call you in the morning," she said quickly, "I'm on my way to the hospital."

"Hospital? What for?"

"Dad's been injured. Oren says he may have been hit by a car. I've got to go, Simon. Talk to you later."

"I'll meet you at the hospital."

"No, Simon . . ." she began, but the line had already gone dead.

Hit and run! The latent implications of the catastrophe struck her full force as she sped through the dark streets. Why had he been walking on that lonely stretch of road at night? Had the act been accidental, or—she shied away from the word—deliberate? Surely no one would have reason to want to hurt her father.

She pressed her fingers against her forehead and tried to think calmly. Would someone at the hospital make certain his clothing was bagged properly to preserve any evidence? She stopped at a phone booth, told the Crime Lab what had happened, and asked that someone alert the emergency room staff.

When she arrived at the hospital, she found the emergency room packed. A woman with a bruised face leaned against one wall, a couple of men with blackened eyes and split lips glared at passersby. A man with a bloody head wound had wedged himself in a corner and gone to sleep. Others, either waiting or with unseen problems, stood in groups of two or three, some wept noisily, some silently, some muttered angry words.

A couple of jeaned and booted young men with bands around their heads shoved her aside and strode toward the reception desk. In their wake staggered a sobbing girl wearing a black nailhead jacket, short skirt, and purple leotards. Her electric blue hair stuck straight up. Black eyeliner made teary spider tracks down her chalked face.

Amy observed the chaotic scene from where she stood beside the door. During the portion of her internship she'd spent here, Friday and Saturday nights had always been a zoo. Worst yet, a continual aroma of alcohol, vomit, and rank sweat seemed to pervade the atmosphere. Yet, offensive as the smell was, she'd found the constant air of hostility harder to bear.

Amy gradually worked her way to the desk, found someone she knew in charge and within a few minutes she was on her way to the surgery floor. As she hurried down a corridor, she caught sight of her aunt in the distance. Although only an inch separated them in height, she always felt a child beside the tall, erect woman who'd been a mother to her even in the years before her own mother had left her and her father.

Later, when she took pre-med, she'd read about the importance of bonding, and realized there'd been no such relationship between her and her mother. As a consequence, when she needed comfort, she'd always gone to Auntie Helen.

She loved her aunt's plain, ruddy face, the dusting of freckles on cheeks and nose, and her wavy cap of graying reddish blonde hair. Despite the woman's angular body, she had a wonderfully soft and ample bosom and Amy had lost track of the times she'd pillowed her head there.

Helen rushed to her and wrapped her in an embrace.

"You're home, thank heavens for that." A second generation Scot from Canada, she still rolled her r's.

The familiar soft burring sound brought tears to Amy's eyes, and she clung to her aunt. "I'm so glad you're here."

Helen held her at arm's length and gasped. "What happened to your face, child?"

"I'll tell you later. How's Dad?"

"Both legs are fractured and he has a concussion. He's in surgery." Helen led her to a thinly padded ivory Naugahyde settee.

As they huddled together, the details of Amy and Simon's visit to White Bird came out. Amy left the bits she'd learned while at the Lewistown newspaper office until last.

Helen's face became set and expressionless. "Elise helped people and wrote human interest stories?" She knotted her hands in her lap. "That's hard to be—"

Simon came through the door and she rose to greet him. He put out his hand to shake hers, but she ignored it and embraced him as she had Amy. "Sorry I missed you on Wednesday," he said.

"My goodness," she said, when she let him go. "You do look a sight. Sit down and tell me how you've been."

He stayed standing. "Helen, I'm to blame for what happened to Amy." He swung to face Amy. "And probably what's happened to B.J. too."

Helen shook her head. "Simon, Simon, it's been four years since you stayed at our house while you wrote that piece on the Senator, but you're still trying to carry the weight of the world on your shoulders."

Simon waved her remark aside and focused on Amy. "My editor liked the profile I did on B.J. He bumped another article and ran it in the November edition. The magazine hit the news stands this morning and the *Times* ran a blurb on the profile in the afternoon edition."

He clumped the length of the room and turned. "I didn't mention Oren's case, but Elise's killer now knows the man viewing Lomitas Island's crime evidence is no ordinary medical examiner." He came to stand in front of her. "Amy, I may have set up your father."

Ten

Saturday, October 29

At 2 a.m., the nurse let Amy see her father for a few minutes. She tiptoed in and peered down at him. Bandages covered his head and both legs were in casts.

With his tremendous vitality stoppered, he looked fragile and as if he'd suddenly grown old. All her life, he'd been her anchor. How could she get along if he . . . Fear tightened her chest until she could scarcely breathe.

She lay her hand over his. "How're you feeling, Dad?"

He opened his eyes, attempted a meager smile and failed. "I've been better."

She leaned closer. "What happened?"

"Calder's new deputy called from the marina. Said a fishermen had found a body." His voice faded out and he stopped to swallow.

"Don't tire yourself. You can tell me tomorrow."

He grasped her hand and struggled to raise himself. "You have to know now."

"All right but you mustn't overdo it." She eased him back on the pillow.

"My car wouldn't start, tried to call the sheriff's office, but the car phone didn't work. Didn't want to fuss with the alarms to use the one in the house. Figured on a Friday night there'd be people headed for the harbor, so I decided to hoof it."

"Did you see who hit you?"

He shook his bandaged head and groaned at the movement. "Happened about a quarter of a mile beyond Prescott's Byway. Damned thing came out of the darkness. No lights and going like hell."

She hesitated to ask the next question. This case had enough complications already. "Do you think it was intentional?"

"Might have been. Phone Tom and find out if his deputy called me about a body." He winced and closed his eyes.

She patted his shoulder. "I'll take care of everything." She leaned down and kissed him. "Try to get some rest."

When she returned to the waiting room, Simon rose and came toward her. "How is he?"

"Not too comfortable." She glanced around. "Where's Helen?"

"She decided to spend what was left of the night at a friend's house."

"Good. She looked awfully tired."

"She said she'd see B.J. later in the day."

Amy nodded and they started toward the elevator. On the way down, she repeated what her father had told her.

Simon's face became grim. "It's all my fault. I never should have written that article."

She grabbed his shoulders and gave him a shake. "Will you stop blaming yourself for every thing that happens."

When she and Simon exited from the building, half a dozen flash bulbs went off. "Good God," Simon muttered. "This is all we need."

She swore under her breath, remembered their bruised faces and swore again. Reporters and TV cameras closed in on them. Simon had said his article would give her visibility. It had certainly done that all right. She'd met a number of the media while working with the Crime Lab's mobile unit, but few of them had known her name—until now.

A TV anchorwoman thrust a microphone at her. "Is your father badly injured, Miss Prescott?"

As soon as she got that question answered, a dozen more were shouted at her from every direction. "That's all I can say," she said and backed away.

"Were you with your father?" the woman persisted. "Is that where you got the bruises on your face?"

"No comment," she said and kept repeating it, but still the woman kept prodding.

"Leave her alone." Simon put his arm around Amy. "Can't you see she's worn out?" He tried to guide her to the edge of the pack.

"What's your interest in the Prescotts, Kittredge?" somebody yelled.

"Yeah, Simon," chimed in another. "A friend of the lady's give you that shiner?"

"Get behind me and hang on," Simon said, and began to work his way through the crowd.

When they were clear, she directed him to her car and they piled inside. She started the motor. "I'll take you home."

"No, I'll call a taxi from the lobby of your apartment building."

They didn't speak again until she pulled into her parking stall at the back of the apartment.

"Could we talk for a minute?" Simon asked.

"Might just as well, I'm too jittery to sleep." She stretched and rubbed her eyes.

He leaned toward her, his face tense. "What if the body that was found is Elise's?"

She drew in a shaky breath. "I'm trying not to think about that right now. First, I want to talk to Oren."

"Ask him about Elise's car and whether or not she still had a bunch of expensive jewelry."

"Right. Then, I'll get in touch with the sheriff and find out what's been going on."

"Let me know what you learn." He put his hand on the door latch, changed his mind, and turned to face her. "Do you mind if I call you around ten just to make sure you're all right?"

A smothering sensation came over her. "How would you feel if I checked up on you?"

A shocked expression spread over his face. "Don't be ridiculous, I can look after myself."

"That's no more true for you than it is for me. Things can happen over which we have no control." She sat silent for a moment, then went on. "When I chose my profession, I knew what to expect. Neither Dad nor I are content to do routine forensic work. We like the excitement of fitting pieces of a puzzle together. And when you unearth things people want to keep buried, you put yourself in danger. As an investigative reporter, you accept that—so do I."

Simon glowered at her. "Well, be careful then, dammit." He thrust out his chin. "Friends are hard to find."

After several hours sleep, Amy contacted the detective who'd promised to check Dr. Tambor's account at Sibleys. "The pendant was solid gold with the inscription, 'To my blue-eyed darling,' " the detective said with a chuckle. "The coat mentioned on the slip was cashmere."

"What size?" she asked and crossed her fingers.

"Ten," he said.

She let out a yell, thanked him, and dialed Oren. "Mom

just called from the hospital," Oren said. "She says B.J. is already talking about coming home."

"Wouldn't you know it. Doctors are the world's worst patients." After discussing her father's condition and her trip to White Bird, she asked him if he'd heard anything about the body that had been found.

He inhaled sharply. "Who—whose body? Where? When?"

His labored breathing blurred the sound of her own voice as she repeated what her father had said about the phone call he got.

"When Calder came by to tell Mom and I about B.J., he didn't mention anyone finding a . . . a . . . he didn't say a damned thing about . . . about . . ." He fell silent.

Minutes passed and she grew worried. "Are you okay?"

Oren cleared his throat. "Does B.J. think it's . . . Elise?"

Images of submerged bodies she'd seen in the past rose before her eyes. "Identification takes time," she said quickly and changed the subject. "Did Elise have a car?"

"Sure. A red Mazda RX-7. License number OEK-199. I told the sheriff."

"Has he located it?"

"Who knows? The man won't tell me anything."

"Did she drive her car that day?"

"She must have, she was at the apartment when I got home."

"She could have walked from the ferry dock."

"Elise walk eight blocks in high heels—no way. Besides, there aren't any sidewalks and it was pouring rain. She had to have driven. Only thing is, I can't remember whether her car was parked in front of the apartment or not."

Her stomach began to churn. "I should have stopped

by when I got off the ferry." She grimaced. "I hoped your problems might seem less serious to you in the daylight." She cleared her throat. "Sorry I let you down."

"Talking wouldn't have helped. I know that now." He sighed. "The cracks in our relationship had grown too wide." He sighed again. "Elise acted strange that whole damned week. She was home every evening, but during the day I couldn't reach her. She wasn't at work, or at our town house in Seattle, or at our apartment here on the island. Friday night, when I tried to pin her down, we really got into it."

Amy took a breath and plunged in. "Simon and I have evidence that Dr. Tambor purchased an expensive coat and pendant. We're almost certain they were for Elise."

"I don't believe it. She couldn't have. I'd have known it if she . . . if she . . . Oh, God . . . Why, Amy?" He let out a low moan. "I've gone over and over the months we were together and I can't make any sense to her actions. Why did she do the things she did?"

"What kind of things?"

"They aren't important now."

"You can't know that for certain. Whatever motivated her might provide a clue to her disappearance."

"Simon and I have agreed not to discuss Elise unless we find there's no other recourse."

"Oh, that's great. Just great. Dad and I are trying to unravel a mystery and all the while you and Simon may hold the key."

"It's my life I'm risking."

"Like hell it is. What if the attempt on Dad is related?"

"Now you're being ridiculous. What does Simon think?"

"He's scared. Damned scared."

"You're both off base. There's no way Elise's disappearance and B.J.'s accident could be connected."

131

Amy curbed the impulse to argue with him. "Simon says Elise used to own some expensive jewelry. Does she still have it?"

"So far as I know. She . . . she loved sparkly things. Some nights, she'd dress up and put on a regular style show with all her diamonds and emeralds."

"Dad and I didn't find any expensive jewelry at your Lomitas apartment. Has the sheriff checked your town house?"

"I suppose so, he has the keys. But the stuff should have been here on the island. Elise always carried her jewelry with her when she traveled."

"All of it?"

"She was funny about her possessions. Wanted everything right where she could see it. Wouldn't even consider a safety deposit box."

Amy frowned. "Did she regard you as another of her possessions?"

"Butt out, Amy. You know all you need to know," he said, and hung up.

She dreaded calling Tom Calder. His resentment of her father had probably doubled since Simon's article was published. She planned her strategy carefully.

When she reached him, she asked whether someone had tampered with her father's car.

"Doubt it," Tom said. "I found a coil wire hangin' loose, but that coulda happened by itself."

"You dusted for prints, didn't you?"

"Nah, waste of time considerin' the crowd millin' around your yard. Hell, half the islanders had their fingers on B.J.'s Ford before the helicopter took off."

"Dad says the person who ran him down was speeding and that he was driving without lights. Sounds to me like he didn't want Dad to see him. Did you find any tire tracks?"

"Good God, no. How could I? Westridge Avenue turned into a parking lot as soon as word got out about B.J."

She clamped her jaw closed and counted to ten, then took a new tack. "A friend and I just returned from White Bird, Montana—the town where Elise Dorset lived before she came to Seattle."

"What the hell you think you're pullin'? You and your big-town smarties better not mess things up for me. Ya hear? I already know who the killer is."

She made a line through an item on the pad in front of her. With his closed mind, Tom would jeer at the meager bits they'd learned about Elise's background. "Oren says Elise drove a red sports car. Have you located it?"

"That punk's really got you and Doc snowed, hasn't he? It so happens the woman sold her car the week before he done her in."

Elise sold her car. Amy stared at the words she'd scrawled and apprehension chilled her. Oren lied. Why? Why? Her mind clenched shut. "How'd Elise get to the island that Friday night?"

"By bus, I suppose."

"You *suppose?* Didn't any of the drivers remember seeing her?"

"No, but that doesn't mean she wasn't on it."

Feeling as if she were slogging through knee-deep mud, Amy inhaled and began again. "Elise owned some expensive jewelry. Dad and I didn't find any of it at their apartment."

He drew in air and blew it out. "One of you tight-lipped Prescotts coulda told me. Wasn't a thing worth diddley damn at their place in Seattle." She heard his fist smack the desk top. "Hell's bells now I gotta check the pawn shops. More damned time and money down the toilet. And for what?"

His voice lowered. "I know what goes on in them hotel rooms at political rallies. Your cousin could have used that jewelry to buy sex-u-al favors." He mouthed the word as if it were a succulent piece of candy.

She glowered at the receiver. The horny old nincompoop would be drooling on his tie in a minute. "Speaking of affairs," she said. "Dad and I think Elise and her employer were romantically involved."

Calder made a sound of disgust. "You're off your trolley."

"Oh, yeah? He bought her . . ."

"Can it, Prescott. Smear tactics aren't gonna clear Oren. Now, I got work to . . ."

"Hold on, Tom," she said before he could hang up on her. "The person who called Dad last night claimed to be your deputy. He said someone at the marina had found a body. You know anything about it?"

"Jee—sus! What you gonna come up with next? Musta been some joker tryin' to pull B.J.'s leg. He shoulda known better'n to go off half-cocked."

She knotted her fist. "Yeah. Sure. And I suppose the same joker put Dad's cellular phone out of commission?"

"Ah, those stupid things are always goin' on the fritz. Besides it could have been out of order for hours. I've noticed B.J.'s gettin' a tad senile lately."

Senile! Dad's wits were sharper than that pea-brain's any day of the week. She slammed the receiver into the cradle. To hell with Calder. The attempt on her father's life had been planned. She'd almost swear to it. She jumped up from her chair. If someone wanted him dead, he'd try again.

Snatching a coat from the closet, she rushed to the Crime Lab. Her father's clothes remained her only hope of finding a clue to his assailant. She met Gail Wong as she walked in.

"Sorry about your father," Gail said. "I've been assigned to go over his clothing. I'll try to give them first priority."

Amy gripped her hands together. "I can't wait, Gail. I have to find out who did it—and fast." She hung up her coat and reached for her white jacket. "Let's get started."

Gail put her arm around Amy's shoulders. "Sorry, no can do. The chief knew you'd be in. He says your father's stuff is off limits to you."

"Damn, doesn't anything get by him?"

"Not in the time I've known him." She studied Amy's face. "Geez peez girl, you're a certified mess. What happened?"

Amy gave her a brief account of their frightening experiences in White Bird.

"Good grief," Gail said when she finished. "That place sounds like something out of a horror movie." She grinned. "But traveling with a good-looking hunk like Simon probably made it worthwhile." She regarded Amy from under stubby lashes. "Right?"

Amy let out an exasperated breath. "You and Dad should start a matchmaking business. Being alone isn't all that bad you know."

Gail wrinkled her face. "No, just God-awful dull."

"Better to be bored than married to the wrong man." Amy slipped her arms into her coat. "Call me if you find anything significant. If I'm not at the apartment, try the island." She hurried out.

When she reached her father's hospital room, she found Simon sprawled in one of the two chairs. He had a new light weight cast and had evidently graduated from his crutches. She greeted the two men, drew her chair close to the bed, and reported the results of her phone calls.

"So there wasn't a body at all," B.J. said. "I sure bobbled that one."

Simon sat bolt upright. "Bobbled? Holy hell, B.J., someone's out to get you. You ought to have a guard outside your door. Anybody in a white uniform could walk in here and . . ."

B.J. held up his hand. "Don't get all steamed up. I'm already working on a plan to get out of here."

Amy sprang to her feet. "You can't do that."

"Why not? I'm in stable condition. You're a doctor, I'm a doctor. What more do I need?"

She raked her fingers through her hair. "Good God, Dad, you've got a short leg cast on one leg and a long leg cast on the other. I can't get you in and out of bed, you're too damned heavy."

"I was thinking of sweet talking Calder into letting Oren stay at the house."

Her lips tightened. "With sensitive evidence on his case in the basement? No chance, Dad."

Simon stood up. "I could do it."

She swung to face him. "You have a job and responsibilities of your own."

He met her level gaze. "Let me worry about that."

B.J. beamed at both of them. "Now that that's settled, let's get on to more important matters. Did Tom mention the name of the person who bought Elise's car?"

Amy shook her head and sank onto a chair. "I doubt he even asked. If it threatens to shake his case against Oren, he's not interested. You should've heard him howl when I told him about Elise's jewelry." She grimaced. "But, he is going to contact the pawn shops."

"Hm-m-m." B.J. punched a pillow into place and raised the head of his bed. "If the guy's a pro, he'll fence the stuff and it will never be found." He turned toward Amy. "Would you contact the Department of Motor Vehicles about the car?"

She nodded. "Did you get a chance to go over the material from Oren's van?"

"Yep. Nothing worth pursuing."

Simon rested one hip on the edge of the bed. "How about me going to see Dr. Tambor again?"

B.J.'s gaze swung from Simon to Amy. "Tom show any interest when you told him about Tambor and Elise?"

Her lips tightened. "None. The jerk figures we're digging up dirt to muddy his case."

"Then go to it, Simon. Just be sure you get the interview on tape. Looks as if it'll be up to you and Amy to do the leg work if we're going to clear Oren."

Amy tucked her purse under her arm and got up to leave. "Well, Dad, since you're set on going home, I think I'll head for the island this afternoon. There's lots to be done and the animals need to be fed."

"Amy, you can't," Simon said.

He flushed when she turned and stared at him. "Why not?"

"Your place is so isolated. It's not safe for you to be out there all by yourself." He shifted his feet. "Can't you wait until B.J. and I go?"

She lifted her chin. "As I told you earlier, I don't need a keeper."

"Now, now, kitten," B.J. said. "Simon has a point."

She eyed him sternly. "I'm going. End of discussion."

She stomped out of the room. Men. They thought you couldn't survive without them. Dangerous or not, it'd take a tidal wave to keep her off that island now.

From the hospital, she drove downtown and asked one of the officers in the traffic division to run a make on Elise's license plates.

After a long wait, he returned. "Owner's name is Roger Norman. No traffic or criminal offenses on our books."

He scowled. "And no record of a Washington State driver's license."

The piece of paper he handed her listed Roger Norman's post office box and social security number. She thanked him and asked to use a phone book. When she didn't find the man listed, she turned to the City Directory. He wasn't there either. She filed the information in her purse. Roger Norman would have to wait. A full scale search would take time and she didn't have any to spare right now. She phoned her father and passed on the few bits of information she'd learned.

"Things are beginning to move," B.J. said. "Simon just called. Dr. Tambor's agreed to see him. They're going to meet in the doctor's office at eleven on Sunday morning."

Her stomach went suddenly hollow. "Sunday morning! Has Simon gone nuts? The place will be deserted." She pressed her hand against the widening void in her midriff. "Dammit, Dad, the man could be a killer."

"My words exactly. Simon claims he'll take a friend along." B.J began a long list of precautions for her to follow when she got to Lomitas.

"Yes. Yes, Dad, I'll remember." She hung up and tried to dismiss Simon from her mind. Nevertheless, as she traveled to her apartment, pictures of a guilt-crazed man attacking Simon filled her mind. Blast it, Simon had no business making her worry. She had enough troubles without him adding more.

She caught the three o'clock ferry from Anacortes. As soon as they were under way, she left the car and climbed to the upper deck. She bought a sandwich and settled herself at a window seat.

The sky had cleared, but a cold wind scuffed the green quartz sea into white-tipped waves. With only an occasional shudder, the ferry threaded its way through Thatcher Pass where breakers bunched and rolled. Swells built and struck Blakely Island's steep, rocky sides, exploding in salt white plumes that soared forty feet, drenching a fringe of evergreens. Off to the northeast, the day beacon on Lawson rock blinked a warning.

She finished her sandwich and sat back to observe the other passengers. A man and his young son occupied the booth across from her. The man had taken off his shoes, pillowed his head on his packsack and closed his eyes. The little boy smiled to himself, slipped his feet into his father's shoes and clumped up and down the aisle.

As she watched, her mind returned to the plaster footprints in her father's basement. An idea popped into her mind and a tingling sensation went through her. It would have been so simple—so devilishly simple such a thing hadn't even occurred to her.

With an effort, she reined in her soaring spirits. She'd have to enlist Oren's help, make more casts, and do some complex calculations. But maybe, if she could prove this one point, it'd be the breakthrough they needed.

When she disembarked at Faircliff, she stopped to buy groceries and a copy of *Global News*. She told herself she only wanted to read the article Simon had written about her father. Way down deep she admitted to a more selfish reason. What had he said about her? Did he think her chosen profession diminished her femininity? The errant thought surprised her. In all her years of training, she'd never considered such a possibility—nor had she really cared. She squared her shoulders. That kind of thinking had better stop right here and now. She put the station wagon in gear and started for home.

Along Westridge Avenue, whorls of mist coiled in lochs and estuaries and long, murky strands interlaced the thoroughfare like a massive web. When she passed by, the skeins trembled as if a giant spider lay waiting in the gloom.

She made a left hand turn and slowed as she passed her father's house. He had been gone only a day and already the old place looked deserted and forlorn.

With a heavy sigh, she parked in her own driveway, got out of the car, and set her groceries inside the screened back porch. "Cleo," she called, and expected to see the small, black cocker come leaping out of the underbrush with her ears flopping and her tongue lolling.

She walked around to the front veranda, and whistled. No answering sound except the roar of the surf. A faint uneasiness gathered at the back of her mind. Cleo seldom ventured far on her forays. Stopping to whistle and call every few steps, she circled the mist-smudged cottage.

Shadows deepened at the edge of the woods. "Cleo," she called again and heard a creaking sound. She turned, saw something dark swaying in the wind, and the hair rose on the back of her neck. Slowly, fearing what she might see, she moved forward.

"Cleo." Her voice broke. From a thin wire twisted around a maple tree limb, the dog's body swung lazily in the evening breeze. "Bastard," she shouted. "You dirty rotten bastard!"

She rushed to the house for the wire cutters and lowered the cold, stiff body to the ground. "Cleo, Cleo," she moaned and stroked the little dog's head. *I'll get him. If it's the last thing I ever do, I'll get him.*

Her fingers touched a scrap of paper tucked under the leather collar. She unfolded it, peered at the printed scrawl and her chest squeezed tight.

You're next, Amy.

Eleven

Amy wrapped Cleo in a rug and buried her on the slope below the cottage. By the time she'd finished, night had fallen. A thick gray mist shrouded the trees and muffled all sounds except the fog horn off Shag Reef.

She trudged into the dark, cold house. In a numbed daze, she turned on all the lights, locked the doors, and checked the windows. Then she huddled in a chair.

I should call and tell Dad. She shivered and wrapped her arms around herself. She couldn't. He'd insist on her returning to Seattle. If she phoned Helen she'd be there within minutes, but she and Oren had enough burdens to bear.

Simon? She hugged her chest tighter and rocked back and forth. *He'll tell me I should have had better sense than to come here by myself.*

She pushed herself out of the chair and turned on the furnace. Maybe she shouldn't have been so stubborn, but she was here and she'd handle it. One thing for sure, the note and how Cleo had died would have to be kept secret. If anyone found out her life had been threatened, she wouldn't be free to do what she must do.

She made tea and forced herself to drink some of the hot brew. A weapon, she thought suddenly. Her cup clattered against the saucer. She must have some means of protection. Several years ago, at her father's insistence, she'd learned to use a pistol. After completing her training, she'd put the holster and .38 in her father's closet and hadn't thought about it again. She picked up the poker and went upstairs.

After a quick shower, she put on pajamas, got under the covers and rolled up—knees to chest—in the middle of the double bed. Despite her bravado she felt the dwelling's emptiness and at the base of her consciousness lay an unnerving awareness of the distance between her cottage and the nearest neighbor. Every creak and pop of the house's old timbers caused her heart to leap and set her pulse racing.

She pulled the blankets over her ears. The person who'd killed Cleo had left the note to warn her off. He probably wouldn't actually do anything—unless he discovered she intended to finish her father's work.

A sudden chill shook her and in the midst of it she recalled how Simon's body had surrounded her with warmth two nights ago. Sweet, gentle, Simon. For an instant the gnawing ache inside her swept aside all else. Careful, her more sensible self cautioned, he could hurt you much worse than Mitch did. She pummeled her pillow, settled her head on it and did deep breathing exercises in an attempt to relax her muscles.

A soft tapping at the window brought her upright. She sat stiff and alert, clutching the comforter to her as if it were a body shield. When she thought her nerves would surely snap, a gravely mee-o-o-w sounded and she sagged with relief.

She turned on the lamp, jumped out of bed, opened the window and took Marcus in her arms. She hugged him to her and buried her face in his fur.

"She's gone, Marcus. Our Cleo is gone." Her tears

overflowed and Marcus bumped his head against her cheek as if he understood.

Sunday, October 30

Next morning, she automatically reached for her glasses on the night stand. After groping around for several minutes, she remembered she'd lost them in White Bird. She muttered an oath. Contacts might be more flattering but they didn't mix well with blowing sand. Venturing out of her warm bed into the early morning chill, she located another pair of dark-rimmed glasses and went into the bathroom to wash her face.

The phone rang as she was combing her hair. She answered and found her father on the line.

"Just thought I'd give you a jingle," B.J. said, his tone carefully casual. "How're you doing?"

She cleared her throat and hoped her voice wouldn't shake. "Cleo got hold of some poisoned food. She . . . she's dead."

"Dead! Good God . . . What's the matter with that vet? Why didn't he . . . You did take her to the vet, didn't you?"

Her mouth went dry. Lies. They always got her into hot water. "She'd been dead for quite awhile when I found her."

"How long, Amy?"

Damn, she should've known he'd try to pin her down. "Come on, Dad. You know rigor mortis varies depending upon conditions."

"I don't like it, Amy. Awful fishy her getting poisoned just after the hit and run. You'd better do an autopsy. Or have the vet do it. Her liver, kidneys, and stomach contents should be analyzed."

Amy searched her mind for a believable excuse, found none and decided to be halfway honest. "Dad, she's already buried. Let her rest in peace."

"That's sloppy investigating."

"Maybe, but she's my dog and that's what I want to do."

"Well, you be damned careful. Hear?"

She promised, bid him goodbye, and hoped he'd given Simon the same precautions. Tension gathered at the back of her neck. Simon may have said he'd have a friend accompany him to his interview with Dr. Tambor, but knowing his go-it-alone attitude, she doubted his word.

She dressed and went down to the kitchen. Keeping her eyes averted from Cleo's dish, she made coffee. While waiting for it to perk, she stood at the counter and read Simon's article.

Even if Dr. B.J. Prescott hadn't been her father, she wouldn't have been able to lay the magazine down. Simon grabbed her interest in the first sentence and never let it lag for a second. The man was good, damned good. Anyone who could turn out such a superb story in a few hours had to be a top-notch writer.

She poured herself a cup of coffee and sipped it as she scanned the article again. Simon had talent, no doubt of that. If he put his mind to it, his name could be up there with the rest of the literary giants.

After breakfast, she set a tote bag on the counter. Inside, she stuffed the packaged and labeled evidence she'd gathered the night before: Cleo's collar, the threatening note, and the wire she'd cut from around the spaniel's neck. Her preparations completed, she left the cottage and started up the hill to use her father's lab.

She hadn't gotten far when she heard the sound of a motor. Seconds later, Helen's car came barreling down the road with Oren at the wheel.

When he saw her, he jammed on the brakes and jumped out of the car. "What're you doing here?" He came to a stop in front of her, feet planted wide apart, his elbows akimbo.

She scowled at his hostile stance. "This is where I live. Remember?"

His expression changed, became veiled and remote. "I'm supposed to feed the animals." He glanced around. "Where are they?"

She gulped. Face to face, people always saw through her lies. "Marcus has had his breakfast." She scuffed yellow maple leaves into a pile at her feet. "Last night I found Cleo by the back porch." Amy moistened her lips and raised her gaze to meet his. "She'd been poisoned."

"Poisoned?" He said, his face curiously blank. "How . . . peculiar."

She stared at him. She didn't know the man he'd become. They'd been apart too long. "Is that all you can say?"

"Perhaps you were right." He peered into the distance. "Maybe . . . there is a killer roaming the island." Moving in a jerky fashion as if his limbs were pulled by invisible strings, he got into his car and sped away.

With a vague feeling of alarm, she trudged up the driveway in his tire squealing, sand spurting wake. When they were teenagers Oren had been solid as a rock. Well, reasonably stable—most of the time. She chewed her lip. No sense lying to herself—emotional stress had always torn him to pieces.

When she reached the lab, she dusted both sides of the threatening note for prints and found none but her own. That out of the way, she set to work in earnest. The four by six inch sheet had machine sliced edges on three sides. Remnants of a printed heading still remained intact along the torn upper edge—a "T" several spaces to the right of center and a "P" an inch from the right hand border. A lead—slim, and next to impossible to trace, but better than no lead at all.

In a somewhat more optimistic mood, she tested the paper content—twenty-five percent cotton fiber bond—a type commonly used for scratch pads. A trace of padding gum clinging to an edge substantiated her conclusion.

To avoid being distracted, she'd kept the note face down. A kernel of dread gathered as she turned the paper over and studied the killer's printed scrawl.

In mystery stories, writers often spoke of a certain place or thing having an aura. In the past, her scientific mind had rejected the theory. Now, her skepticism vanished. The black smeary letters emanated malevolence.

Not being a handwriting analyst, she could only guess at the implications of the intense pen pressure, the erratic right and left slant of the letters. More samples of the person's writing would be needed before a graphologist could attempt a personality profile.

She reread the data she'd recorded. Before the graphic depiction of crimes on TV, the absence of fingerprints on the note and dog collar would have signified a clever criminal. These days, even the rankest amateurs wore gloves—unless the crime had occurred in the heat of anger.

A couple of ominous questions rose to blot other concerns from her mind. Had the dog been garroted to keep her quiet, or had the killing been an integral part of a premeditated plan?

She repackaged the note, hid it on one of the shelves, and unwrapped the wire used to strangle Cleo. Much to her disappointment, the wire turned out to be 16 gauge aluminum, a common variety available in any hardware store.

She sighed and noted the time—ten o'clock. Simon

should be on his way to his appointment with Dr. Tambor. She massaged the back of her neck, moved to a nearby table and gazed down at casts of the footprints she'd found near Prescott's Byway the day after Elise disappeared. Only time and a great deal of work would prove the true worth of the idea she'd had yesterday while watching the little boy on the ferry.

After checking the prints from all angles and taking minute measurements, she turned her attention to plaster impressions of the striations discovered near the dinghy in Orca Narrows. Microscopic examination of the tiny horizontal grooves revealed brownish shreds, thready plant fibers and bits of black seeds.

She glanced at her watch. By now, Simon should be riding up to the fourth floor in the elevator. A hard, cold knot formed in the pit of her stomach. *Keep him safe.*

Her hand trembled as she set the impressions aside and snapped off the microscope light. She had to get outside, do something physical that'd keep her mind totally engrossed. If she stayed cooped up, her fear for Simon would grow until she could think of nothing else. She decided to revisit Orca Narrows and gather pieces of shrubbery for comparison with those that she'd found.

She returned to the cottage to stow clippers and storage bags in a packsack. As she cut cheese for a sandwich, the light glinted on the keen-edged blade, the pointed tip. She remembered sitting only a few feet from Mrs. Demetrius while she fingered a deadly looking letter opener. A fine trembling began inside of Amy. Cornered killers did terrible things, Simon should know that.

She jammed an apple in her jacket pocket, snatched up the sandwich, and set off for the trail along the cliff's edge. If she kept moving, perhaps she wouldn't dwell on him.

Gray clouds scraped tree tops protruding from wisps

of swirling mist. Below her, a heaving pewter sea smashed into massive boulders, turning them slick and black as seal skin. On a pinnacle, out of reach of the spray, perched long-necked cormorants spreading ebony-hued wings to dry.

Ordinarily, she enjoyed watching them. In her present mood, they put her in mind of black-caped mourners. A shudder ran through her. What kind of a person would deliberately kill a warm, loving animal like Cleo just to send a warning? The answer came to her with stunning force. A brutal one.

She stood stock still and squeezed her eyes tight shut. She hadn't said a real prayer in a long time and even here with only the crows and black birds to hear, she felt shy and ill-at-ease.

She looked up at the forbidding sky. "Please, I'll do anything. Just don't take Simon too," she whispered.

After a few minutes, she shook herself and started off again, resolving to do what she came to do. As she marched along, her gaze swept from side to side. A week ago Saturday, when she'd been searching for the dinghy, she hadn't had time to properly assess the area.

Where a small rivulet trickled between cattails and tall swamp iris spears, she knelt to study some footprints on a muddy bank. A number of other people had traveled this path since she'd been here. She frowned. Little point in her taking a scientific approach at this late date. Nevertheless she didn't want to overlook something her father, Tom Calder, or the deputy had missed.

All along the way, she clipped bits of huckleberry, beach pine, and juniper, packaging and labeling each before storing them in the packsack. When she reached the rim of the bluff where she'd previously seen broken twigs and crushed foliage, she searched for them. But in the seven days since she'd seen them, wind and rain had erased all trace.

A little farther on, she noticed several short, ivory-colored strands caught in a crevice. She plucked them out with needle-nosed forceps and deposited them in an envelope. Her deductive mind insisted nothing on the cliff could possibly be linked to Oren's case. Still, she'd been taught criminals don't always act in a logical manner.

Twenty minutes later, she arrived at the precipitous slope she'd scrambled down to look at the overturned dinghy. Farther along, she knew there should be a much easier route. She decided to chance it.

On the other side of a rocky knoll, a patch of Scotch broom narrowed the footpath. Dry seed pods rattling like castanets, the shrub's green wandlike stems surged and dipped in the wind. She paused long enough to snip off some sprigs before squeezing by. A few yards beyond, she discovered the trail she sought.

The path led downward through a deep cleft in the rocks to the crescent-shaped cove. Here, by some trick of wind current, the mist had cleared, filling the narrows with sunshine. It glistened on clumps of slick olive-green kelp where gulls fought over beached crab.

At the far end of the cove, an orange plastic ribbon marked the spot where the dinghy had rested. She scanned the expanse of sand. No shrubbery within thirty or forty yards of that particular section. Bent in a half crouch, she did a foot by foot scrutiny. Sometimes she got down on all fours. Once, she lay on her stomach and rested her cheek on the salt-crusted sand to get an ant's eye view. Satisfied that she'd eliminated all the possibilities, she hurried toward home.

After leaving the bluff trail, she plodded up the long incline leading to the cottage. Halfway there, she heard the phone ringing and broke into a run. She took the steps two at a time, dropped the key and swore. "Don't hang up." She flung the door open, snatched up the receiver and said hello.

"Where the hell have you been?" Simon barked. "I've been trying to reach you for over an hour."

He was all right. She collapsed in a chair.

"Well?"

His dictatorial tone sent her temper soaring, until she noticed his agitated breathing. "What happened?"

"I screwed up. That's what happened. I knew I should have insisted on seeing Tambor last night."

She ground her teeth together. Why did he think he had to be perfect. "Just tell me will you. I'm not going to grade you on your performance, for God's sake."

"I'm trying to, dammit. The lights were off and the elevator out of order when I got there."

Her heart thudded against her ribs. A good reporter wouldn't let a dark building keep him from a good story, and the doctor knew it. "So you acted like an idiot and walked up to the fourth flour. Right?"

"Why not? For all I knew, his suite had a separate fuse box." He exhaled and went on. "From the looks of Tambor's office, he'd really hung one on. Whiskey bottles everywhere, but no sign of him."

"So the man got scared and took off. Just our luck."

"That's what I thought . . . until I saw the open elevator shaft."

She caught her breath. "He . . . he didn't, did he?"

Simon swallowed noisily. "The police . . . found him . . . at the bottom . . . of the shaft."

"Do they think he fell"—she shuddered—"or . . . or jumped, or . . . Oh, my God! They don't think someone else did it do they?"

"Hah! *They* aren't saying *anything*. *I'm* the one who's

150

been doing all the talking for the last two hours. You know a Lt. Joseph Salgado?"

"I've heard the name."

"Jesus! The guy has a broken nose and eyes like a Doberman. And he acts like I did it."

"You told him why you were there, didn't you?"

"Of course I told him, or tried to. I doubt the man believes his own mother. So I took him to the condo and showed him the picture and master charge slip we found. He gave me holy hell for poking my nose in where it didn't belong."

"I'm to blame too. Didn't you tell him that?"

"Of course not. What good would that have done?"

Silence stretched between them and she knew he must be fighting to regain control. Finally, his breathing slowed. "Sorry I yelled at you," he said quietly. "But after seeing Tambor dead, then not being able to reach you, I went a little crazy. I just knew you'd got yourself hurt, or . . . or worse with one of your damn fool stunts."

His remark rasped her taut nerves. "Takes one to know one, Simon."

"Don't start that addle-headed business about being able to look after yourself. It's dangerous out there and you know it."

Of all the arrogant, high-handed, stiff-necked . . . Her irritation fizzled away. He'd worried about her. Cared enough to keep calling. "Let's skip it, okay? Besides, Dr. Tambor's death may clear up this whole nasty mess."

"I hope so, but—" He broke off and sighed. "I talked to your Dad. He's arranged to rent a van. We plan to arrive on the early morning ferry tomorrow. Amy," he said in a soft, wheedling tone. "Couldn't you get someone to stay with you tonight?"

"Simon, will you stop"—she filled her lungs and began again—"I'll sleep at Aunt Helen's. What kind of trouble are you planning on getting into?"

"Don't worry about me, I can . . ." A flat, humorless laugh burst from him. "I'll be well supervised. The lieutenant put a tail on me."

"Smart man. Remind me to send him flowers." She hung up and hastened to repack her suitcase. If she arrived at Helen's house before dark, perhaps she could get casts of Oren's footprints. She'd need some of him empty-handed and others with him carrying a heavy weight. If she could prove reasonable doubt of Oren's guilt, then perhaps the authorities would realize Dr. Tambor could have had a motive to do away with Elise.

She sagged against the bed. The evidence against Oren was so damning and this one factor so complex and difficult to substantiate even her father had overlooked it—or had he? She wandered into the bathroom and stood looking into space. Perhaps, in her eagerness to find something that'd clear Oren she'd made an error. She tossed her hair dryer and make-up bag into the suitcase and closed the lid. One doubtful item was better than none at all.

She loaded the car with needed equipment and drove up the hill to put her shrubbery clippings in the lab. Once they were stored away, she checked the windows, locked the doors, and turned on the alarm. If anyone tried to get in or tamper with the security system, a buzzer would go off at the sheriff's office.

On her way out of the driveway, she passed her father's car and made a mental note to call Virgil's Auto Shop. Over the years Virgil had performed miracles on the old clunks she'd owned—he'd know if the Ford's motor had been sabotaged. If it hadn't, the hit-and-run might have been accidental. However, an inner voice told her there was faint hope of that.

Her scalp prickled. Suppose Elise's death, Cleo's strangulation, and her father's assault weren't related. That would mean more than one killer prowled the island. She shuddered at the thought.

Monday, October 31

The next morning at breakfast, Helen read aloud the report of Dr. Tambor's death. Before Amy, Oren, and Helen had an opportunity to discuss it, Tom Calder arrived and demanded to know where Oren had been Saturday night.

After the sheriff had fired several questions at him, Oren fixed him with a hard, cold stare. "I didn't push that doctor down an elevator shaft, if that's what you're driving at."

"You'd better come up with more than that, Prescott. Your word isn't worth beans."

Oren flung down his napkin. "Next you'll be saying I ran down my uncle." He got up and went to stand at the window.

The sheriff bunched his fists on his hips and jutted his head. "Wouldn't surprise me none. None at all. I've seen cold fish in my time, but you top the list."

"Go to hell," Oren said without turning around.

"Look a here, hot shot, you can't—"

"Stop it, Tom," Helen said. "You too, Oren. The two of you squabbling isn't accomplishing anything."

Amy set down her cup. She would have preferred not to get into it with Calder but someone had to set things straight. "What makes you think Dr. Tambor was killed?"

"He was carrying on with your cousin's woman, wasn't he?"

She regarded him with a scowl. "That's all you've got?

153

When I tried to tell you about the doctor and Elise on Saturday, you didn't give a good God damn."

A muscle knotted along his long-jawed face. "So what? The picture's changed."

"Then you'd better get your facts straight." She stood up and regarded him with a level look. "The doctor was drunk. He could've jumped, or fallen down that shaft."

The sheriff's eyes flickered and widened ever so slightly. Then he caught himself and his lip curled into a sneer. "Yeah, and he could have been pushed too." He turned and stalked out.

Later that morning, B.J. and Simon arrived on the ferry and for the next few hours the big house was a flurry of activity. After lunch, they gathered in what used to be her father's bedroom, but now more closely resembled a jungle gym.

Under B.J.'s direction, Simon had rigged up pulleys, ropes, and grab bars. With these in place, B.J. hoped to be less dependent on her and Simon. She eyed them without enthusiasm. Two nights ago, he'd undergone surgery to relieve a concussion. What if he fell?

"Watch this, Amy," B.J. said. With Simon beaming in the background, he raised himself, swung his long leg cast off the bed, followed with the short leg cast on his right leg, caught hold of a metal railing and pulled himself up enough to get his crutches into place. "How about that?"

She smiled wryly. "Great, Dad. Just great. Now get back in bed."

Simon winked at her and she frowned in annoyance. "Don't help him with anymore of his hare-brained schemes. Okay?"

154

Simon flung up an arm as if to ward off a blow, and grinned at her from behind the cover. "Aye, aye, sir."

He was always so serious his clowning took her by surprise. She kept her face straight, but knew her eyes betrayed her amusement. "I mean it, Simon," she said with as much force as she could muster.

His grin broadened into a heart-melting smile. "I know. know."

B.J. plopped back on the bed and settled himself among the pillows she'd stacked. "Lighten up, kitten. I know my own limitations."

"That'll be the day."

He reached for her hand and gave it a squeeze. "Get your notebook. It's time we had a buzz session."

She set up his easel and brought out the huge pad of newsprint he always used.

"Fine. Fine. Now you do the honors."

An uncomfortable feeling came over her as she stepped into the spot where he always stood and picked up the soft leaded pencil. "Where do you want to begin?"

"Let's start with Elise."

She drew a circle in the center of the sheet and labeled it.

"Okay, let's see what we've got kids." He tugged at his beard. "Here's a woman who impressed me as being quiet and soft spoken.

Amy listed the qualities beside Elise's name.

B.J. nodded his approval. "However, Helen found her to be cold as a clam."

Amy wrote as he talked. "She was also moody and unpredictable." She glanced at Simon. "Isn't that right?"

He nodded. "Also self-centered and short-tempered." His features darkened. "There wasn't an ounce of truth in those stories she told that Mrs. Michaels at Dr. Tambor's office. So why'd she lie? I've never met anyone so . . . so"—he waved his hand—"forget it."

B.J. flung him a benevolent glance. "I can understand you and Oren having sore spots. I went through it myself when Amy's mother left without telling me she was going, or why."

His eyes clouded for a moment, but he recovered quickly and went on. "However, if either of you are holding something back that we should know, I'm not going to take it kindly."

Simon sat up straight, folded his arms and concentrated his attention on the opposite wall.

When Simon made no comment, B.J. took up his recital once more. "In White Bird, you learned Elise had been kind to a retarded boy and his mother."

"Perhaps something happened there that changed her." Amy printed "White Bird" and drew a circle around it. She remembered an oversight and said, "Dr. Tambor's office manager is bound to be a key witness against Oren. We need to find out if she's trustworthy or just one of those people who likes to grab attention." She headed a column with a large question mark and put down Mrs. Michaels's name.

"Ah." B.J. smiled and rubbed his hands together. "Now, we're beginning to get somewhere."

"Heard anything more about Elise's jewelry?" Simon asked.

Amy shook her head. "Calder isn't noted for his speed and efficiency." She made a number "one" off to the right and wrote "jewelry" after it.

Simon put his hands behind his head and stretched out his legs. "The Seattle police are involved now. Maybe they'll get faster action."

"What about her car, Amy?" B.J. said. "Found out anything more?"

"Only what I told you on Saturday." She picked up her notebook and turned toward Simon. "A man named Roger Norman bought it." She jotted his name under Mrs. Michaels, then began to write his social security number. She'd put down the first three digits when she stared at them and gasped. "He's from Montana."

Simon sprang from his chair and joined her. "How do you know?"

"The first three digits of the social security number indicates the area of the country where the person first applied for a card."

"Yes, yes, I know," Simon said. "Social Security's geographical divisions are the pits. I've found it next to impossible to pinpoint a number." He peered at her figures. "How do you know 516 indicates he's from Montana?"

"Oh, ye of little faith." She grinned. "Montana's numbers can start with either 516 or 517. A private investigator I know has separated the numerical divisions into individual states. I checked with Social Security. They said anyone with access to the right information could work out an exact break down. I've monitored the man's system and it hasn't been wrong yet."

Simon swept off his imaginary hat to her. "Wow, this is terrific." He paced the length of the room and came to stand at the foot of B.J.'s bed. "Norman being from Montana could be just a coincidence, but considering what we ran into in White Bird, I doubt it. What do you think, B.J.?"

"I'd say we'd better find out just how, or where he fits in the puzzle."

"It'll take some digging," Amy said. "I've already checked the city directory and phone book."

"Let me give it a shot," Simon said. "I'm good at turning over rocks." He came to her side and studied the chart.

"I called Gail at the lab," she said. "No one's heard

157

the results of the postmortem on Dr. Tambor." She glanced at her father. "She found some flecks of paint on your clothing."

"Good for her. Has she done a laser analysis?"

"She can't get to it today. That place is a mad house on Mondays." She made a question mark, then darkened and shaded the lines. Her dog's name belonged on the 'To be investigated' list. A feeling of impotent frustration came over her. She must not let Cleo's death get shuffled aside.

Twelve

Amy was standing at the kitchen sink paring carrots for dinner when she became aware of Simon watching from the hallway. He'd become so adept with his cast that he no longer clunked when he walked. A distracting tremor began in her midriff.

She inhaled and let her breath out slowly before glancing over her shoulder. "Something I can get for you, Simon?"

He smiled and shook his head. "Sure smells good in here. He joined her at the counter, found a paring knife, and picked up a potato.

"You needn't do that. I can manage."

"I want to pull my weight. My being here makes more work for you."

Simon's body seemed much too close, the big country kitchen much too small, the air too rarefied to sustain her. To add to her distress, the warm, steamy confines intensified the faint woodsy odor of his aftershave. Her sideways glance took in his fitted sage green shirt and matching trousers. Nice. They complimented his chestnut hair and his slim body. Her glasses fogged and a film of perspiration broke out on her upper lip.

She moved quickly to the stove, lifted the domed lid

of the iron kettle and picked up a sharp tined fork to check the meat inside. Simon leaned in beside her to get a look, his arm brushed hers, and she nearly dropped the lid.

He sniffed noisily. "Ambrosia. Pure ambrosia. They should make a perfume and call it essence of pot roast." He watched her push the fork into the meat in several places, giving the tines a little twist each time. "You do that like an expert."

She hunched her shoulders slightly, drawing into herself. "I've been the only woman in this house for seventeen years."

"Know what? I don't believe I've ever known a woman who could cook." He frowned. "Isn't that ridiculous? I love good food."

So Julie couldn't cook. The "perfect wife" wasn't quite as perfect as Simon had led her to believe. She resettled the lid on the kettle. "These days girls only learn what they want to learn." Returning to the pan of vegetables, she began to pare another carrot.

He peeled a potato, dropped it into a pot of water in the sink, and started to chuckle. "If you dabbed that essence of pot roast behind your ears, men would flock around you in droves." With each word his voice had grown more harsh. "Then you could find that perfect guy B.J. wants you to have."

She turned to look up at him. To her surprise, his eyes held a strange, bleak expression. "You guessed what he was up to?"

"It wasn't difficult. He's always talking about you."

"Sorry. I didn't know how to warn you." She concentrated on cutting the stock and root ends off an onion. "Dad's fifty-five and he wants a grandchild."

"You're very close, aren't you?"

160

She nodded and peeled away a flap of the onion's russet-colored skin. "I guess it was bound to happen."

"I envy you. My father and I never did mesh."

"Not even after you grew up?"

He shook his head. "I'm not a doctor, a lawyer, or a business man. So he figures I'm piddling my life away."

"But you're a good investigative reporter. Doesn't he know that?"

Simon made a face. "No, and neither do I."

She dropped the onion she held into the pan and swung around. "Come off it, Simon. A good writer digs below the surface. He makes you think. I read the article you wrote about Dad. It was damned good. You made me realize what an exceptional man he is."

"You really liked it?"

She ran water on the vegetables and began to cut them into quarters. "Uh huh." She gave him a sideways glance. "Except for the remark you made about me. 'Intelligent brown eyes hidden behind scholarly dark-framed glasses.' Are they that bad?"

He flushed and pulled at his shirt collar. "We—ell, there are glasses and—glasses. At first, I wondered why you didn't wear contacts or select something more attractive."

He leaned his elbow on the counter, rested his chin on his hand and tilted his head to look at her. "Now, I realize you're shy. You don't want people to notice you, so you hide behind your glasses." He lifted an eyebrow. "Right?"

He'd found her out. Heat flared in her cheeks. "My, my, an amateur psychologist. Just what we need." She grabbed the pan of vegetables and hurried to the stove.

That evening after they'd finished eating, Simon helped B.J. settle into his easy chair in the living room. Simon sat on one end of the couch, she perched on the other.

B.J. sighed and patted his stomach. "Good dinner, Amy. Sure beats hospital fare."

"Delicious," Simon said. "Tasted as good as it smelled."

Could Simon fit a "sensual, attractive, intelligent" cook into his life? Amy removed her glasses and unveiled the smile her father swore would melt stone. "Thanks. I haven't done much cooking the past few years." Her voice thinned and she came to a stop. *Say something clever. Don't be so damned dull.* She wet her lips and struggled on. "Nice to know I haven't lost my touch."

Simon stared at her for an instant, then glanced at B.J. who beamed at them in a paternal manner. "Suppose it is," he mumbled and picked up a magazine.

Scared him. She put on her glasses and settled the bridge into place on her nose. *I never did know how to flirt.*

B.J. adjusted his propped leg to a more comfortable angle and leaned back against the cushions. "Something I better tell you two so you won't be expecting any help from Sheriff Calder. He's buckin' for a cushy job and I suspect he's willing to do most anything to come out of this case a winner."

Amy made a face. "God help the justice system. Talk about a narrow mind. Tom's convinced of Oren's guilt. If someone else came in and gave the old buzzard a signed confession, I'll lay odds he wouldn't accept it."

Simon put down his magazine. "Wait'll he learns about Dr. Tambor."

"Oh, he already has. He showed up at Helen's house this morning breathing fire. He not only accused Oren of doing in Dr. Tambor, but of running down Dad as well. Crazy. Absolutely crazy." She glanced at her father. "Can you picture Oren doing such a terrible thing?"

"Um-m-m," B.J. mumbled without meeting her gaze.

She stared at him in dismay. Had he begun to doubt Oren's innocence?

B.J. gnawed his lip and peered over at her. "You ask Virgil to look at my car?"

"He'll be here in the morning."

"What about my cellular phone?"

"I'll take it into Anacortes tomorrow." She frowned and changed the subject. "Those blood-stained articles have to be analyzed, Dad. Time's running out."

B.J. ran a hand over his face and stirred restlessly. "I talked to the prosecuting attorney while you were getting dinner. The town council had an emergency meeting. They've arranged for a medical examiner from Olympia to replace me for a few weeks. Dr. Laroche is a good man." His shoulders drooped and he took in a deep breath. "Problem is, he can't get here until next week."

Amy noticed his increased pallor and stood up. "What say we get you to bed?" She expected him to protest, but he didn't.

After she and Simon had made him as comfortable as possible, she leaned over and gave him a kiss. "Have a good night." She turned to Simon. "You'll enjoy the guest room. My great grandfather brought that carved four-post bed from Madagascar or some such exotic place."

Simon avoided meeting her eyes. "Uh, B.J. and I thought"—he threw her father a beseeching look—"we were thinking it might be best if . . . Oh, hell, B.J. you tell her."

She folded her arms across her chest. The two men had been conspiring again. "Spill it, Dad."

B.J.'s brows met in a fierce scowl. "Now don't get all huffy, Amy. I knew damned well you wouldn't move in here, so"—he raised his chin in a belligerent gesture—"I persuaded Simon to sleep in the spare room at the cottage."

She glared at Simon. "Of all the crazy, asinine ideas. Just because you're a guest here doesn't mean you have to go along with everything Dad suggests, you know."

Simon digested her comment with a grave expression. "I'm not a guest. B.J. insisted on putting our arrangement on an employer/employee basis."

For an instant, Amy experienced a curious sense of loss. She firmed her jaw to halt the traitorous tremor of her lips.

"Besides," Simon went on hastily as if expecting an outburst from her. "His idea sounded sensible to me. Once the alarm is on, nobody can get near B.J."

"Well, I'm not going along with it."

"Come on, kitten. You know how flimsy the locks are at the cottage. It's not safe for you to be there by yourself."

"You shouldn't be alone either. What if you should fall?"

"We have our intercom. If I have a problem, I'll call you."

She blew out her breath. "You promise?"

"Yes. Yes. Now, run along. I'm tired."

She stood at the door looking back at her father. "I still don't like it."

Simon took her arm and eased her toward the front hall. "Probably won't be for more than a couple of nights. We should hear about Dr. Tambor soon." He took his suitcase from the hall closet, helped her on with her coat, and put on his windbreaker.

"We'll need a flashlight." She located one, rejoined him and went through the door he held open. Rain drummed on the front porch roof. She sighed, returned to the coat closet and brought him a yellow slicker. "You'd better put this on or you'll get soaked."

He backed away. "I'll be all right."

She doubled up her fist and shook it under his nose. "Put it on, dammit, or I'll sock you one."

"Yes, ma'am." He took the coat from her.

Her face grim, she selected one of the keys that hung on a chain around her neck and turned on the alarm.

Simon moved closer. "Sorry, we ganged up on you. I had to agree to his scheme. He's worried something will happen to you."

"I know." She pulled up the hood of her raincoat. "It's too dark to take the short-cut through the trees. We'd better follow the driveway."

When they moved away from the protection of the house, water pelted them. Cold needlelike spray stinging her face, she skirted the grove of Douglas fir where wind thrashed sweeping branches and tossed limbs in their path.

She grasped his hand. "Watch your step, the grass is slippery." She guided him down the slope.

They reached the cottage's glassed-in back porch and clambered up the steps. She flipped on the light and grinned at his sodden appearance. "I'll bet our rain is wetter than England's."

Simon laughed. "Could be. London's is a grimy puree." He hung the borrowed slicker on a wooden rack in the corner and looked around. "Where's your little black cocker? I haven't seen her since we arrived."

She turned so he couldn't see her face and hastily unlocked the back door. Simon saw too much. Heard too much. Lying to him packed a risk. She switched on the light. "Let's get a fire started. My ancient furnace can't compete with the drafts." She set off down the short hall.

With him at her heels, she stopped briefly in the kitchen to point out the plate rail above her great grandmother's pine table in the dining alcove. In the living room, she knelt on the hearth and began to crumple newspaper and lay kindling on top.

Simon stooped to examine a deacon's bench and straightened her bedraggled Raggedy Ann doll in one corner. "You've got a neat place here." He sat in a padded glide rocker and smiled contentedly. "It fits you."

She struck a match and ignited the paper. "Does that mean I'm ancient, antique, and plain?"

He smiled. "None of the above."

She arranged logs on top of the crackling cedar kindling and closed the fire screen. "Bring your bag. The guest room's upstairs. Nothing fancy, but the bed is comfortable."

As they passed her room, she paused at the sound of a loud meow. When she was home, she usually left her window open so Marcus could come in and sleep on her bed. She swung the door inward and he marched into the hall with his head held regally erect.

"Well, now, who's this?" Simon bent down on his knees and began to make small chirping noises. Within minutes, he had the yellow Manx purring and rubbing against his leg.

Amy watched in astonishment. "His name's Marcus Aurelius. Marcus for short. He's usually not friendly to strangers."

He smiled up at her. "Perhaps he knows I'm a friendly stranger." He sobered and got to his feet. "What happened to your dog, Amy?"

Her up-flung hand failed to muffle her startled gasp. "She . . . uh, she died." She ducked her head and tried to brush by him.

He caught her arm and swung her to face him. "When?"

A cold lump gathered in her stomach. "I . . . I'm not sure."

166

His grip tightened. "Before or after B.J.'s accident?" His eyes bored into hers.

How far could she go without him guessing? "The same night." She wet her dry throat. "I . . . I think."

The lines in his face deepened. "How?"

Her nerves drew taut. "P—poison." He continued to stare into her eyes and her nervousness increased. Unable to stand his stern appraisal any longer, she stooped, picked up Marcus, and pressed a burning cheek against his fur. If Simon suspected the truth, he and her father would turn the place into a prison.

Simon folded his arms and scowled at her. "That's all you know?"

She didn't trust her voice so she nodded.

He exhaled deeply. "You and your mulish independence. It'd be just like you to keep something to yourself."

"That'd be stupid, wouldn't it?" She set Marcus free, hurried into the spare room and began to fluff pillows and turn down blankets.

He stood at the door observing her. "Yes, it would, Amy," he said quietly. "Real stupid."

Thirteen

Amy placed her forefinger under the sentence she'd reread five times in the last twenty minutes and went over her conversation with Simon. She squirmed uncomfortably. The man had a knack of making her doubt the wisdom of her decisions. She heard a sound and looked up as he came down the stairs.

"I'm going for a walk," he said, and took off for the back door.

She stared after him. Evidently he'd decided to set the rules for tolerating confinement with his employer's daughter. Number one: I'll stay out of your hair and you stay out of mine.

She sighed, wriggled tensed shoulder muscles and looked down at the book in her lap. This was not the time to dwell on Simon. She'd have to hit the books if she expected to finish her evening forensic specialty class with the rest of her group.

An hour passed, and she became so engrossed that the sound of Simon shouting from the back door startled her.

"I'm all sand and sea spray. What do you want me to do?"

"Hang on a second." She joined him and opened a recessed door on one side of the hall. "One of my more ingenious ancestors solved the sand and salt problem. Follow me."

She flipped the light switch and descended wooden steps. Gray cement walls absorbed what little illumination the dangling low watt bulb put out. "Sorry for the mess. This is where most of my cast-off junk lands." She gestured to a shadowy corner where two three-legged chairs teetered on top of a paint-smeared chest of drawers. Clam guns, shovels, and fishing poles of various sizes occupied another corner. Cans of paint, jars filled with nails, screws, nuts, and bolts ranged along a shelf mounted beneath hinged half windows.

She pointed to overhead wires. "I hung my wash down here until I got my dryer. Over here"—she walked to a raised cement structure set in the middle of the wall—"is the gray ghost's coffin." It was oblong, about the size and depth of a bathtub and a short piece of hose dangled from a mixer faucet.

"You just drape your slicker over that hanger up there, give the whole thing a good spraying and let it drip dry." She stood by as he followed her instructions.

"Works like a charm," he said, when he finished.

She handed him a towel to dry his hands. "Yep. The pit's ugly as sin, but using it sure saves your neck and wrists from getting chafed with hardened salt spray."

Simon's eyes glinted above wind-reddened cheeks. "You inherited good genes." He followed her up the stairs. "It's spectacular out there with the great white plumes of sea water exploding against the cliffs. I could learn to love your island."

"You should see Otter Inlet by moonlight, or on a blue and gold day."

His expression grew solemn. "It's not good for a journalist to get attached to a place . . . or a person." He increased the distance between them. "I . . . uh . . . have

169

to get to work. My head's teeming with words. I'd better get them on paper." He ran up to his room, returned with a blue spiral notebook and disappeared into the dining alcove.

She drummed the couch's wooden arm with her fingers. He wasn't what you'd call a stimulating companion. She picked up her book. At the end of half an hour, she found she'd read and reread the same page and couldn't remember a word. She gave up, and stacked the record player with some of her 1940's big band collection. The sounds of Benny Goodman, Jimmy Dorsey, and Harry James always put her in a dreamy, senior-prom sort of mood.

Simon appeared before the first tune ended. He shuffled through the dust covers she'd stacked on the table. "You've got some great ones. I didn't know you were a collector too." When the smooth notes of a Glen Miller classic began, he held out his hand. "Let's not waste this."

She hesitated. "What about your ankle?"

"No problem. I'm practically pain free."

She lay her glasses on an end table and went into his arms. She'd done little ballroom dancing and she felt like a stick. Simon made no comment, and as she relaxed he maneuvered her into more intricate steps. However, the crowded furniture prevented him from doing anything too fancy so her lack of skill didn't matter.

With each tune, the space between them lessened. His nearness muddled her thoughts and made her tremble inside. He rested his cheek on her hair, put both arms around her, and swayed to the music. She held him close, enjoying the wonderful warmth of his body, the thunderous beat of his heart against her ear.

His hands slid down her back, pressing her into the contours of his body. *So good.* Her chest swelled until

170

she could scarcely breath. She longed to belong some-where, to feel needed. Could she make him care for her as he had for Julie?

"Oh, damn." He drew in a deep breath, then another and another, each more tremulous than the last. "Amy?" He moved her gently against him. Before she could react to his unspoken question, he put her from him. "I'd better get back to my writing."

She sank onto the couch and waited for her pulse to return to normal. As she huddled among the cushions, her thoughts battered her brain. He wanted her, but it meant nothing. Men found it easy to desire a woman—any woman. Love and affection they gave much more selectively.

She hugged a pillow to her. In White Bird, he'd made it clear he was unavailable. She buried her face in the pillow's velveteen softness. *I don't need him. I don't need him or any other man.* A sick feeling settled in her stomach. Perhaps, his rebuff in White Bird was the real reason for the attraction she felt. Did she, for some psychological reason, program herself for rejection? She made a face—considering the outcome of her marriage, it would certainly seem so.

She heard Simon's chair scrape, then his footsteps as he went to the kitchen. Glass clinked against glass. Water gushed from a faucet. Footsteps returned to the alcove. His chair creaked as he sat down.

A long silence, then he got up again and came into the living room. He shoved his hands deep in his pant's pock-ets and regarded her from beneath drawn brows. "We're friends. Right? And . . . and friends should be straight with each other. Shouldn't they?"

She felt a tightness in her chest and realized she'd been holding her breath. She found her voice and spoke with careful phrasing. "It makes for less problems."

He sprawled on the opposite end of the couch and an uneasy silence fell between them. Finally, he exhaled and rubbed the palms of his hands on his pant legs. "I haven't been able to forget that night we were together in White Bird. I've tried"—he ran his fingers through his hair—"but when I'm near you, your smile, the fragrance of your hair, the way you move gets to me."

The sound of her pulse roared in her ears. She peered at him. "Gets to you?"

He frowned. "I haven't been with a woman in a helluva long time. Okay? And . . . and you turn me on." He lifted his chin as if challenging her to debate the point.

Her thoughts skittered wildly. Was it better to be desired because of her body than not to be wanted at all? She wrapped her arms around herself. *He could make me feel alive again.*

She stretched her lips into the semblance of a smile. "Why shouldn't you get turned on? You're a normal, healthy male." Her nails dug into her flesh—and she was a normal, healthy female. She straightened her shoulders and folded her hands loosely in her lap. "That monument you've erected to Julie won't crumble if you react to another woman."

His features turned wooden. "Who says I've built a monument?"

She rose to her knees on the couch cushion and gave him a long level look. "I do. You've made her into a saint. No live woman could possibly compete." Their gaze locked in an angry stare.

He sprang to his feet. "That's crap. Pure crap." Holding himself ramrod stiff, he got his notebook from the alcove and stalked up the stairs.

She caught the early morning ferry to Anacortes. In addition to her father's phone, she'd brought along the gray fibers found in Oren and Elise's apartment. If she could complete the errand for her father quickly, she hoped to go on into Seattle.

At Cellular One, Inc., the clerk said the phone looked as if someone had smacked it with a hammer. He gave her a transportable unit in its place. Her initial goal accomplished, she drove to Seattle and took the elevator to the Crime Lab.

She was hanging up her coat when Gail came in. After they'd exchanged greetings, she asked Gail if she'd completed the laser analysis on the paint flakes found on B.J.'s clothing.

Gail flopped into a chair. "Did it first thing this morning. The vehicle's had three paint jobs." She bent down a slim finger tipped with pink-pearl nail polish as she ticked them off. "First navy, then cherry red, and finally metallic blue. I'll run them through the National Automotive Paint File soon as I get a chance."

"Nice going, Gail." Amy jotted the information in her notebook. "If we're lucky, that'll give us the year and make." She flung her friend a pleading look. "We need a break right now so speed it up if you can. Heard anything about the autopsy on Dr. Tambor?"

Gail jerked upright. "I read there might be a link between him and Oren's fiancee. Do you think he tried to run your father down?"

Amy shrugged. "At this point, nothing would surprise me. What about the autopsy?"

"Haven't heard a whisper."

Amy frowned. The paper trail usually kept them fairly well informed. "The M.E.'s office must be hand carrying their reports. I wonder what they're trying to keep under wraps?"

"I'll give you a jingle if I find out." Gail got up and started for the door. "You going to be in the area at lunch time?"

"Depends on how long it takes to go over the physical evidence I brought in."

In the lab, she mounted gray fibers found at Elise and Oren's apartment and slid them under the polarizing microscope's objective. Hm-m-m, surface scales—that eliminated wool. Long smooth sides on the filament suggested a synthetic. The infrared spectrometer verified her hunch.

She had just finished writing down her conclusions when the director came up to her. "I hear you're doing a bit of moonlighting for your father."

"Only until Oren's case is cleared up." She picked up her notes. "I brought in some modacrylic polymer fibers. They're straight, a lustrous gray in color, and somewhat thicker in diameter than Orlon rug fiber. Got any ideas what they might have come from?"

He shook his head. "They're using synthetics for everything these days." He patted her shoulder. "Good luck, and tell your father I wish him well."

Gail came over and leaned on the counter. "How about a wig or hair piece?"

Amy clapped her on the back. "You're a genius."

"But of course." Gail grinned and tossed her head. "Need anything else?"

Amy shook her head. "Not right now. After I talk to the detective in charge of the Tambor case, I'm going to run by the apartment then dash back to the island. I hate that evening traffic."

Gail studied her with a concerned expression. "Try to get some rest, Amy. Remember, you're on vacation."

Amy twisted her mouth into a wry smile. "I'd almost forgotten." She picked up the receiver and dialed a friend in the police department. He gave her a number. She called and reached Detective Lieutenant Joseph Salgado. She identified herself and asked what she wanted to know.

"Can't tell you much, Dr. Prescott. They've put a tight lid on this one. And speaking of lids, who the hell does that sheriff on Lomitas Island think he is? A guy has to pull information out of him a strand at a time."

She spent the next ten minutes answering his questions. When he'd learned all she knew, he said, "Thanks, you've saved me a lot of foot work." He tapped his pencil on the desk. "I have only one good lead. On Friday, the doctor withdrew ten thousand dollars from his bank account." He made a sound deep in his throat. "Some messy can of worms, eh?"

"Cash or check?"

"Hundred dollar bills."

"His wife know anything about it?"

"Nope. Didn't have an inkling."

"Any trace of the money?"

"Negative."

"Did it look as if he planned on leaving town?"

"No bus, airline, or boat reservations, but there are other ways out of this burg."

"Perhaps the elevator shaft seemed easiest." When the lieutenant made no reply, she went on. "Do you know the time of death?"

"Late Saturday night or early Sunday morning."

"Anything more you can tell me?"

"I've already said more than I should have." His pencil began to tap again. "Keep me posted, doc. I don't like surprises."

On her way to pick up some extra clothes at her apartment, she pondered the bits of information she'd accumulated. An illicit affair, a gray wig, and ten thousand dollars—she could easily fit them into a scenario involving Elise's murder.

Whoa girl, enough of that kind of nonsense. At the beginning of her training, she'd often made assumptions on insufficient evidence. She tried not to fall into that trap anymore.

When she arrived at her apartment, she fit her key into the lock. At her touch, the door swung inward and a putrid odor assaulted her nostrils.

Death. The familiar smell jammed her heart against her ribs. "Oh . . . God." Not here. Not here too.

She forced herself to assume the observer mode she'd learned when she'd assisted with autopsies. From this above-the-scene position, she could see, hear, observe, and catalog without the odors affecting her as much.

But, despite her dogged professional approach, a chill climbed her spine. The building hadn't had many burglaries. Few of the tenants had possessions worth ripping off.

She scanned the kitchen and living room and saw no one. Her muscles clinched tight, she ventured a few steps farther. A wave of heat hit her in the face. Her gaze swung to the thermostat. Someone had turned the switch as high as it'd go.

On the floor, a few paces away, her great grandmother's cobalt blue wine carafe lay shattered into bits. Some of the pieces had been ground into fine glass splinters.

He always destroyed the thing she cherished most. Apprehension rippled along her skin. How did he know?

She swallowed and the dry clicking noise sounded loud in the hot silence. On tiptoe, she started down the hall. When she neared her bedroom, she wavered. Cornered burglars killed.

Crouched in a ready-to-run stance, she listened. No sound. No sound at all.

The door stood ajar. She gave it a hard boot with her foot and flattened herself against the wall. A foul repulsive stench belched forth nearly tilting her stomach.

Nothing in the room had been disturbed. Perspiration beaded her forehead, her upper lip. Could he be in the closet? She plucked up her courage and yanked open the door. Empty, except for her clothes.

The source of the odor must be in the bathroom. Clamping her jaws together to control the waves of nausea, she headed for the half-open doorway.

The mirror came into view and she gaped at it. In red marking-pen, someone had scrawled across the glass surface. *SNOOPERS GET DEAD. VERY VERY DEAD.* Below he listed their first names: hers, her father's, and Simon's—each one with a slash mark through it. She quivered. She'd nearly lost her father. Would Simon be next?

She moved closer and her scalp prickled. The same writing. The smeary letters slanted erratically right and left as they had in the note she'd found under Cleo's collar.

On her left, a yellow flowered shower curtain screened the tub from view. The body must be there. She braced herself and jerked open the curtain.

In the partially-filled tub floated three, very dead, hideously swollen rats.

She gagged, bent over the toilet, and lost her breakfast.

Grabbing a towel from the rack, she staggered out of the apartment. The police had to be told. To protect the crime scene, she made her way to the public telephone on the first floor and phoned Lt. Salgado.

"You'd better bring a photographer," she said, after she'd explained her reason for calling. "You'll need pictures of the message he left."

"I know that. Believe it or not, the police department does manage to function without supervision from the lab."

"Oh . . . sorry. I didn't mean to imply—"

"Forget it. I'll be there as soon as I can."

When he arrived, she noticed Lt. Salgado's appearance didn't match his tough, hard-edged voice. He was tall, stoop shouldered, and had thinning black hair. Pendulous bags under his eyes spoke of sleep loss and chronic overwork. Earlier in his life, someone's fist had redesigned his nose. It now meandered over his lined face.

He questioned her in the hall while his men dusted the apartment for fingerprints and snapped pictures. This time circumstances compelled her to reveal the true facts of how Cleo had died and about the threatening note left with the body.

After the technicians had finished and the dead rats were carted off to the lab, Salgado motioned her into the bathroom. "We're dealing with a sick person here," he said. "One that knows you, your father, and Kittredge."

She stared at the ominous message. "How do you figure that?"

"In each message he's left you, he's used only first names."

"But I've never met Dr. Tambor. Neither has my father."

He narrowed his eyes and his features took on a sly, secretive appearance. "I was thinking of your cousin."

"No, no." She shrank against the wall. "No, not Oren. We're friends. True friends. Have been since childhood." Her voice gathered strength. "He couldn't have strangled Cleo and he wouldn't have done a thing like this."

He raised an eyebrow. "That's an emotional opinion, Dr. Prescott, not a scientific one."

She wrapped her arms across her chest and clutched

her elbows as if she were freezing. *He's found new evidence. Something that links Oren to more than just Elise's death.*

His gaze probed hers. "A person in your profession should know people are seldom what they seem to be."

After he left, her stomach continued to churn, triggering jets of fiery acid. Oren wouldn't do anything that'd hurt her, or her father. He . . . he just couldn't have.

She rushed down to ask the apartment manager to have a new lock put in, then she hurried back upstairs. *Keep busy, don't think.* When the shock wore off, she'd be able to sort things out in a more rational manner. She telephoned the island and arranged for installation of dead bolts on the cottage doors.

The locksmith said he could be at the cottage by 2 P.M., so she dialed her father's number. She hoped he wouldn't ask a lot of questions. He'd have to know what had happened, but she had a feeling he was already beginning to doubt Oren. Perhaps, if they were together when she told him, she could explain—she shivered—explain what?

Simon answered the telephone on the first ring. "He's taking a nap," he said when she asked for her father. "You want me to give him a message?"

She sighed. Simon would put her on the hot seat regardless of whether he heard her story now or tonight. She recounted her day starting with the more mundane events and finishing with the horror in her apartment. But, she remembered to omit Salgado's reference to the previous message she'd received.

When she finished, he didn't say a word for a long anxious moment. Finally, he cleared his throat and asked softly, "Are you all right?"

His gentleness caused tears to gather in her throat. "I was pretty shook up at first, but I'm okay now."

"Are you sure?"

"Yes, I'm"—her voice broke—"that's a lie. I'm scared, real scared. He's targeted Dad, now you . . . Simon, what if it wasn't Dr. Tambor?"

He drew a ragged breath. "Come home, Amy. Lock your car doors and keep them locked. And don't get out of the car while you're on the ferry. Do you"—his voice dwindled, and he started again—"do you have a gun?"

Oh, hell! After Cleo died, she'd searched for the damned thing, but hadn't found it. Since then, she hadn't found the right moment to ask her father if he had the .38. She inhaled and let the air trail from her mouth. "Yeah, I have one, but I don't have it with me."

His breath trembled in and out. "Just come home. Come home *now*."

"I will. I'll leave as soon as I hang up."

"Be careful, Amy. Don't trust anyone, whether you know them or not. Not anyone, you hear?"

The journey frayed her nerves but proved uneventful. Nevertheless, when she reached home, she parked in her father's driveway to assure her car wouldn't be vandalized. He had flood lights outlining the paved semi-circle. Unfortunately, he seldom remembered to use them and she suspected they weren't on the night his car and phone were sabotaged. She made a mental note to lecture him. From now on, his grounds must be kept well lighted. And if she intended to spend time at the beach house, they'd have to have an electrician put in some outside lights.

She stared through the windshield at ragged clumps of purple chrysanthemums and scowled. It wasn't right. They shouldn't have to make their homes into fortresses.

She locked the car and entered the house, expecting to find Simon waiting anxiously by the front door. He wasn't there and didn't answer her call. She set the box containing the cellular phone in the hall closet and went to see her father. He had to know about the dead rats and the chilling message on her mirror.

That evening, they gathered in her father's room while she stood at the easel. She turned to the page labeled Dr. Tambor, wrote each of their names in individual circles, then listed the possible links Simon and her father suggested. The sketch was as smudged and confused as her mind when they finished.

"Better start a page on Roger Norman," Simon said. "I had a friend do some checking. Norman doesn't have a telephone and has never had a utility account."

"He could be staying with someone." She chewed a fingernail. "Why would he buy a car? The fellow I had go through the files says he doesn't have a driver's license."

"A lot of people drive without licenses," B.J. said. "Besides, he may have wanted it for parts."

"The car's not that old, B.J." Simon drummed his fingers on the arm of the chair. "Oren says he took it in for a fifty thousand mile check-up three weeks ago. The mechanic said the car was in tip-top shape. Wanted to know what Elise would take for it. Oren said she laughed when he told her."

Amy wrinkled her forehead. "Yet, she sold it a week and a half later without a word to him. Would she do such a thoughtless thing?"

Simon's mouth pulled in at the corners. "Oh, yes." He massaged his clenched knuckles. "Without a second thought."

"How could you and Oren . . . ?" She stopped and forced a smile. "Guess what? Gail says the hit-and-run vehicle has had three paint jobs—navy blue, red, and metallic blue."

"Has Gail run it through the NAPF?" B.J. asked.

"Not yet." Amy studied her scrawled notes on the sheet of newsprint with a feeling of impotence. "We'll have to watch our step until we find out who's at the bottom of all this."

"Looks that way," B.J. said. "But in my opinion, we'll be fairly safe so long as we're on the island. A person would have to be crazy to risk coming here again."

"Even if he's using disguises? I don't know, Dad." She noticed the weary droop to his shoulders and set the easel in the corner. "You'd better get some sleep." She paused in the doorway. "What'd Virgil say about your motor?"

"Pulled coil wires. He had to tow it in anyway, so I told him to do a tune-up at the same time."

As she and Simon went down the hall, he squeezed her hand. "Glad you're home." His cheeks and the tips of his ears turned faintly pink. "You're a comfortable person to have around."

Comfortable! She didn't want to be comfortable. She wanted to be alluring, intriguing, or seductive. Any damned thing *except* comfortable.

He stooped to peer into her face. "Why the odd expression?"

"You're adept at giving back-handed compliments."

He thrust out his chin. "I've recently discovered how restful a comfortable woman can be. Julie was seldom quiet." He ran his hand over his face. "Pushing, always pushing. Change jobs, move to New York, make a name for yourself. Drove me nutty."

"Oh . . ." She broke into a smile. "In that case, thank you." Her smile broadened. "Thank you very much." Score one point for her. She laughed out loud when he blinked owlishly at her confusing comment.

After making a thorough security check of the house

and making certain the outside lights were on, she opened the front door and started out.

Simon pulled her back. "I'll go first."

She scowled at him. "Since when are you bullet proof?"

Simon met her fierce gaze with his own. "Either you do it my way or neither one of us goes out that door."

She blew out her breath. "Wait until I ask Dad where he put my gun."

"Forget it. He's already upset, he doesn't need any more excitement right now." He turned off the lights in the foyer and on the porch. "I'll let you know when to turn them back on."

She clutched the sleeve of his jacket. "You shouldn't be taking such a chance."

He disengaged her fingers. "Good investigative reporters don't let danger stop them." He slipped out the door.

She stood in the darkness listening to the heavy fearful beats of her heart. Five minutes passed, then ten. She felt pain and realized her nails were digging into the palms of her hands. She jumped at a soft knock on the door.

"All clear, Amy."

He was safe. Her legs went weak. She clung to the umbrella stand for a half minute before she could close up the house and join him.

During the walk to the cottage, he stayed close to her side. When they arrived, she locked the new deadbolts while he checked windows, pulled drapes, and closed the shades. That done, they smiled tentatively at each other and settled down.

Evidently, they'd marked out their space the night before. Simon claimed the dining alcove and she the living room. Radio reception on the island was poor so they worked in silence. She thought briefly of playing records, but decided not to risk it. She felt much too vulnerable.

If he put his arms around her tonight, she might do something she'd regret.

At ten o'clock, she set her textbooks aside. She knew she should call good night from a safe distance. Instead she went to the kitchen, ran water, filled a glass, and drank it slowly. When she finished, she sauntered into the dining alcove. Trailing her fingers along the edge of the table, she said, "I'm going to bed. It's been an exhausting day."

He blocked the progress of her fingers with his own. "I started my book today."

She smiled at him. "I'm glad for you."

His forefinger stroked the length of hers. "You people give me room to breathe. Julie never did."

She opened her eyes wide. His second criticism of his wife in one evening.

"Whenever I was in the study writing, she'd come in and want to discuss the bills, or some project of hers." A muscle bunched along his jaw. "Our marriage had lots of cracks. I'm not sure it would have survived much longer."

She sighed. "I know the feeling." To her surprise, he pulled her over to where he sat and rested his cheek on her breast. Warmth suffused her body. She caressed his hair and let her hand glide to his face. How could she want him and not want him at the same time? She closed her eyes. *Our egos are fragile, Simon. We must be very, very careful.*

Simon turned until his lips brushed her palm. "You and I are kind of like recovering alcoholics. Only we're luckier. Since we're friends, we can lean on each other."

He lifted his head. "I don't want you to misunderstand, so I'll try to say this right." His earnestness sharpened the lines of his face. "Amy, if you should ever need a . . . a man for . . . for any reason. I'm . . . I'm available."

For a second, she didn't know whether to laugh or cry. She forced a chuckle, snatched a fly swatter from a hook, and tapped his shoulder. "I dub thee, Sir Simon of the kitchen table."

The corners of his eyes and mouth crinkled, but he kept a straight face. "Dammit, woman, I'm serious."

"I know, and it's incredibly sweet of you." She touched his lips with hers, said good night, and hurried up the stairs. If she'd stayed a second longer, she'd have been lost.

She undressed, put on thick, flannel pajamas, surveyed herself in the mirror, and discarded them in favor of a foamy sea-green satin nightgown. After getting into bed, she found herself too keyed up to sleep. She took a pocket book mystery from her night stand drawer and began to read.

Three pages into the story she found she didn't have the faintest idea what she'd read. Each moment that passed her consciousness of Simon's presence increased. At last she heard him coming up the stairs. His footsteps stopped at her door. She held her breath and willed him to come in. If he took her into his embrace and kissed her, her cautioning inner voice would be silenced—for the time being at least.

"Night, Amy," he called.

She sank back on the pillow and closed her eyes. Another opportunity flubbed.

At 2 A.M., the shrilling of the phone awakened her. She fumbled for the receiver and said, hello.

"This is White Bird, Montana," the operator said.

The words jolted Amy wide awake. *The trustee at Marchmont Hospital. It had to be her.* A picture of the skittish blonde file clerk flashed through her mind, and brought her upright. She snapped on the light. "Yes?"

"Will you accept a collect call from Francine Anseth?"

185

"Yes. Yes. Put her on."

"This is Francie Anseth," a faint voice said. "Do you remember me?"

Amy's heart gave an excited leap. She must take great care. The woman frightened easily. "Of course, I asked you to call me about Elise."

"I can't talk long. It's not safe." Jerky little breaths underscored her words. "I warned her, Doctor. I . . . I warned Elise about him, but I was too late. He'd already gotten to her."

"Who Francine?"

"Bull, the randy old bastard. She wasn't the first, nor the last."

Amy began to shiver. Make sure. Make very sure. "Bull? Who's that?"

"That fine, upstanding sonuvabitch Wade Marchmont, that's who." Francie gulped air and rushed on. "She didn't want the abortion, but he insisted."

Amy's mind reeled. "Did Dr. Yates do it?"

"Mona and me crawled into the ventilator tube and watched the whole thing. Yates was boozed-up as usual. Kept telling Marchmont she was too far along. Then the damned old fool passed out before he was finished."

Before he was finished! Good Lord. Even under ideal conditions an abortion had some risk. "W-what—" She fought to control her shaky voice. "What happened?"

"Bull grabbed an instrument and did something inside her. God, you never saw so much blood. It just gushed out of her. Nearly made us sick. She—" A rustling noise came over the line. "I think somebody's coming."

"Wait, Francine. Is the abortion why she left the hospital and came to Seattle?"

"Left the hospital? That's a laugh. Only one person has ever gotten out of this hell hole. I gotta go."

"But Elise did get away. She came to Seattle."

186

"Elise didn't go nowhere." Francine's voice thinned to a thready whisper. "She died. She died right there on that table four years ago."

Fourteen

She had to tell Simon. Amy threw back the blankets and dashed into the hall. Light shone from beneath his door. She tapped lightly and stepped inside. In his restless tossing, Simon's bed covers had slid off. He lay half on his side, his left leg hooked over the rounded fiberglass curve of the cast on his right.

She stared at the naked length of him. Russet, tightly curled hair spread across his chest, dwindled to a fine line, and spread once more in the shadowed pubic area.

She tried to evaluate him with a strictly professional eye, and failed. God, what a beautiful body—lean, muscular, not an ounce of flab. That night in White Bird he'd been wearing long underwear and she had scarcely seen or touched him.

An overwhelming desire to lie down next to him held her immobile. A warm rush jolted her at the thought. After gazing at him for another moment, she sighed and swung around to leave. In turning, she blundered into a table stacked with books and several of them thudded onto the floor.

Simon reared up on one elbow. "Huh?" He focused on her. "What is it? Has something happened?"

"I . . . I must talk to you." She shifted her feet and

curled her toes into the braided rug. "I have to talk to you r-right n-now."

He flipped the sheet over the lower portion of his body, lowered his head to the pillow and regarded her with a gentle expression. In the silence, she grew conscious of her rapid breathing and equally rapid pulse. His gaze trapped hers and held it, a mute question in their depths. After an interminable moment, he stretched out his arm, turned his hand palm up, and curled his fingers slightly.

His gesture started a throbbing deep inside her. So easy. Join hands, join bodies. The fierce longing increased. *He wants you, you want him. Isn't that enough?*

She shook her head as if answering her own question and backed away. "Put on some clothes. I'll meet you in the kitchen."

In her room, she caught sight of herself in a mirror. Her eyes, her mouth, her breasts, her clinging gown, every part of her betrayed her desire—no wonder he'd thought what he did. How could she have been so dumb? She stuck her feet into slippers and put on a floor-length robe of peach-colored fleece. The bulky garment camouflaged all her curves.

Good going, Prescott. You're great at locking the gate after the horses have gotten out. She made a face and hurried to the kitchen.

She set a jug of water in the microwave, punched in the time, and spooned cocoa mix into yellow mugs. Despite an intense effort to keep her mind centered on Francine's shocking announcement, she couldn't. Instead, she kept seeing the hurt in Simon's eyes when she'd backed away from him.

His footsteps sounded on the stairs and he stalked into the kitchen wearing a frayed T-shirt and droopy sweat pants. Legs spread, elbows akimbo, he scowled at her. "What the hell kind of a game are you playing?"

189

Stiffening her muscles so she wouldn't shake, she put bread in the toaster and pushed down the lever. "I got a phone call." Her teeth began to chatter and she clamped them shut. At that moment, the microwave bell went off. Glad for the interruption, she took out the hot water and stirred it into cocoa mix.

"And . . ." he said gruffly, continuing to glower.

She handed him a mug. "I wanted to talk it over with you."

"That's not what it looked like."

The toast popped up. She snatched a knife and began to spread butter. "Yeah . . . well . . . I didn't know you'd be"—warmth flooded her face—"or that I'd . . ." She glanced up and found herself looking straight into his eyes. Deep in the irises, tiny green specks shimmered.

Her lip quivered and she caught it with her teeth. "I'm sorry, it won't happen again." His belligerent manner didn't soften an iota.

She gave an inward sigh. Her actions had been needlessly thoughtless. She shouldn't have gone to his room.

She sprinkled cinnamon flavored sugar on the toast, and cut each piece from corner to corner. Now, things would probably never be the same between them again. Suddenly she felt drained, exhausted beyond all reason. She put more bread in the toaster, picked up her mug and the short stack of toast. "Let's sit down."

She had intended to dramatize Francine's announcement of Elise's death. Instead, she blurted it out and waited for Simon's reaction.

Simon fixed her with a cold, sarcastic eye and bit off a piece of toast. "Obviously, the woman has some cogs missing."

Amy took a sip of her cocoa. "I know it sounds wild, but we can't just dismiss it either."

"Why not? We know her story isn't true. It can't be."

He flung out his hands. "I lived with Elise for three months." He rose to his feet, put both hands on the table and leaned toward her until they were only inches apart. "Three months, Amy. No way could I live with a woman that long and not know who she was."

"Really . . . ?" Amy set down her mug. "You said she lied. What makes you think she told you the truth about anything?"

He swayed, turned slightly pale. "This whole damn thing is crazy, too crazy to even consider." He sank back onto his chair. "Holy Jesus, if she wasn't Elise, who the hell was she and why did she take Elise's name?" He shuddered. "Don't answer that because I don't want to know."

Amy found a tablet and recorded the phone conversation as accurately as she could. Below it, she wrote Wade Marchmont's name, and pushed the tablet over to Simon. "Let's start with him. If Francine's telling the truth, he's guilty of murder."

Simon read the words over twice. "She implies it wasn't the first time he'd gotten one of the staff"—he grimaced—"or maybe even one of the patients, pregnant."

"Wouldn't surprise me. That creep who tried to rape me hinted that he'd been intimate with some of the women patients." She shuddered. "Perhaps it's one of the ways Marchmont repays the men for keeping their mouths shut about his own peccadilloes."

She cradled her mug in both hands, took a drink, and gazed at him over the rim. "Perhaps there were other wrongful deaths. That grounds keeper at the Marchmont cemetery said, 'Nobody's allowed in here except Mr. Marchmont.' He must have wanted to conceal something. Otherwise, why would he have given such an order?"

Simon's eyes widened. "That would account for him

getting shook-up when he saw the newspaper article about Elise's death on Lomitas." He took a gulp of cocoa and picked up another piece of toast.

"And Dr. Yates' reaction, and also why Marchmont sent those two goons to kill us." She went to the kitchen, buttered the toast that had popped up, and brought it back to the table.

"Good God, Amy, you're right. That Svengali has everyone in White Bird in his pocket." He gazed into space for a second, then excitement lighted his face. "If the right people on the outside got wind of what he's been doing—"

She put up her hand. "Hold it. Don't start twitching your investigative nose. We have to be careful. If Francine's story is true, and Marchmont finds out she knows, her life'll be in danger."

"Ah,"—Simon cocked his head and held up a cautioning finger—"now there's another reason to mistrust her. According to what she says, all this happened four years ago. Why would she take the risk now?"

He yawned and stretched. "We'd better try and get some sleep." He rose to his feet. "You go on up, I'm going to check the doors and windows again."

She took a few steps, then turned back. "Do you feel it too?"

"Feel what?"

His voice sounded casual, but she noticed the lines in his face had grown deeper. "An air of foreboding. It's as if there's some formless monster out there manipulating us. Whenever it suits him, he spins a bit more web and ensnares another victim."

He laughed—hollow, tight, devoid of humor. "With an imagination like that, you should be the writer." He started toward the back door.

Next morning, at breakfast she reported Francine's phone conversation to her father.

"Don't put too much faith in what she says," he said. "Law enforcement people get hundreds of calls like that."

"True, but it still intrigues me." She watched as he smoothed a cautious hand over his shaved scalp. The last of his sutures had been removed, but his fringe of hair would never cover the scars. They would always show as a grim reminder.

B.J.'s fingers touched a tender spot on his head and he puckered up his face. "This case is a real Tartar. I've seldom had one with so much confusing evidence."

Simon poured him more coffee and refilled his own cup. "Think you and Amy could get along without me this afternoon?"

"We can manage." He lifted an eyebrow at Amy. "Can't we, kitten?" At her nod, he went on. "I've been feeling guilty about taking up your time anyway. Yesterday, I talked to Helen. She knows a gill-net fisherman who injured his left hand. He can't fish, but he's got a family and needs money. Helen says he'd be able to handle my needs until I get these damned casts off."

A wretched empty feeling settled in Amy's chest. Was Simon anxious to get away from her? She glanced at him through lowered lashes and his deflated look puzzled her.

"You're not taking up my time, B.J.," Simon said. "I like being here with you and Amy."

B.J. sat forward. "Your work is important, Simon. You should be out in the world where you can make a difference."

"A difference? Not a chance until I get out of the slump I'm in. I've written more meaningful words in the past week than I have since Julie died." His gaze darted to her and back to B.J. "But if you'd rather get someone else—"

"No no, son, I enjoy your company. I just don't want to be selfish. Now, what were you about to say when I interrupted?"

"Nothing important." Simon glowed as if he'd been awarded the Edward R. Murrow prize for exceptional journalism.

"Okay, if you say so." B.J. disappeared behind his paper.

Simon spread a thick layer of strawberry jam on his toast and took a huge bite. "Delicious," he said when he swallowed. "Almost as good as the cinnamon toast you made last night." His gaze touched hers, moved down to her mouth, then upward to capture her gaze again. Slowly as if searching for a stray bit of jelly, he ran the tip of his tongue along his lips.

She felt as if a steel band had tightened around her chest. She took a quick, open-mouthed breath and without thinking touched her lip with her tongue. Simon's eyes changed from hazel to smoldering mahogany and his features took on a sensual look. Heat flooded her face. Mating games weren't her strong point. They made her uneasy. What if she couldn't, or wouldn't follow through?

The corners of Simon's mouth curved in a half smile. Regarding her tenderly through half-closed lids, he tilted his chin ever so slightly—once, twice, three times—in subtle invitation.

Perspiration dampened her neck and still he held her captive with his gaze. From a long way off, she heard her father's paper crackle.

What am I doing?

She broke eye contact with Simon and sat gripping her shaking hands in her lap. *Does he mean it, or is he only getting even for last night?*

194

She jumped up and began to clear the table, giving him a wide berth. He rose and began to help. When their bodies accidentally brushed, both of them jerked back as if burned.

He mumbled something about making an appointment with Mrs. Michaels at Dr. Tambor's office and hurried out of the room. In a short while he came back. "She won't see me. Says she knows who I am now and that I'm just as rotten as Elise said I was." He leaned against the cabinet. "She blames me for everything that's happened. Everything. Can you beat that?" He went to help B.J. back to bed.

When he returned, Amy finished wiping off the counter and set the sponge under the sink. "So how about getting at Mrs. Michaels from another angle?" She dried her hands, took a pad from beside the kitchen phone and wrote down a number. "Maybe you can get the answers you need through Lt. Salgado."

"I doubt it, but I'll give it a shot." He tore off the sheet and started out.

"He's more cooperative if you have something to trade. But don't tell him about Francine." She grinned. "He has enough to cope with as it is."

Simon grinned back. "Gotcha."

She finished her cleaning and went down to the lab. After thumbing through all their reference books, she reviewed the collected evidence. Finally, she decided she needed more proof to support her theory. She went upstairs in search of Simon.

She found him in the library working at his laptop computer. "Do you have a pair of sneakers I can borrow for a little while?"

"Sure do. What're you up to?"

"I'm going over to Prescott's Byway. That's where I

discovered the clearest footprint. I want to run a controlled experiment."

"Could I come along?"

She remembered the charged atmosphere at breakfast. With him watching her, she'd be all thumbs. "We—ell, I really—"

"I can be your gofer." He shut down his computer and came around the desk. "You'll need equipment, won't you? I promise to keep my mouth shut and not get in your way." He raised three fingers in the Boy Scout oath. "Honest."

If she turned down his offer, he'd link it with her actions last night. She shrugged. "I can always use an extra pair of arms. I want to check in with Dad first."

"Good idea." Simon followed her down the hall.

She found B.J. propped up in bed with a stack of forensic journals on either side of him. He grinned as they came to stand beside him. "Don't let all this fool you, I've been beating a few bushes and I have news."

Amy regarded him with a severe expression. "Don't go pushing yourself."

B.J. gave her arm an affectionate squeeze. "Hush, girl. I'm too old to change my ways. Now, listen. I talked to a medical examiner in Billings, Montana. We met at a seminar several years ago. He's retired now. I told him about Wade Marchmont and asked him to nose around."

Amy puckered up her forehead in a worried frown. "Did you tell him Francine Anseth could lose her life if he happens to talk to the wrong person?"

"You bet I did and also that asking questions could land him in hot water." He smiled. "The guy is going nutty with nothing to do. He welcomed the excitement." He sobered. "But he's no fool. He'll step lightly."

"I sure hope so." Amy told him where she and Simon were going and they left the room.

Outside, a temperature inversion had given them unseasonable weather for November. The warm, humid air felt heavy and she found it difficult to get a full breath. Overhead, the sun penetrated gauzy cloud cover, spreading a muted, hot house glow.

She rummaged in the car and handed Simon two forensic kits. Pushing her hair off her perspiring forehead, she said, "I'll meet you in front of the cottage." She stowed her unneeded jacket in the car and went in search of a bucket.

When she rejoined Simon, smile lines crinkled around his eyes. "This is great. We haven't had a chance to be . . . er, ah . . . to see much since I came. Now, you can point out the walks you enjoy, the views you like. Oren told me once that you and he have explored most of Lomitas." He handed her the shoes and picked up a satchel in each hand. "Wither way, Captain?"

"Just follow me." She tied the sneaker's laces together and slung them around her neck. Taking care not to spill water from the bucket she carried, she set off down the hill. Where the steep sandstone embankment bordering the beach blocked the way, she set down her burden to watch their ketch ride heavy swells. "Something's brewing."

"What makes you think that?"

He stood behind her and she imagined she could feel his body heat. She forced her mind back to his question and pointed to three silent crows in a bare-limbed alder. "Normally they'd be making a terrible racket." She looked up at the gulls circling overhead. "Even they are quieter than usual."

"Ah, just as I suspected, you *are* a witch."

"Don't be silly." She turned, found him so close her breasts pressed against his chest and her mouth went dry. "D-don't you feel the"—she glimpsed the throbbing pulse at the base of his throat and gulped air—"the strange tension? It . . . uh . . . it feels like the whole world is . . . holding its breath."

"Um-m-m-m." His voice made a mellow vibration in his chest.

She risked an upward glance, found herself gazing into his eyes, and began to tremble. He brushed his knuckle along her jaw, teased a tendril of hair into place and stroked her ear lobe. Her heart speeded up and her breathing kept pace.

The color of his eyes deepened and she felt her cheeks grow warm. He took her face in his hands. "Amy, it's okay for you to react to a man." He smiled a gentle, lopsided smile. "You're a normal, healthy young woman."

For some unaccountable reason, *her* words coming from *his* mouth irritated her. "I have work to do." Pushing him aside, she headed down a trail winding through wind-twisted Sitka spruce and low growing shrubbery.

In the sun-warmed tunnel created by the evergreens, the scent of rosin and Simon's cologne mingled. The combination brought on an infectious sensual languor and she struggled to keep her senses about her.

On the dunes, winter-browned salt rushes tufted the area she'd marked off with bright orange crime-scene-tape twelve days before. She directed Simon to put her supplies some distance away and got down on hands and knees to study the ground. After a ten minute search, she found a similar combination of soil outside the marked area. She wet it thoroughly with the water she'd brought.

She straightened and became aware of Simon. He sat in the lea of a large dune staring out across Rosario Strait. Did he think she was as mixed up and unpredictable as Elise?

She plopped down on the sand near him. "Sorry for my rotten disposition. The pressure is getting to me."

He turned and regarded her with a somber expression. "All men aren't bastards, Amy."

She picked up a handful of sand and let it trickle through her fingers. "I know, Simon."

"Damnit, I wish I could be of more help. Do something to take the load off you."

"But you do. You're wonderful . . . with Dad."

"He's a great guy." He moved closer. "I learned some more about Roger Norman this morning."

Simon shifted position and his bare forearm grazed hers. She felt the brief contact to her fingertips.

"The man doesn't belong to a labor union." Simon picked up her hand, placed it on his jean-clad thigh, lay his hand on top, and went on talking. "He hasn't applied for a professional license, nor has he registered to vote. I sent a query to IRS and I also wrote to request his military record, if he has one."

"Good going." She pasted on what she hoped was a self-assured smile—only a naive romanticist would get all warm and trembly about someone holding her hand. Her cynicism failed to slow her racing pulse. "Norman must have some type of income. He couldn't have purchased Elise's car if he was on welfare."

A horrified expression spread over Simon's face. "Welfare! God, I hope not. Getting information from them is like trying to get into Fort Knox." He rubbed the palm of her hand against his smooth shaven cheek.

"K—keep up the—" Her voice cracked and refused to squeeze through her constricted throat. She coughed and began again. "Keep up the good work. You're doing great." She gently withdrew her hand and began taking off her shoes. "I took casts of Oren's footprints the night I stayed at Helen's."

She slid her bare feet into Simon's Adidas. They felt warm as if he'd just taken them off and to her utter dismay, she got an erotic reaction. Weird. Lately, everything about him turned her on. The thought saddened her. Since her divorce, she'd come to realize her attraction to Mitch had been purely sexual. She didn't intend to make a mistake like that ever again.

She shoved the thought aside and went on with her conversation. "The problem is Oren's prints don't tell me everything I need to know."

She stood and took a step. Her foot came out of the shoe.

"You'll need socks." Simon pulled some from his pockets. "Here, let an old hand show you how it's done."

She sat down and supported herself on braced arms.

He knelt in front of her and rested her heel on his leg. "Nice feet." He worked a thick white sock over her foot, tested the fit of the shoe and added a second sock. "You looked beautiful when you came to my room last night." He kept his head bent and worked nonexistent wrinkles from the knitted fabric.

Picking up her other foot, he held it in his warm hand and ran his fingertip down the arch to her toes. He raised his eyes to hers. "Lovely as a . . ." He licked his lips and swallowed. "As a sea nymph."

The air trembled between them. No one around. No one to stop them. She dug her fingers into the sand. Why not give in? Why not let it happen?

The color in his face heightened, his eyes grew heavy lidded. "Amy, could we . . . ?"

Without warning, a searing memory of her ex-husband's final, and most devastating betrayal, burst inside her skull. Him in their bed with her best friend. She passed a hand over her face. Better to feel nothing than to risk that again. She took the other pair of socks from him, put them on and got to her feet.

She lifted the heaviest satchel in her arms thereby bringing her total weight to 135 pounds and made a set of footprints. To back up her calculations, she had Simon pile driftwood on top of the satchel, then she made some more prints. When the casts hardened, they gathered them up.

On the trail back, she stopped on the embankment. "You can go on up to the house if you like." She took a flashlight and a magnifying glass from one of the kits he'd set down. "I'm going to our boat shack on the beach."

"I'll come along, if it's all right with you."

They stacked everything beside the trail and went down the wooden steps. The barn board shed had been built against a sheer rock face above the high tide mark. Years of salt spray had bleached the eight foot square building almost white.

Amy pushed open the door. A couple of crab pots teetered in one corner, giving off a pungent odor. Broken jam cleats, blocks, and turnbuckles lay atop a torn sail in another.

"In September, I bought a spindle roll of 3/8 nylon rope." She got down on all fours. "After Elise disappeared, Dad noticed the rope was missing." She glanced over her shoulder at Simon who stood in the doorway. "Of course, someone could have taken it weeks before her death." She snapped on her light and began to examine the floor where the spindle had rested.

She'd been scrabbling around for five or ten minutes with her tail in the air and her nose inches from the floor when Simon cleared his throat and said, "Anyone ever tell you you've got an incredibly nice tush?"

Amy flung him a dirty look. "No cute remarks, fella. This is serious."

"Uh huh, so am I."

"Sure you are." She wiped fogged glasses on her shirt tail and peered through the magnifying glass once more. "Could be," she mumbled. Taking tweezers and an envelope from the pocket of her jeans, she pulled several strands of filament from a splintery board, then rose to her feet. "I'm through."

When they got back to the house, she made herself a sandwich, and retreated to the lab. After hours of calculating weight versus depth and pressure, she trudged upstairs to find the table laid, her father at ease in a recliner chair and Simon getting dinner.

B.J.'s sharp, observant gaze swept her face. "Simon told me about your project. Learn anything new?"

She massaged aching temples. "The killer wants us to believe Oren walked from the van to the beach the night Elise vanished. Right?"

B.J.'s chest rose and fell. "What other conclusion is there? His shoes match the casts exactly."

"Yes, they were Oren's shoes." She paused and looked from B.J. to Simon. "But someone with shorter, narrower feet wore them. Someone who weighed between 130 and 140 pounds."

"The doctor!" Simon shouted. "He was about five foot eight and had a slight build. And"—Simon used the large kitchen knife he held to emphasize his point—"his shoes caught my eye right away. They were narrow, pointed things. Patent leather like women wear."

"I don't know, Simon." B.J. scratched his beard. "I can see a number of loop holes. Elise appeared to be a fair-sized woman. I can't see a small man carrying her body through ankle deep sand."

Simon scooped chopped green pepper into a bowl.

"Maybe he couldn't under normal circumstances, but I'll bet if I were scared enough, I could lift *twice* my weight."

"Perhaps, weirder things have happened."

"Unless my figures are wrong," Amy said. "And I don't think they are. He didn't carry her to the beach and probably didn't even have her body in the van."

Simon stared at her. "He must have, Amy, otherwise how did the bloodstains get in the dinghy?" He took a platter of sliced roast beef, baked potatoes, and a salad to the table, poured milk for everyone and seated himself. "Do you think he dumped the rug and sheet in the bottom of the boat, then changed his mind?"

"No, that can't be. Splashing occurs when fresh blood spurts from a wound. Spatters happen when partially co-agulated blood is disturbed, perhaps by a blow." She took a small slice of meat from the platter Simon passed. "The stains in the dinghy were a peculiar mixture of splash, spatter, and pool."

"And drips from a rain-dampened sheet would not have made the same pattern," B.J. said. He slathered horserad-ish on his roast beef, took a bite, and nodded in satisfac-tion. "Besides there's no point in us letting the stains in the dinghy sidetrack us. For all we know they could be animal blood."

Simon speared a wedge of tomato from his salad, chewed thoughtfully, and looked over at Amy. "So you think the mired van, the footprints, and the stuff thrown into the ravine are all part of a frame?"

She nodded. "That's my opinion . . . at the moment." She smiled faintly. "But I reserve the right to change my mind."

B.J. slit the jacket of his baked potato and added butter. "By gosh, you could be right, Amy." His cheeks flushed with excitement. "Once you toss out the obvious, all sorts of possibilities pop up."

"No lie," Simon said. "Why would Oren, or anyone else for that matter, bring the body here to dispose of it? The killer must have had his own car. There's a lot of water and country roads between here and Seattle. He could have gotten rid of the body anywhere."

"My thoughts exactly," Amy said. She sipped a little of her milk, but it didn't sit well on her nervous stomach. "The whole set-up seems too pat."

"Can you prove it?" B.J. asked.

"No, not yet," she said wearily. "A lot of pieces are still missing."

"That's for damned sure. How did the man know Oren would be gone and how could he be sure he could get the van?"

"Questions, questions, my head's teeming with them," she said and sighed.

B.J. put out a hand and touched her shoulder. "Patience, Amy, it'll all come together in time."

Their conversation dwindled and finally stopped altogether. After they finished eating, Simon helped B.J. to his room so they could start the bedtime routine.

Sunk in gloom, Amy did the dishes and straightened the kitchen. Her body felt weighted, and every in-drawn breath took an effort. She rested her head against the cupboard and let her shoulders sag. Another wasted day. A weary sigh escaped her.

When a hand touched her hair, she jumped and wheeled around. She hadn't realized Simon had come into the room.

"Don't be discouraged," he said. "You and B.J. will solve the puzzle." He grinned rather weakly. "Shoot, between the two of you, you know everything about forensic science."

"That'll be the day."

"Salgado called back this afternoon."

She searched his face. "Anything interesting?"

"Mrs. Michaels has two referral letters Elise gave Dr. Tambor. One was from a doctor in Idaho, the other from one in Oregon." His expression became grim. "I called the numbers he gave me. Neither doctor exists."

"That makes Francine's story seem more believable." She glanced at the clock. "Are you through with Dad?"

"He's tucked in with a gory mystery." Simon walked over to the refrigerator. "You scarcely touched your dinner. Wouldn't you like to take a sandwich to the cottage?"

"It'd probably land in a lump in the pit of my stomach and stay there." She searched for a flashlight and didn't find one.

"My fault," Simon said. "I forgot to bring it up this morning." He peered out the window. "Doesn't seem as dark as usual. We can find our way." He switched on the outside lights and opened the door.

Overhead, moonlight glowed eerily behind seething masses of indigo clouds. Lightning glinted in strobelike flashes and thunder rumbled in the distance.

She moved closer to Simon. "We seldom get much lightning."

He took her hand. "Some day we'll take a trip to Idaho and I'll show you a real lightning storm."

Plans. In the space of ten days, they'd developed a past, a present, and now a possible future. Shaky as the prospect seemed, the thought cheered her.

Simon stood very still his eyes searching the shadows. "Run as fast as you can. Stay clear of the trees and head down-slope across the lawn. Okay?"

His apprehension escalated her own. "No way. I'm staying with you."

"Doggone it, will you do as I say for once?"

"No." Hooking her arm through his, she matched his uneven stride. They arrived at the cottage out of breath, and stood on the unlighted front porch looking out at the night.

"You're a stubborn, exasperating woman, Amy Prescott. But I'll never forget you."

Him and his back-handed compliments. Her throat filled until it ached. "I won't forget you either."

Suddenly, he enfolded her in his embrace, crushed her to him, and brought his mouth down on hers. Her lips parted and she responded with all the yearning locked inside her.

Her blood humming in her veins, she fastened her arms around his neck and strained against him. They kissed, their mouths open, exchanging fierce, hungry kisses. He held her so close their shuddering breath came out as one and his trembling became hers.

His lips left hers and traveled down to the hollow of her throat. "I need to touch you, to make love to you. Please, Amy, I'm half out of my mind with wanting you."

His voice broke the spell.

She pulled away from him. "This isn't real, Simon."

"The hell it isn't." He reached for her.

She kept her distance. "Please, Simon, we have to go slow. This is like"—she searched her mind for the right simile—"like being in a war. Because of the danger our emotions have encapsulated and intensified. Feelings seem deeper, more significant than they would otherwise."

She squeezed her hands together. Somehow she had to make him understand. "You . . . you trigger urges in me."

"Good. I'm glad I'm not the only one."

"But I'm not like that, Simon."

He laughed. "You could have fooled me, kid."

She scowled at him. "It's the pressure we're under. We'd be foolish to trust what's happening between us."

He shoved his hands in his pockets and hunched his

shoulders. "That's not true. At least, not for me. When you're not around I get this grinding emptiness inside me until I hear your footsteps. 'She's here,' I think, 'now I can concentrate on my writing.' "

He walked to the railing and stood there for a moment before turning back. "But then I feel the need to be in the same room with you. And that isn't enough—I have to be beside you. And . . . and that's the worst of all. Aching to touch you, knowing that won't be enough either."

She blinked back the moistness in her eyes and tasted salt in her throat. "Oh, Simon." She touched his face with her fingertips. "You're such a fine, gentle, wonderful man."

He jerked his head away. "Knock it off, Amy. You're trying to boost me onto some stupid pedestal and I'm standing here lusting after your body."

His choice of words stirred her wry sense of humor. She peered up at him. "Lusting?" She grinned. "Old fashioned, renaissance-type lusting?"

"It isn't funny, Amy. Cold showers don't help a god-damned bit."

She smiled gently and lay her palm against his cheek. "When all the danger has passed, if you still feel the same, perhaps I'll let myself do a little lusting too."

Fifteen

Laughter eased Amy's jitters. "We'd better get inside." She unlocked the door and flipped the light switch. Nothing happened.

Simon tried a table lamp. "Lightning must have knocked out a transformer. Let me take a look up the hill." He stepped outside. "Nope. B.J.'s porch light is still on."

"Probably a fuse. The cottage's wiring is ancient. When too many appliances go on at once, one blows."

"I'll get the flashlight." An arm outstretched, Simon shuffled into the kitchen. "I know right where I left it." Banging and clattering followed and the sound of breaking glass. "The damned thing isn't here."

"No problem, Simon. I keep candles handy." She rummaged in a drawer and found what she sought. After using the last three matches in the small box, she got the candle lit. "I'll dash downstairs and put in a new fuse."

He set his jaw. "No, I'll go."

"All right let's compromise. I'll hold the candle, you change the fuse." She led the way down the basement stairs.

"What's that odor I smell?" Simon asked.

She sniffed. The air held a rank, musky aroma. "Perhaps, the septic tank backed up."

"No, this is different. It reminds me of"—the timbre of his voice changed—"a story I did. Amy," he said sharply. "Go back upstairs. I'll take care of the problem here."

"Don't be silly. The fuse box is just over there in the middle of that outside wall." The candle flame fluttered. She cupped one hand around it and hurried across the room.

A few feet from her objective the candle flickered and went out. Instantly, the basement became a foreign place. A cold, black, murky cave. "Don't worry. I have matches here somewhere." She spoke in a hushed voice, not knowing why she felt the need.

She was about to stretch out her hand and feel along the shelf in front of her when she heard a thumping noise. She peered in its direction. In a faint glimmer of moonlight, she located the cause. Alarm clutched her insides.

She reached back and took hold of Simon's sleeve. "The window's broken. The latch is undone."

"Sh-sh." He gripped her shoulders and brought his mouth close to her ear. "Don't move. Something's in here."

Her scalp prickled and she strained to hear, listening with held breath. A whisper. Skin against skin? Cloth against cloth?

Simon's grip on her shoulder tightened, his quick breaths loud in the darkness.

Her nerves crawled, scritchity as beetle legs. She had to have light. She swept her hand along the shelf. One of the precariously stacked cans tumbled off and crashed onto the cement floor. A beat of silence—close, thickly matted—then a chilling, whirring sound. Her mind refused to comprehend, yet she knew it well from hikes in the hot, sagebrush dotted hills of Eastern Washington.

"Rattlesnakes," Simon breathed. He made a move toward her and the whirring increased in volume. Dry. Brittle. Deadly. The sinister sound seemed to come from everywhere. "Dozens of them."

Icy terror settled into the base of her spine. In her mind, she could see their writhing coils, the upward-held bodies—their taut-scaled "S" shape ending in flat, triangular heads with flickering black-forked tongues. Their slithering bodies made ominous whisperings on rough cement.

She clenched her teeth hard, made herself be calm and think. Finally, she eased closer to Simon. "Help me grab the clothes line wire. I can use it to get to the pit."

He held her to him. "It'll break and you'll fall right in the middle of 'em."

"It's all we have."

He swore half under his breath. "For God's sake, be careful. Soon as you're safe, I'll make a dash for the stairs."

"No no no, you mustn't move. I have an idea I want to try." She squeezed his hand. "Ready?"

He bent, clasped her below the hips and hoisted her up. She waved her arms above her head, searching for the wire. Her movement overbalanced him and he staggered.

A menacing rattle, so close this time it raised the hair on the back of her neck. Cold sweat gathered on her skin.

"Jesus, God! He struck my cast. Grab the wire, Amy, grab it quick before he strikes again."

Not Simon. Not Simon. She located a rafter, traced its splintery side until her fingers closed on the line. "Got it." The wire twanged and creaked. The thin metal strand was old and brittle, and with her lack of agility, chancy as hell. She lifted her weight off Simon and started hand over hand toward the tublike structure farther down the wall. Fasteners holding the wire popped and cracked. *Please. Please. A few more feet, just a few more feet.*

"Amy? You all right?"

With a rending screech, the wire let go at one end. She hung onto the swinging line with both hands and pawed the air with her feet. Her toe banged the side of the pit. Two more inches—two—only two and she'd be inside. Sweat stung her eyes, fogged her glasses, slicked her hands. No sound in the cool gloom except her harsh breathing.

She pushed off, pendulumed out, started the return arc. Her hands started to slip. Not yet. Not yet. She flung her body forward, hitting her shins, her arms, and her head as she fell. No matter. "I'm in," she called.

She righted herself, snatched up the hose and turned to assess the situation. Dim gray light now filled the basement. She could make out Simon some twenty feet away. "Are the snakes still there?"

"All around me. All within striking distance."

"I'm going to try sweeping them away with water."

"Snakes swim you know."

Panic clawed at her stomach. "Hot or cold water?"

"Cold. The colder the better."

Score one. Lomitas's water made a person's teeth ache. "Stand very still, Simon." She turned the tap on full bore and a blast of water shot from the nozzle. Moving the hose back and forth, she aimed at black blobs on the floor at Simon's feet.

Time ticked by, seconds seeming like minutes. Would the water make them aggressive? She squinted, trying to see into the deep shadows concealing the floor where Simon stood.

"You did it." Simon started toward her. A loud whooshing hiss stopped him in mid-stride. "No! No! Oh . . . my God."

Moonlight shafted through the window. In its silvery gleam swayed a snake. Black. Shiny as black satin. Hood spread, its body swaying, the cobra hissed again.

Her blood seemed to congeal. "What'll I do?"

"Nothing. Above all don't move or make any loud noises."

She shut off the water. The snake still stood poised, primeval eyes agleam. The distance between him and Simon seemed to have lessened.

Suddenly a gust of wind caught the broken window, punched it inward and sucked it back. Wood smacked wood, a fragment of glass shattered on the floor.

The cobra drew its head back and opened its mouth wide. "Duck, Amy, duck."

She felt something wet hit her glasses.

"Jesus, Jesus, Jesus." Simon writhed on the floor digging at his eyes.

Venom. She groped for the faucet. *Hurry. Hurry.* Her hand found the handle, gave it a yank and sprinkled him with a fine spray. "Hold your eyes open. Let the water fall in." Her heart beat in big, terrifying beats. Cobra venom affected nerves, paralyzed heart and lung muscles, caused blindness. She must get to him.

She switched off the cold faucet and turned on the hot. The pipes clattered and thumped. Built up steam belched forth with the stream of scalding water she directed at the snake. *Make it work. I have to get to him.*

The snaked whooshed, sprayed her with another shot of venom and slithered off to a far corner.

She took a handkerchief from her pocket, soaked it with water, vaulted out of the pit, and ran to Simon.

"My eyes, my eyes." He thrashed his head about. "God, oh God, the pain."

She braced his head. "This'll help some." She forced open his lids, squeezed water from the cloth and let the drops fall in. From all around her came an almost inaudible shu-shu-shu. Fear rippled along her skin.

She knelt and tugged his arm around her neck. "Try to get your legs under you." She straightened and brought him up with her. "Can you walk?"

"Feel funny." He swayed and let out a low moan.

She got a better grip on him and started toward the stairs. Two wriggling serpents cut her off. She swung him around. Step by wobbly step, she moved him back until she reached the pit, leaned him over the edge and lifted him in.

She tumbled in beside him, dripped more water in his eyes, rinsed off his face and her own. What to do? Light from the moon had disappeared and with it had gone any chance of getting Simon across that hazardous stretch.

She felt for his hand. "I have to get help."

He clung to her fingers. "You can't"—his body contorted and his breath made a whistling sound—"you can't go . . . out . . . there."

She willed steadiness into her voice. "I'll make it." Quaking inside, she picked up the hose and sent a blast of frigid water along the pathway to the stairs. Back and forth. Back and forth. Uncertainty gnawed at her. Was Simon right about the temperature? The hot water had worked on the cobra.

Soon as she turned off the water, the formidable whirring took over. The noise reverberated off the walls until she couldn't tell from which direction it came. White naked terror gripping her chest, she put one leg over the edge of the pit.

Simon clutched her shirt. "Don't. You won't have a chance."

She freed herself and raced for the stairs. As each foot

213

touched down, she expected fangs to jab her leg. *Simon will die if I don't make it.* Something glanced off the water-soaked leg of her jeans. Adrenalin pumping, she leaped, and leaped again. Where the hell was she? A board caught her across the shins and she fell forward.

"Simon . . . Simon, I found the stairs." She rubbed a throbbing shin bone.

His sigh filtered through the gloom. "Be . . . careful."

She took a deep breath, held it for a couple of seconds, then slowly exhaled. She made her voice light. "You hold the fort. I'll be back soon." Her wet shoes squishing with every step, she clambered upward and took hold of the door knob. Had the killer put snakes in other parts of the house?

She felt around for a broom she sometimes kept in a corner and found nothing. Seconds sped by. Time wasted she didn't have to spare. She pulled the door open, sped to the kitchen, found a candle and a match. Light at last. She scanned the floor and sucked in a relieved breath. Safe—for now.

Oren could get to the cottage in ten minutes. She'd alert her father, have him contact Oren while she gathered some flashlights. Between the two of them, they could get Simon to safety.

She lifted the receiver of the intercom and pushed the button. Dead. Her inner trembling began again. *Keep going. Don't think.*

She fitted the candle into a holder. With it in one hand and a push broom in the other, she inched into the living room. The phone on the desk had no dial tone. She flung it from her. "Bastard. Dirty, rotten, sadistic bastard."

Seething with fury, she surveyed the room. No snakes, at least none in sight. She set the broom where she could get at it easily, took the poker from its stand and hurried up the stairs. In her night stand was a flashlight with fresh batteries.

She entered her bedroom, set the candle holder on the dresser and happened to glance in the mirror. A scream tore from her throat.

A gray sinuous ribbon rose slowly from the middle of her bed. The cobra swayed, his black eyes gleaming in the candle light. He hissed, flared his hood, drew back his head.

She let out a howl of rage and swung the poker. The iron rod struck the snake broadside, flinging it against the wall. The cobra's body landed with a plop, slid to the floor and lay still. She resisted an urge to pound it to a bloody pulp.

Snatching up the flashlight, she ran down the stairs and out to the ship's locker on the back porch. Glory. Glory. Two torches. Their batteries were a little weak but they were usable. She put them in a sack.

With the sack in one hand and a broom in the other, she rushed back to the basement stairway. She positioned the torches to light the floor below and a shudder ran through her. A dozen snakes slithered between her and the pit.

Minutes crept by. How long had Simon had the venom in his system? Her pulse speeded up another notch. "I'm coming over."

He lifted his head. "Forget it. There's no way."

She grabbed the push broom. "Oh, yes, there is. I'm going to make one." Talking continuously, she started across. "You underestimate me." She shoved a sleek side-winder aside. "When I get mad, I'm the fiercest damned woman you ever saw, fella, and"—she gave another a shove before it could strike—"and don't you ever forget it." She sprang in beside him. "See, I made it."

He clasped her in a weak embrace. "Amy, love . ." He

215

took a breath. "I don't think I'm . . . going to get out of this one."

"Oh, yes, you are." She got her arms around him. "You and I are bailing out of this snake pit."

"My legs won't work."

A dark, panicky anguish filled her. "Yes, they will." She heaved him upward and he slid back. *Dear God he has to be able to walk. I can't drag him.* She tried again and failed. A whirring noise near the pit froze her, but only for a millisecond. A lusty clout from the broom sent it flying.

Now. Right now, or never. She wet the tea towel she'd snatched up in the kitchen, folded it and tied it over Simon's eyes. "We're going for it, Simon." She got him over the side and tried to get him on his feet.

"Can't . . . make . . ."

"Yes you can." She hooked her hands under his arms and began to drag him. Midway a movement at the broken window brought her up short.

Simon went taut in her grasp. "What is it?"

"Marcus. Oh, Simon, his head's all bloody." The Manx sprang to a shelf, sat there growling for a moment, then crept out of sight.

She returned to her task of moving him along a few feet at a time. "Won't be long now. We're almost to the stairs." A snake wriggled from beneath the bottom step. Before she could move, the rattler coiled and reared its body!

At the same instant a ball of yellow fury leaped out of the shadows. The two animals blurred together in a snarling mass of tawny fur and writhing serpent. Gripping the huge diamondback just behind its head, Marcus repeatedly clawed the fat, undulating coils with his powerful back legs.

When the snake finally went limp, the cat rumbled

deep in his chest and took a last baleful look around. Satisfied, he dragged his prey into a corner.

Simon lurched to his knees. "What's going on, Amy? Are you all right?"

She drew in a shaky breath. "Marcus got the rattler."

"Thank God." He sagged against her.

She urged him forward. "We've got it made now." He managed to creep up the stairs one at a time, but collapsed at the top.

Fear gripped her. He couldn't die. "You hang on. You hear?" Grabbing his arms, she dragged him out onto the front porch, ran back inside for blankets, and tucked them around him.

Simon groaned through clenched teeth and yanked at the cloth over his eyes.

She gripped his hand. "I'll get help."

She rushed up the slope, tripped over a root, fell sprawling, scrambled to her feet and hurried on. When she reached her father's house, she raced into the living room and jerked the receiver off the hook. The line was dead.

Dead. Just like Simon was going to be. A high, keening cry escaped her. She clapped her hand over her mouth. *Think, you silly idiot!*

The cellular phone.

She rummaged in the closet, tore open the box, dashed down the hall and burst into her father's room. His light was on and he was sitting up in bed. "What the hell's going on?"

"Snakes. Snakes everywhere," she gasped. "Rattlesnakes, cobras." She told him about Simon.

B.J. blanched and reached for the phone she held. "I'll call the hospital. Can you set flares for the helicopter."

She jerked her head and turned toward the door. "Is there anything I can do for Simon?"

"Pray, Amy. Pray like hell."

Sixteen

The nurse on Airlift Northwest refused to let Amy go with Simon in the helicopter. Determined to be with him, she managed to catch the 8 P.M. ferry from Lomitas with only minutes to spare. With fear for Simon pursuing her, she paced the windswept deck.

The minute Simon was out of danger—she fingered the holstered pistol her father had given to her before she left—she'd find the rotten slimeball who'd done this. If Simon died—she clutched the rail and stared into the darkness. *I can't lose him now. We've only begun to know each other.*

The instant she drove off the ferry, she floored the accelerator. Unmindful of speed limits, she burned up the freeway during the eighty-mile drive to Seattle.

When she parked her car in the Harborview Medical Center lot, she glanced at her watch—10 P.M.—three hours since the cobra's venom had entered Simon's system. She had to learn his condition, find out the results of his work-up, pry a prognosis out of someone.

She thought for a moment. Since she was no longer on staff here, the hospital personnel would view her as a disruptive snooper. It'd be hours before anyone bothered to give her a progress report. So, she'd have to use a more devious plan.

She took a rumpled lab coat from the back seat, tousled her hair a trifle more and draped a stethoscope around her neck—now she fitted the role of a harried intern.

Inside, she didn't ask about Simon. No one, except attending physicians and accredited personnel, gained admittance to the Intensive Care Unit. However, during her internship, she, like the others, had learned the back stair routes.

Once on the floor, she didn't have to wonder if he was still alive. The sound of his harsh, dry voice crying out her name filled the corridor. Her heart twisted. He'd begun to hallucinate while they waited for the helicopter.

She saw a familiar figure coming toward her and lengthened her stride. "Cam. Cam Nguyen." She hugged him. "Thank God you're on duty."

The slender, white-coated man hugged her back. "Your father called to brief us on what happened. He said you were on your way in." He gestured toward a door. "Kittredge's been doing that ever since he arrived."

She gripped his arm. "How is he?"

His expression became grave. "Neurotoxic venom can cause a multitude of problems, the most devastating being cardiovascular changes and respiratory distress."

The triage drilled into her during her internship took command. "Is the heart-lung machine set up?"

"Yes, Doctor," he said, sliding into the brisk routine they'd once had.

"Good. What about the antivenin? Has it been ordered?"

"A shipment of snakes arrived at Woodland Park Zoo last week. One of the cobras zapped a handler." A smile softened the tense lines of his lean, fine-boned features. "So we had antivenin in stock."

She slumped against the wall. "When did you administer it?"

"About two hours ago."

She swallowed into a dry throat. "How soon do you expect to know if . . . if it's going to work?"

He peered at her from under thick, dark brows, his brown eyes soft with concern. "That's difficult to say, Amy. It depends on his physical condition and how much venom his system absorbed." He put an arm around her shoulders. "And, as you know, there's always a possibility of his being allergic to the antivenin."

She turned her face into his shoulder. "Don't let anything happen to him, Cam. He . . . he's important to me."

He squeezed her arm. "I'll do my best. God knows you deserve a shot at happiness."

"Yeah. Sure." Her lips thinned. "But I doubt if the All Mighty is keeping score." She flinched as Simon's voice echoed through the hall again. "Can't you sedate him?"

He blew out his breath. "With the possibility of respiratory problems facing us"—he lifted his shoulders in a shrug—"I don't dare."

"May I see him? Perhaps, I can get through to him and relieve his mind."

Dr. Nguyen motioned to a nurse. "Put a chair beside Mr. Kittredge's bed."

The nurse stiffened. "That's highly irregular, Doctor. We really can't permit—"

"Get the chair," he said quietly. "No one in the unit can rest until he calms down."

Amy lingered at Cam's side and he looked at her questioningly. "Something else bothering you?"

"I'd like to keep this out of the papers."

"Information leaks out of this place like water through a sieve, but I'll do what I can."

"Thanks, Cam, the less the person who pulled this knows, the better."

She opened the door and edged into the brightly lit room. Despite her familiarity with the heart monitor's bobbing green blip and the throaty "um-m-m huff-f-f" of the respirator, her heart still beat in heavy, apprehensive beats. I.C.U.'s gave her a feeling of powerlessness. Here, only plastic hoses and electric cords tethered patients to life.

She moved to where Simon lay. The color of his face matched the bandage covering his eyes. His legs and head moved in restless torment.

As she started to lower herself onto the chair beside him, he jerked upward nearly tearing his IV from its moorings, and cried, "He's going to strike. Amy! Amy! Oh, God . . . oh, God."

She eased him back on the pillow. "It's over, Simon." He tensed and started to rise again. She lowered the rail on her side, stretched her arm across his chest, and grasped the opposite rail to hold him down. "Easy now." With her other hand, she brushed back his perspiration-dampened hair and stroked his forehead.

He struggled to get up. "I gotta help her." He fell back. "Can't. Can't. Oh, Jesus God."

She leaned over him until her breath feathered the fine hair by his ear. "I'm here Simon. Right here beside you." She turned him on his side, massaged the knotted muscles in his neck, and worked her way down his back. All the while, she kept up a running patter, telling him of the places they'd go and the things they'd do, when he got well.

By the time he finally relaxed, her hands and arms ached. She sank onto the chair, sagging with an exhaustion so profound it penetrated to the marrow of her bones.

How long had it been since she'd had a full night's sleep? Her mind refused to calculate.

Simon stirred, murmured her name, and put out his hand. She bent over him and held his palm against her cheek. "I'm here."

At last, he fell into a restful slumber, yet worries continued to flood her mind. The venom might affect his eyesight, his heart, his lungs. He hated being dependent on anyone else. Ill health could shatter him, and his dream of being a novelist.

She sighed and rested her head on the bed.

Thursday, November 3

It seemed to her she'd just closed her eyes when someone shook her shoulder roughly. She straightened and her startled gaze took in the big clock on the wall—6:30 A.M. Good Lord! She reached to check Simon's pulse.

"What are you doing here?" a stocky nurse hissed. She grabbed the back of Amy's chair and tried to wrest it from under her. "This sort of thing is not allowed in ICU."

Amy stood and fixed the granite-faced woman with an icy stare. She detested doctors who pulled rank, but sometimes circumstances made it necessary. "*I* am Dr. Prescott. Mr. Kittredge is a special patient, and he's going to get special care. If you have a problem with that, call Dr. Nguyen."

The woman's cheeks turned a mottled purple. "Humph! We'll see." She marched off muttering about officious doctors.

"Go get 'em, tiger," croaked a voice behind her.

She bent and clutched him to her. "You made it through the night." She kissed his forehead, his cheeks, and finally

222

his fever-parched lips, wetting him with tears in the process.

He brushed her face with shaky, translucent-appearing fingers. "Go home." His hand settled back onto the sheet and he slipped into deep sleep again.

She made her way to the apartment. The last time she'd been here the rooms had been filled with the stench of death. Fortunately, her bone weary tiredness kept her from dwelling on the fact. She undressed, flopped into bed, and fell asleep immediately.

When she awakened around noon, her first concern was Simon's welfare. After the head nurse informed her he seemed to be stabilized, Amy's thoughts turned to her father. Last night, Helen had stayed with him. Today, Arne Olafson, the gillnet fisherman would take over.

She dialed and got her father on the line. "The nurse says Simon has . . ."

"I know, I called." His tight, keyed-up voice betrayed his agitation.

"What's wrong, Dad? Didn't they tell me the truth?"

"The Seattle Police arrested Oren this morning."

"Arrested him?" She clung to the telephone receiver as if it were a life line. "Why? What possible reason could they have?"

"They found a baseball bat behind Dr. Tambor's building." B.J. let out a trembling sigh. "Oren's fingerprints were on it."

"No!" The harsh cry wrenched from her throat. "Not Oren. He's not—" She curbed her angry frustration. "What're they charging him with?"

"With . . ." B.J. cleared his throat. "With Dr. Tambor's murder."

"They can't! He's innocent, Dad. Did you tell them about the footprints?"

"Of course, but Lt. Salgado scarcely listened. He

223

thinks Oren blamed the doctor for everything that's happened to him. He stole Elise's love, and that drove Oren to take her life."

"If that's true, then who set up the frame, and why?"

"Are you certain of your findings, Amy? I sure as hell wish I could get downstairs. I'd like to go over your calculations."

Suddenly, she felt fragile as blown glass. Keeping her tone as steady as possible, she said, "Are . . . you . . questioning my ability?"

"We—ell . . . no, of course not. I . . . uh . . . I'd just like to . . . check for myself."

"I see." *He didn't trust her.* She swallowed but couldn't dislodge the golf-ball-sized lump in her throat. Now she had to prove her skill to him as well as everyone else.

B.J. coughed and broke the stiff silence. "Someone opened a big gash in Marcus's head last night."

"Yes, I know. I forgot to tell you."

"The vet says the cat evidently got in some good licks too. He had several badly torn claws."

"He killed one of the rattlers. It might have happened then."

"Possibly, but he also could have scratched the person who hit him. Scratches from cats who kill and eat wild animals can cause serious infections."

"I hope so, Dad. The person deserves to get sicker than hell."

"I have to agree with you on that."

In her mind, she pictured snakes slithering through the deserted cottage, hiding in all the narrow inaccessible places. "What're we going to do about the beach house?"

"A herpetologist from Seattle's zoo will be out today. He says rattlers should be in hibernation this time of year. He thinks they've been kept warm so they'd stay active."

"Does he know any local dealers?"

"He gave me the names of the reputable ones. He says some pet shops are fronts for thriving black markets in exotic animals of all kinds. It won't be easy to track down the person who bought the snakes."

"I'll find him." She clenched her fist. "I'll find him if I have to hit every outlet between here and the island."

"Easy, kitten, don't go off half-cocked."

"My brain's never been more clear. Did Calder find any evidence?"

"Fresh tire tracks in Prescott's Byway. I told him to make some casts." He let out an exasperated breath. "But I doubt he'd know a clue if he fell over it."

"Has Elise's jewelry turned up yet?"

"Calder and Salgado both come up with zilch. I do have one piece of good news though. The medical examiner who's going to take my place will be here Monday."

"Finally! The very idea of not letting bloodstains be examined until two weeks after a crime—it's dictatorial, totally unprofessional, and absolutely absurd." She got the wild animal dealers' names from him and said goodbye.

She drove to the Public Safety Building and found Gail having lunch at her favorite restaurant. When Gail spotted her, she beamed and waved.

"You must be psychic. Boy have I got news."

Amy took the chair opposite her. "Great, I could sure use some." She motioned to the waitress, asked for a cup of coffee, and ordered a roast beef sandwich.

Gail's smile faded. "What now?" She shuddered when she heard of Amy and Simon's horrifying experience. "Good God, Amy, somebody better find that psycho before he wipes out you and your family."

"Lt. Salgado will probably blame Oren. He's charged him with Dr. Tambor's murder."

"Yeah, we were discussing it at the lab." Gail crushed

her paper napkin into a ball, then without looking at Amy carefully began to smooth out the wrinkles. "What do you think?"

"Oren isn't capable of—" Gail's steady-eyed gaze stopped Amy's blustering outburst. She pressed her fingers against her aching head. "Hell, I don't know what to think anymore. Tell me your news."

"I ran those paint chips through the NAP file. Your father was struck by a Mazda RX 7 that had recently been painted a metallic blue."

"The same make and model as Elise's." Amy lowered her cup to the table and leafed through her note book. "You did say the car was once cherry red, didn't you?"

Gail nodded.

"It's gotta be the car Elise sold to a man named Roger Norman." Amy leaned forward. "He and Elise are both from Montana. What if—?" She paused, unsure whether to reveal that the woman she called Elise might not be the "real" Elise at all. Better not, she had no proof. "What if Norman had been her lover and she moved to Seattle to get away from him?"

"Hey, terrific." Gail shoved her fingers through her short-cut hair. "The guy comes here, finds out she's engaged to Oren, and kills her." Her dark eyes widened. "And it might have been him, not Oren who clubbed the doctor over the head and shoved him down the elevator shaft."

"You're forgetting the baseball bat had Oren's prints on it."

All the animation left Gail's face. "Sorry."

Amy lifted her shoulders and let them fall. "Did anyone process the rats from my apartment?"

"Oh, yeah." Gail held her nose and acted as if she were about to throw-up. "Cause of death—strangulation. Probably a fine wire by the way it cut into the animal's skin."

Strangulation. The same method used to kill Cleo. The hair rose on the back of Amy's neck. "Any fleas on the bodies?"

Gail tapped her forehead. "Smart thinking, old girl." She grinned. "Nary a one and their stomach contents bears out our conclusion—they weren't alley rats."

Amy drew in a deep breath and let it out slow. "Whoever did it has easy access to animals."

"And hates them," Gail added. "Rats aren't exactly appealing, but geez, what kind of a person could . . ." She grimaced. "Gives me the chills just thinking about it."

Could Oren? Amy's appetite vanished. She wrapped the remainder of her sandwich in a napkin and stood up. "I've a lot of leg work to do." She gazed down at Gail with an earnest expression. "Thanks. You've been a big help."

Gail rose and walked to the door with her. "Watch your step. This character may already have committed two murders. He knows who you are and where you live. A third killing wouldn't faze him."

Amy touched the slight bulge underneath her arm. "Dad insisted I pack some fire power and I thought I'd figure out some sort of disguise."

"Not a bad idea." She patted Amy's shoulder. "Take care."

Amy found a print shop that'd give one day service. She chose Emily James as her name, Animal Supply Inc. as her business, and made up a California address.

Next, she bought a wig, a beige blonde one streaked with gray. In the dressing room, she added age lines under the eyes and around the nose and mouth, as she'd learned to do when she'd acted in a college play.

Still not quite satisfied with her appearance, she took off her dark framed glasses and put in her contacts. A few more details and her disguise would be complete. A thrift store provided her with two changes of clothes and several styles of glasses. When she came out, she looked twenty years older and a good deal fatter.

Pleased with her transformation she set off for the animal supply houses. She could have phoned them, but she had an ulterior motive for wanting to visit each establishment in person. Although it was definitely against standard protocol, she'd brought the note left by Cleo's killer to Seattle. Now, she intended to find the scratch pad from which it'd been torn.

By late afternoon, she'd seen everything from tarantulas to Tasmanian tigers and an acrid odor of animal dung clung to her clothing. Unfortunately, none of the people she questioned had cobras or rattlesnakes for sale, nor had they sold any recently. Nevertheless, her time hadn't been entirely wasted. She'd managed to leave each supply house with a sheet of their scratch pad paper.

After talking to the last dealer on her list, she returned to the car and removed her disguise. With her sheaf of pad samples in hand, she hurried to the Crime Lab to analyze the paper and check their lettering against the fragments left on the torn top edge of the killer's note—none matched. She curbed her disappointment. Tomorrow, she'd start canvassing the pet shops.

Seventeen

Amy showered, changed clothes and went to the hospital. She inquired about Simon at the information desk and learned he'd been moved from ICU. Humming a joyful tune, she entered the elevator. Simon had weathered the critical phase, now if he could cope with the aftermath, he'd be home free.

The door to his room stood open. Inside, the lights had been dimmed. Simon was propped up in bed, but he wore dark glasses so she couldn't tell if he was awake. As she hesitated in the doorway, someone called her name. She smiled when she saw Cam coming toward her.

He grasped the hand she extended. "I think he's over the hump, Amy. We're not sure about his eyes yet, but aside from some residual muscle weakness, he's managing well systemically."

"Thanks to you, Cam." Her mouth curved into a smile. "Payment in full for the night calls I took while you were out romancing Mai."

He laughed out loud and slipped his arm around her waist. "How're you doing these days, old buddy?" His fingers probed her ribs, and he frowned at her. "When are you going to learn to stop and eat occasionally?"

She grinned and shrugged. "Can't be helped, I don't have you around to nag me." She jerked her head toward Simon. "Is it all right if I go in?"

"Sure. He's awake. I was just in there."

She smiled and went to Simon's bedside. "How're you feeling?" She stretched out her hand to touch him, and tell him how happy she was to have him alive.

"What are you doing here?" he said in a sharp tone without turning to look at her. "Who's taking care of B.J.?"

She recognized the voice, the stiff set of his features, and snatched back her out-stretched hand. He'd crawled into his icy cocoon again. "Arne Olafson will be staying with him."

"Fine. Now each of us can get on with our own lives."

Her insides began to quiver and she slumped onto a chair. Silence, taut and uneasy stretched between them. She squared her shoulders. She'd not make it easy for him to get rid of her. "Would you like me to read to you?"

He snatched off his dark glasses and glowered at her. "I don't need you, or anyone else babysitting me."

She came to her feet. "You're right. A good boot in the rear would do you more good." Hot tears ran down her face. She brushed them away as more took their place. The exasperating show of weakness made her even angrier. "Damn you and you're hard-headed independence. It wouldn't hurt you to lean on someone for a change."

"Yeah, look who's talking. Well, count me out."

Her chest hurt, her body hurt, her throat felt as if a tight band had closed around it. "You . . . you bastard. You stubborn, arrogant, egotistical bastard." Holding her head high, she walked out.

When she reached her apartment, she prowled through the rooms. Finally, she pulled everything out of the kitchen cabinet, filled a pan with soapy water, and began to clean. Several hours passed before complete exhaustion drove her to bed. Even then she didn't fall asleep until dawn.

Friday, November 4

Next morning, before leaving the apartment, she divided the city map into grids. Then, with the Yellow Pages in one hand and a red felt pen in the other, she marked the location of thirty pet shops within the city limits.

Her gut feeling told her the person she sought lived in the Seattle area and not one of the nearby towns. She fervently hoped her hunch was right, if she didn't find him soon, he'd strike again.

After picking up her phony business cards at the print shop and donning her disguise in a public restroom, she started with the outlying stores and worked her way inward. She soon devised a system. Following a walk through the store to size up the employees, she'd present her card and start asking questions.

Hour after gray-filled hour, she kept at it and every step of the way Simon's words throbbed inside her head like a sore tooth. She felt empty, cast adrift, and wished she'd never let down her guard.

Finally, when her tortured nerves quailed at the thought of hearing one more screeching parrot, or the frenzied barking of another Pompoo or Shih Tzu, she went home. As she neared her apartment door, she heard the shrilling of the phone. She unlocked the door and snatched up the receiver. Her heart plummeted when she recognized Cam's voice. "What's wrong?"

"That's what I'd like to know. Did something happen between you and Simon last evening?"

"Why?"

"After you left, he spiked a temp and was restless all night. That shouldn't have happened. He's been on antibiotics since he arrived. So there must be some other reason why he suddenly started going sour."

"We quarreled. He . . ."—her voice broke, she swallowed hard and went on—"he insists he doesn't need me, or want me around."

"And you believed him? Ah, come on, Amy, you've had enough psychology to know what's bugging him. Sure the man acts macho, but my guess is, he's damned insecure. You saved his life. How do you think that makes him feel?"

She flung her purse at a chair, missed, and swore under her breath. "He saved my life once and I was damned grateful. Why should this be any different?"

"I shouldn't have to tell you the answer to that. How about the two of you trying a reconciliation?"

"Why should I?"

"Because, I think you may love the guy. Love doesn't happen often, Amy. Don't toss him aside lightly."

Love Simon? She sprawled on the couch. No way would she love another man, especially one whose moods shifted as capriciously as Simon's. It hurt too much.

"What about it, Amy? His system can only stand so much. And you know as well as I do, medicine's no cure-all."

She sighed. "I'll give it some thought."

"Don't let me down, old friend. I need your help."

After Cam hung up, she lay staring at the ceiling. The thought of calling her father to update him on her progress crossed her mind, but she pushed it aside. He'd question her about Simon and if he sensed the two of them were having problems, he'd worry.

Why did everything have to fall apart at once? She

went into the bedroom, undressed, and stepped into the shower. Hoping to wash away her cares, she turned on a cold needle-spray and let it beat against her skin. Her strategy didn't, work—an achy sadness still weighted her down.

When she reached Simon's floor at the hospital, his room lights were off. Panic squeezed her heart. Had they taken him back to ICU? Gradually, her eyes became accustomed to the darkness and in the glow from the street lamps she saw him sitting beside the window.

She went in, closed the door behind her, and eased into a chair near him. when he didn't acknowledge her presence, she stirred uneasily and gave an anxious cough.

"B.J. told me about Oren," Simon said quietly. "Do you think we're wrong about him?"

"I won't let myself even consider it."

After several minutes, Simon let out a noisy breath. "So you're out there looking for the crazy nut who dumped the snakes in your basement, aren't you?"

She thought of lying, but knew he wouldn't buy it. "Yes."

He smacked the vinyl upholstered chair arm with his palm. "I knew it."

"There may be two people responsible for what's been going on, Simon. I have to find out who it is before someone else gets hurt."

"God dammit, Amy, that someone else is you. Don't you realize that?"

She let the matter lay and briefed him on the information Gail had given her about the hit-and-run car. "This Roger Norman could be a likely suspect," she finished.

"It's possible," Simon said. "I made some calls today. Montana's Department of Labor and Industries has a file on him. He injured an ankle while working as an orderly at Marchmont Hospital."

"Marchmont! So he must have known Elise, or whatever her name is."

"I suppose. Strange thing is, the IRS doesn't have any records for the last three years."

"Not everyone files an income tax return."

"No, but employers have to turn in employee deductions."

"Maybe he was doing itinerant work."

"Perhaps."

Simon said nothing more, and since she couldn't think of anything that'd ease the cool politeness between them, she got to her feet. "I'd better go. I don't want to tire you." She took her time going to the door, hoping he'd give her some excuse to stay.

Her hand was on the knob, when he said, "Amy . . ."

Now he'd tell her he hadn't meant what he said the previous night. "Yes?"

"Uh . . . thanks."

Her lip quivered. "For what?"

In the quiet darkness, his breathing sounded loud and agitated. "For . . . for coming by."

She waited, but he remained silent. "I was in the"—her voice trembled and threatened to break—"I happened to be in the neighborhood," she said quickly and left.

Saturday, November 5

The following morning as she was finishing her breakfast, a knock sounded at the door. Surprised, she hurried to answer and found Lt. Salgado standing in the hall. Adrenalin speeded her pulse. "Good grief what's happened now?"

"Let's talk inside." He pushed the door open and walked into, her living room.

She gripped her elbows and pressed folded arms against an agitated stomach. "Tell me, for God's sake."

He tossed the paper he carried onto the coffee table, took off his tan raincoat, lay it over the arm of the couch and sat down. "I'm here about you."

She collapsed onto a chair. "Me? What're you talking about?"

He rested his hands on his thighs and leaned forward, squinting at her through narrowed eyes. "Where do you get the idea you can do better than the police?"

She stiffened. "I don't happen to think my cousin is guilty. I'm not waiting until you come around to my way of thinking before I do something. Has someone complained?"

"Yeah, Kittredge. He's been burning up my phone. Wants to know what the hell we're doing. Says you're trying to track down a killer all by yourself."

She felt a rush of elation. Simon cared. Her joy lasted only half a second, then annoyance took its place. The last thing she needed right now was the lieutenant hounding her. "Simon tends to get overly protective. I made inquiries at a few pet shops, that's all."

The lieutenant's stare didn't waver. "If you find where the snakes came from, then what?"

She drew herself up. If she let him intimidate her now, she'd never earn his respect. "I figured if I could show reasonable cause, you might put the place under surveillance."

Salgado threw up his hands. "Great. Just great. Before, I had just a screwed-up case. Now, I got an amateur who's trying to play detective." He wiped a hand over his face. "What next, for Christ's sake?"

"I'm *not* an amateur *and* I'm not playing."

He leveled a finger at her. "You stay the hell out of this, doctor, or I'll make it damned hot for you over at the lab. You got that?"

Eighteen

Amy opened the folded newspaper Lt. Salgado had left on the coffee table. Centered under the headline—JOURNALIST SURVIVES HARROWING ENCOUNTER—a picture of Simon dominated the front page. "Blast it!" She flung the paper in the waste basket. Now, the sadistic freak knew Simon was alive.

She hurried into the bedroom to finish dressing. As she started to slip her arm into her shoulder holster, she stopped. Up until this moment, she'd avoided thinking too deeply about the gun she carried. Now, her instructor's words came back to her, "Don't ever carry a gun unless you're prepared to use it."

She removed the .38 S&W Special and held it in her hand. Would she have the guts to use it? After several minutes of soul searching, she returned the pistol to its holster. She'd better make her first stop the police firing range.

By ten o'clock, she'd gone through ten rounds of ammunition. One of the officers she frequently encountered while on duty in the mobile crime unit was practicing nearby. When she finished and took off the hearing earmuffs, he sauntered over.

"You aren't half bad, Prescott," he said. "From now on I'll think twice before I make a pass at you."

She smiled broadly. "I even surprised myself. Haven't practiced in a couple of years."

His holster creaked as he settled his revolver more comfortably on his hip. "Don't pay to let yourself get rusty." He cocked a knowing eyebrow. "In our business you never know when some nut is gonna make you his target."

She holstered her pistol and put on her jacket. "So I've found out." She picked up her sports duffel and made for the ladies room. Time she got into her wig and hit the streets again.

Four hours and half a dozen shops later, she pulled into a parking lot on Union, pushed money into a metal slot, and started walking south on Second Avenue.

In midblock, she entered Rasmussen's Pet Shop. A bell over the door tinkled and a stoop-shouldered man looked up from his figuring behind the cash register.

"Something I can help you with, miss?" he asked in a heavily accented voice.

"I'd like to look around a bit first, if you don't mind."

"Look"—he made a sweeping gesture—"look all you like."

She took a pen from her pocket and began to search through her purse. "You wouldn't have something I could write on, would you?"

He handed her a scratch pad, then pulled a raveled stocking hat over his sparse gray hair. "I go to my home now." He waved toward the back of the shop. "Darryl, my clerk will help you."

She waited until the door closed behind him before she started her inspection of the place. After spending the last three days in pet shops, she'd learned good lighting, clean cages, and healthy animals were the mark of a thriving

238

business. As she wandered narrow, dimly lit aisles, she saw dull-eyed birds and monkeys in grimy cubicles and knew Rasmussen's didn't fit in that category.

She edged around a reticulated python's glass container and nearly stumbled over a slightly obese man who squatted in front of some shelves. Ah, this must be Darryl. He sat on an unopened carton of dog food, beside him lay a wickedly curved box opener.

He shot a narrowed sideways glance in her direction and mumbled something she couldn't catch. She leaned closer. "I beg your pardon?"

Dark, turbid eyes glittered in the clerk's flushed face. "You spying on me?" he asked in a sibilant whisper.

She drew back. Did he know her? Had he seen through her disguise? Goose bumps prickling her skin, she eyed the box knife and inched by him to a spot where the aisle widened. "I'm Emily James." She held out her card.

Darryl grasped it between thumb and slim forefinger. His nails were bitten and ragged. With a noncommittal grunt, he bent his mop of frizzy brown hair over the card. After a full minute, he cupped the elbow of his left arm and lumbered to his feet. "So?"

"We have a client who's starting a private zoo."

He scratched the pustular red rash spreading outward from the edges of his mustache and frowzy Van Dyke beard. "What they lookin' for?"

He had a low-pitched voice and she had to lean closer in order to catch the words. The unwashed smell of him made her step back a pace. "He wants to begin with elapids and crotalidae."

Darryl pooched out his bottom lip and tossed his head in an effeminate manner. "Cut the technical lingo, lady. I'm no zoologist."

"Oh, sorry. He's interested in acquiring four cobras, some rattlesnakes and two fer-de-lance."

239

"Can't help you." He returned her card and went back to moving cans on the shelf.

She thought fast. "One of the clerks at Pet World said Rasmussen's sometimes filled special orders—if the price was right."

Darryl hunched his shoulders, but didn't turn around. "He's off his trolley."

She shifted her feet. "Why don't I leave my card. Perhaps, Mr. Rasmussen might . . ."

The clerk made a quick movement, and when he rose to his feet the blade of the box knife pointed at her belly. "Leave the old man out of this." He took a quick step forward and she shrank against the gerbil cages behind her. "You got that?"

She edged sideways. "Yes. Yes, of course. I didn't mean to upset you. I'll try another shop." She darted between the display counters and dashed through the front door.

Once outside, she slowed and sauntered toward the parking lot. Darryl was definitely, the flakiest character she'd encountered, but that didn't make him a killer. As she walked along, she mulled the matter over from several angles.

By the time she reached the car, she'd made her decision. Muddy-gray make-up base with deeper age lines and wire-frame glasses changed her appearance. A voluminous black coat, wool head scarf and thick muffler completed her transformation. Pleased with her handiwork, Amy lifted a bulging shopping bag from the back seat.

Head down, her shoulders bent, she trudged to the opposite side of the once-proud street and squeezed into a roofed, bus shelter. Behind her, spray-can graffiti decorated boarded-up windows of a store. In front of her, pink-haired punk rockers in black nailhead jackets, mothers with clinging children and suited-business men stood shoulder to shoulder.

Traffic hurtled by. Grit and scraps of paper swirled in the metallic, carbon monoxide breeze while the pallid afternoon sun crept down crumbling walls, brick by brick.

She'd been watching the pet shop forty-five minutes when the clerk came out, locked the door, and crossed the street at the corner. While following him at a discreet distance, she noticed he guarded his left arm from the bumps of passersby. On First Avenue, he made his way to the bus stop and boarded the Metro bound for Judkins Park. By lengthening her stride, she managed to scoot on at the last minute.

Bounding like a scared jack rabbit, the bus traveled south on First and turned up the hill on Spring Street. She tucked her chin inside her muffler, grabbed the overhead bar to hold her place in the crush of homeward bound commuters and tried to keep her quarry in view. Her venture might lead nowhere, but Salgado wouldn't listen unless she had more than intuition to go on.

The bus wound up Seneca and started south on Boren disgorging passengers along the way. Suddenly, she noticed Darryl's frizzy head among the disembarking throng at the back exit. She clawed her way to the door and leaped off.

Up the block, Darryl caught the green light, ran across the street, and entered a cocktail lounge called Pandora's. As soon as the signal changed, she charged after him.

A raucous happy-hour crowd packed the place. Music blared and strobe lights flashed in sync on silver foil walls. Couples danced with arms locked in tight embrace.

She set her bag on a chair upholstered in lavender with teal velvet trim and gazed around the shadowy interior. A number of the patrons wore elaborate dresses and had meticulously coiffed hair.

One of the women drifted by and Amy's gaze fastened on something a few inches above her remarkable cleavage. *Black chest hair!* Good grief, *she* was a man, and so were most of the others.

She glimpsed Darryl heading in the direction of the men's room and positioned herself so she could watch the door. Men and "women" entered and left, but the clerk remained inside. An hour passed and waiters began to give her hostile glances. She shifted to another spot and waited another thirty minutes. No one stayed in a restroom that long. He must have gotten by without her seeing him.

Pursued by a compelling sense of haste, she grabbed a bus and returned to her car. During the short drive to the Public Safety Building, and while she removed her disguise in the restroom, a vague notion nibbled at her mind. Sometime in the past few hours she had learned something important, only she couldn't pin it down. She shoved the matter to the back of her mind and hurried out.

Upstairs in the Crime Lab, she met her director. He peered down at her and frowned. "You look terrible. Your vacation doesn't seem to be doing you much good."

She scrubbed at the age lines she'd forgotten to remove with a piece of tissue. "Would you mind if I took a few more days off?"

His frown grew more pronounced. "I know what you're doing, Amy, and I don't approve." He sighed and ran a hand over thinning brown hair. "I'll check the schedule and let you know before I leave."

She flung him a grateful look. "Thanks. I'm hoping my investigation will pay off soon."

"Watch yourself. We need you around here," he said and wandered off.

The instant she was alone her disturbing anxiety returned and she began to scurry about. After numbering the day's collection of scratch pad sheets, she checked the printed headings with the note she'd found tucked under Cleo's collar, and analyzed the paper content. From time to time she stopped to massage her aching neck muscles, then rushed on.

She was down to the last of the batch when the director came by to okay her extended vacation. She explained what she was doing.

"Hm-m-m-m." He stared at the off-white page that had Rasmussen's Pet Shop printed across the top, then over at her note. "Both are Times Roman typeface." He placed the original sheet over the newly acquired one and carefully aligned the letters that remained on the torn upper edge. "They're a perfect match, Amy."

Her heart gave a thump and for an instant her chest felt too small to contain it. She steadied her voice. "I'd better check the paper before I start celebrating."

He patted her shoulder. "I'm going home. It's been a long day. Don't stay too late."

"I won't." Her right eyelid twitched and she squeezed her lids together a couple of times before she mixed a small section of the paper with sodium chloride and formed it into a disk. Scarcely daring to breath, she focused the infrared light onto the mixture, and turned on the spectrophotometer. She waited while the machine produced its graph of peaks and troughs, then compared it with the one from the note.

Hallelujah! The pattern of the absorption bands corresponded with those of the note. Darryl must be the culprit!

She scowled and pulled at her lip. How could he be? She'd never seen the man before. What possible connection could he have with her and Simon and her father?

She sat with slumped shoulders trying to fit him into

the puzzle. Only one concrete fact had been confirmed—someone who had access to Rasmussen's animals had strangled Cleo, put the rats in her apartment, and had very likely brought the snakes to the cottage.

Could the clerk's connection to them be through Elise? Amy found a pad of paper and began to jot down notes. If Darryl was gay, surely he wouldn't have killed Elise and the doctor because of jealousy. Whoa, now, maybe he would. What if Dr. Tambor had had a male *and* a female lover?

From what Amy had learned so far, Elise thought little of two-timing a man. However, she didn't sound like a woman who would tolerate being treated in a similar manner. What if she found out about the doctor's duplicity and decided to get even by blackmailing him and his lover. That would explain the money the doctor withdrew from his account.

She stared at the scribbles she'd made. Suppose Darryl resented the doctor's betrayal *and* the doctor felt equally betrayed by Elise? Such a scenario would give each of the men a good reason to do away with Elise. It would also give Darryl ample reason to harbor a smoldering anger against the man he'd thought loved him alone.

Amy shoved the notepad aside—speculation wouldn't do. Quickly, she recorded the results of the tests she'd run and dialed Lt. Salgado's number. She'd established a link between the pet shop and Cleo's death, that should be enough to warrant keeping the place under surveillance.

Much to her exasperation, she found Lt. Salgado had gone out. Despite her protests, no one would tell her where he could be reached.

The needling anxiety at the back of her mind grew stronger. What if she'd tipped Darryl off? Would he leave town, or . . . or would he . . . Oh, dear Lord. She grabbed her coat and hurried out.

Twenty minutes later, she brought the car to a squealing stop in the hospital parking lot. She dashed inside and caught the elevator. On the way up, she took slow, deep breaths and forced herself to be calm.

Her fears for Simon's safety were silly. She glanced at her watch—a half hour before visiting hours ended—plenty of time to rehash what she'd learned with Simon. Perhaps, by now he would have gotten over his resentment, and they could be friends again.

When she got off the elevator and started down the corridor toward his room, she noticed a uniformed policeman strolling up and down but ignored him. Friday and Saturday nights always brought an influx of crime victims and wounded criminals to the trauma center.

She stopped at Simon's door and was about to turn the knob when someone grasped her shoulder.

"What're you doing on this floor?" the pudgy, young officer asked. "Why are you trying to get into Mr. Kittredge's room?"

The blood drained from her face. "Has something happened to Simon?" The officer's blank stare infuriated her. She grabbed his coat with both hands. "Tell me, dammit. Is he all right?"

Her shrill voice raised heads and brought Cam running. Suddenly, the door beside her opened and Simon stood there in his rumpled pajamas. He regarded each of them in turn. "What the hell's going on out here?"

A singing sound erupted inside her head, the room tipped, and her legs gave way. Cam helped her to a chair in Simon's room and held a crushed ammonia ampoule under her nose. The fumes made her eyes water, but her stomach returned to where it belonged.

"Have you eaten anything today?" Cam said.

She forced her brain back through jumbled time. "A piece of toast."

Cam smacked his forehead. "What am I going to do with you?"

She bristled. "I had more important things on my mind." She glanced around for Simon and found him leaning against a nearby wall. His face seemed strained and his eyes held a bleak expression.

The police officer, his arms folded, his features grim, guarded the doorway. Her attention swung back to Simon. "Why is he here?"

Cam left the room and Simon started to move to the chair next to her, but changed his mind and sat on the bed. "At dinner, we had cherry cheesecake for dessert. I didn't want mine, so I set it on the window ledge for the pigeons. Naturally they ate it. Thirty minutes later all four of them were dead."

Nineteen

"Oh, God, how could I have been so stupid?" She stumbled into the bathroom and lost what little food she'd eaten.

After sponging her face with cold water, she joined the others. "Sorry," she said. "Nervous reaction I guess."

Cam, who'd returned with a cup of soup, patted her shoulder. "Sit down. I'll get something to settle your stomach."

A muscle along Simon's jaw bunched, otherwise his expression remained wooden and unreadable.

The policeman came over to her. "I'm Officer Sampson. May I see some I.D. please?"

She fished her wallet from her purse and blurted out how she'd followed the edgy pet shop clerk to a gay bar only four blocks from the hospital. "He may not be the guilty party," she said. "But someone around that store is. My tests prove Rasmussen's scratch pad paper is identical to the note I got when—" Simon's accusing look brought her up short. Damn! She'd blown it.

"What note?" he asked in a steely voice. "You never mentioned a note."

She swallowed. "I got it the day Cleo died." She turned

to the officer. "Cleo was my dog." She swung back to Simon. "I didn't want you and Dad to worry."

"What did it say?"

She carefully avoided meeting his blazing eyes. "About the same thing as the message on my apartment mirror."

"Don't try to feed me that crap, Amy."

She jerked her head up. "It said, 'You're next, Amy.' " She thrust out her chin. "What could you have done if you'd known?"

He stared her down. "So you decided not to tell anyone and play Joan of Arc instead." He glared at her. "Who the hell gave you the right?"

"That's not getting us anywhere, Kittredge," Officer Sampson said. "Have you reported your findings to Lt. Salgado, Dr. Prescott?"

"I tried, but couldn't reach him."

"I'll take care of it right now." He marched out the door.

Cam came in with a glass of lemon-lime soda. "This should do the trick. Sip it slowly."

She thanked him and leaned her head against the chair cushion. What a ghastly, ghastly day. She studied Simon over the rim of the glass and could find no trace of the man who'd looked at her with such desire a few nights ago.

"How soon can I get out of this zoo?" Simon asked suddenly.

Cam's dark-eyed gaze shifted from Simon to her and back to Simon. "It's imperative your eye drops be administered as instructed." His lips twitched ever so slightly. "And the antibiotic injections must be continued. However, I'd consider discharging you tomorrow, *if* you had some qualified person to look after you."

"I could do it," Amy said.

"No way!" Simon slid off the bed and paced back and

248

forth, his trim new cast slipper scuffing the linoleum. He came to a stop in front of Cam. Feet spread, hands on his hips, he barked, "I'm sick to death of being taken care of."

Cam stared back at him, his face stern. "It's either my way, or not at all. Your sight and health are at risk."

Simon glowered at him. "How long would I have to have her around?"

"Have to have her around." He sounded as if he'd been sentenced to share a cell with her. She had to restrain herself to keep from flinging something at him. She certainly hadn't reacted in such a surly manner when her father insisted Simon stay at the cottage.

"Three days," Cam said in a cheery voice, seemingly unaware of the tension crackling around him. "Maybe less if your fever stays normal. Amy's a fine doctor, I trust her implicitly."

"Bully for you." Simon stomped to the far side of the room and sat down with his back to them.

Cam motioned to her and she followed him out. "He can leave before noon, if that's convenient."

"I'll be here."

"The supplies you'll need will be at the nurse's station."

She made a wry face. "How about something to sweeten his disposition?"

He folded his arms and grinned at her. "I've done my part to get the two of you together. The rest is up to you."

Simon stalked up to them. He'd put on a robe and fitted a slipper over his bare foot. "I'm going to your car with you."

She'd have hugged him if she'd thought for a minute he'd have let her. He acted tough, but his caretaker instinct took precedence over his anger. Much as she welcomed the opportunity to make things right between them, she couldn't allow him to take the risk. She opened her mouth to protest, however Officer Sampson's arrival made her protest unnecessary.

He contemplated Simon's aggressive stance for an instant before switching his attention to her. "The lieutenant says I'm to accompany you to your car."

Simon took her arm. "I'll do it."

Officer Sampson narrowed his eyes. "When you get out of here, you can do as you please. Until then, you'll stay in your room."

Simon bunched his fist. "Go to hell."

"Don't make things difficult, Kittredge. Dr. Prescott is my responsibility, not yours."

"No point in making an issue of it, Simon," she said. "I'll be all right." He let go of her arm. As she went down the hall, she glanced over her shoulder. Simon stood where she'd left him, frustration lining his face.

When she reached her apartment house, she found Lt. Salgado waiting for her. She greeted him, but all he gave her in return was a grunt and a scowl. Fine, she could play that game too. They climbed the stairs to her second floor apartment in silence.

Once inside, he pointed to a chair. "Sit."

Ignoring his high-handed command, she hung her coat in the closet and asked him if he'd eaten dinner. He said he had, so she made coffee and heated chicken broth for herself. When she had everything prepared, she sat down opposite him. "Anything new on Dr. Tambor's murder?"

He lifted sagging shoulders and let out a gusty breath. "The man died of a blow to the back of the head sustained while he sat on the couch in his office."

She nibbled a cracker. "So his murderer had to be someone he knew and trusted."

He straightened and eyed her suspiciously. "How do you figure that?"

"It was night time and the building was deserted. Do you think he'd be stupid enough to let a stranger get behind him." She paused to let her words sink in. "And he'd be a downright idiot if he didn't keep his guard up in the presence of his lover's fiance." She ignored his stare. "Especially when he's carrying a baseball bat."

"Cute. Real cute, doctor. But sarcasm won't alter the case against your cousin."

"Has the M.E. fitted the weapon to the skull depression?"

"He's working on it."

"Did you find Oren's fingerprints on anything else except the bat?"

"Well, no." He picked at a pulled thread in the knee of his blue polyester pants. "But the forensic crew's still going over the clinic."

"I see." She blew on a spoonful of soup and swallowed it. "So, the bat is actually all you have."

"Yea gods, the doctor stole his woman. That's motive. Whether or not Oren killed his fiancee is not our concern at the moment. However, if he didn't"—he pointed a finger at her—"your father says you think Tambor killed the Dorset woman and framed Oren. That alone would be sufficient to make Oren want revenge."

She lay her spoon on the coffee table. "Maybe, but this isn't a straightforward case either. You'll soon learn none of the evidence you find is quite what it appears to be."

She took another sip of her soup. "For instance, you know that a man by the name of Roger Norman bought Elise's Mazda RX-7. Right?" At his nod, she went on. "Are you also aware a car of similar make and color ran down my dad?"

"Uh huh, and I won't bother to ask how you got the information."

"Did Simon tell you Norman was an orderly at Marchmont Hospital in Montana where Elise Dorset worked until three years ago?"

"Yes, and all the rest of the stuff he's dug up."

She pressed sweaty palms together. "What I'm about to tell you could put a woman's life in jeopardy. So you must promise you won't repeat the information, or act upon it."

His features hardened. "Depends."

"One of Marchmont's mental patients called me. She claims Elise died at the hospital four years ago during an abortion performed by the hospital's director."

His eyes went wide. "Madre de Dios!" He shot to his feet, leaned over and shook his finger in her face. "I told you not to keep things from me. You're going to be in deep trouble if it happens again."

His angry breathing slowed and he slumped into his chair. "Okay, I'll hold off for now." He searched his pockets for a notebook and pen. "Let's hear about this guy you've been tailing." He flung a stern glance in her direction. "Start at the beginning, and don't leave anything out." He took down everything, including a detailed description of Darryl, the pet shop clerk.

When they reached her lab report, she gave him the note she'd found on Cleo, the scratch paper she'd gotten at Rasmussen's Pet Shop, the graph she'd made, and her written report.

He lined up the print of the note's torn edge with the blank sheet and gave a low whistle. "Holy Jesus." His eyes met hers. "Not a bad day's work, doctor."

She offered a tentative smile. "I'd rather you called me, Amy."

He pursed his lips. "You gonna stop messing around in my investigation?"

"Guess I'll have to. I don't have any more leads." She assumed a disinterested expression. "Do you?"

He ignored the question and returned his pen to an inside pocket of his gray suit coat. "The character you're dealing with is either desperate or off his nut." He cocked his head. "Any gut reaction to this Darryl person?"

She frowned. "There's something"—she gnawed her lip—"something that's off key, only I can't put my finger on it."

He got to his feet. "Let me know if it comes to you, okay? Meanwhile, you'd better watch it, Amy. This guy's playing for keeps." He walked to the door, but stopped with his hand on the knob. "Late this afternoon, the lab crew found a print inside a rubber glove we found beside Dr. Tambor's body in the elevator shaft. It doesn't match up with Tambor or anyone else in his office." He shifted his feet. "This could clinch the case against Oren," he said and closed the door behind him.

Had all of her efforts been in vain? For a few seconds, she could scarcely think. Gradually, her mind cleared and she realized his facts didn't jibe.

She dialed her father and brought him up-to-date. After they'd discussed everything else at length, she told him about Simon's food being poisoned.

"Holy hell, Amy," B.J. said. "Get him out of that place."

"Cam Nguyen says he'll discharge him tomorrow if—" She hesitated, not sure of her father's reaction to the rest of her announcement. "If I'll agree to look after him for a few days." She cleared her throat. "Give him his shots, eye drops, and . . . and make sure he gets his rest."

"Now, that's uh . . . uh a fine idea. A . . . mighty fine idea. Simon's too blamed active for his own good. Won't hurt you to let-up either. You plan on staying at your place or his?"

She relaxed. "His condo will be safer. And there's a chance whoever's after us won't know where he lives." She gave him Simon's home phone.

"I'll call you Monday after my replacement finishes work on the blood stains," he said, and bid her good night.

Sunday, November 6

Next morning, she rose early so she'd have time to wash and curl her hair before going to the hospital. She jeered at herself in the mirror. In his present mood, Simon wouldn't even notice. Nevertheless, she put in her contacts, applied make-up with extra care and donned a matching teal-blue skirt and blouse.

After surveying herself with a critical eye, she added a dab of expensive perfume. Satisfied at last, she tossed the clothes she thought she'd need in an overnight bag and rushed downstairs. An icy wind caught her hair and undid all her efforts. Disgusted, she finger-combed it and took off for the hospital.

She found Simon ready to go. As they waited for him to be discharged, she caught him eyeing her several times, but each time he quickly looked away. When all was ready, an orderly insisted on wheeling him to the car. Simon being Simon protested loudly before subsiding with a scowl.

Neither of them spoke as she put the car in gear and got under way. When she turned onto James Street and started down the hill, Simon stopped dwelling on the passing scene.

"B.J. phoned."

"Oh? . . . I wonder if he tried to get me?"

"I guess you'd already left." His gaze met hers for an instant, then fell away. "That Billings, Montana medical examiner friend of his called this morning."

"Has he learned anything new?"

"From what B.J. said, the man's been busy. Among

other things, he contacted Dr. Yates in White Bird and persuaded him to go to the Attorney General. Evidently, they'd heard rumors about the hospital only didn't have enough facts to warrant an investigation."

Amy caught her breath. "What about Francine? If Wade Marchmont learns she turned him in, God knows what he'll do to her."

"They got her out." He let out a sigh. "Wasn't difficult. She's dying of lung cancer."

"Poor woman. Nobody deserves that kind of rotten luck."

They fell silent and she concentrated on her driving. As usual the streets near Elliott Bay and Pike Place Market were congested. She inched the station wagon through a throng of wind-buffeted sightseers on Western Avenue.

"Look at that, would you?" Simon pointed to a limousine stretched across his condo's garage entrance. "Never fails."

"No problem." Ahead a car pulled away from the curb and she slid into the spot he'd vacated. "I'll move the car later."

On the way up in the elevator, she returned to their conversation about Marchmont. "Did Francine tell them what she told me?"

He laughed a harsh laugh that didn't hold a shred of humor. "Yeah, and then some. Francine had a friend with her when she witnessed Elise Dorset's death. A patient by the name of Mona Sanders."

"Mona Sanders! Oh, my Lord, Francine did say, '*Mona* and me climbed into the ventilator tube and watched it all.' Her story about Elise shocked me so, the name didn't register."

Simon ran his hand over his face. "Seems Mona was very resourceful. She knew Marchmont would have to cover-up Elise's death, so she stole her I.D. and rifled her personnel file. Then she seduced an orderly named Roger Norman, and talked him into helping her escape."

He raked his fingers through his hair. "This sounds like a damned soap opera." He inhaled and went on. "She threatened Wade Marchmont. Told him she'd expose his shady activities."

"Did he toss her in that cage Francine was so scared of?"

He shook his head. "Mona convinced him she'd gotten a letter out to a friend. And if she didn't show up at a certain time, the letter would go to the Attorney General's office." Simon blew out his breath. "So he brought her the money she demanded."

Amy shuddered. "Then he probably sent his goons after her like he did us."

"She outsmarted him. She and the orderly tied him up and took him with them. Later, they dumped him alongside the road and kept his car." He massaged his temples. "I can't believe I lived with a woman like that."

Amy's mouth twisted. "It can happen to anybody. You should've known my ex-husband."

He winced as if her remark had struck a raw nerve. "Doesn't compare, Amy. Mona landed in Marchmont because she stabbed a guy six times with a pair of scissors. She pleaded insanity."

"Dear Lord." Amy sagged against the elevator wall. "Oren was lucky someone killed Elise—I mean Mona." She stopped and put her hand over her mouth. "What a terrible thing to say."

The elevator stopped on the sixth floor and they got out. "Unfortunately, it's true . . . and both he and I know it." He unlocked the door and swung it wide.

She gaped at the marked change his decorators had created. The night they'd brought the doctor's trash bags here, the room had been stripped clean. Now, a Navaho rug softened a stark white wall. The furniture and carpet picked up the rug's colors of muted rose, terra cotta, burnt almond, and turquoise.

She felt him watching her. "You like it?" he asked.

"Oh, yes. Very much." She set down the overnight bag she carried and circled the room. She touched a bronze figurine, studied a picture and tried a chair. "Nice, real nice."

Now they were alone, really alone, she began to doubt Cam's judgment. Simon would surely guess she had an ulterior motive for coming. She gripped the packette of medications she'd picked up at the nurse's station and frantically searched for something more to say. Her mind struck a total blank. She flushed and hurried into the kitchen.

Simon followed her. "You hungry? I have a freezer full of TV dinners."

His presence made the kitchen seem too small. "No," she managed to squeak. "I had a late breakfast." She took in a gulp of air. "Maybe, you should rest a bit before lunch."

He stared at her for a moment. "Perhaps." He started pulling out drawers. "First I'm going to take a real shower." He found a plastic bag that'd fit over his cast. "They tell me if I'll keep the damned thing dry, it won't smell so rank."

She nodded. "I suspect they're right." She accompanied him into the living room. "Call me when . . . when you get in bed." She steadied her voice. "I'll come put some drops in your eyes."

He stiffened. "Don't push it, Amy."

"Cam said . . ." she began.

"I don't give a bloody damn what he said." He stalked into the bedroom.

She sighed. If she got through three days of this, it'd

be a miracle. She hung her coat in the closet and put her holstered gun on the shelf above. She sat down and leafed through magazines without absorbing a word.

Twenty minutes later, when he shouted he was ready, her insides started to quiver. She retrieved the bottle of eye drops from the kitchen and walked down the hall.

Be brisk and efficient, she told herself—complete the task and get out. That was the only way to handle a volatile situation like this.

His bedroom had been redone in burnished gold, green, and cinnamon. She remembered the night she'd seen it last. The black satin spread strewn with pictures of Simon's dead wife and in each snapshot Julie's head had been torn off. She shuddered and stepped inside.

Simon lay in a king-size brass bed with the blanket pulled up to his middle. She kept her head slightly averted until she sat down on the edge of the mattress. Then, her gaze started at his naval and traveled upward, stopping where auburn hair curled damply on his broad chest.

Such a beautiful body. Her stomach swooped. Did he always sleep in the buff?

She swallowed into a dry throat, filled the dropper, and leaned toward him, then drew back in surprise. Desire smoldered in his eyes, softening the lines of his face, and bringing a tantalizing fullness to his lips.

The air became too thin for her to fill her lungs. Why was he doing this? He went back and forth like a yo-yo. She mustn't be attracted by his sensuality. She had to have more than that.

She glanced away and when she looked again, the coldness had returned. Why, oh why, did he insist on everything being on his terms?

He reached above his head and grasped a brass support in the bedstead. "Hold still," she said. Her hand shook as the filled dropper neared him and some of the medication fell on his cheek. "Sorry." She snatched a tissue from a box on his night stand to blot the liquid. Her fingers brushed his skin and her heart felt as if it might leap from her chest. She'd never get through these next few days . . . never.

His grip tightened on the brass rod and he squinched his eyes tight shut. "Get it over with. I can't stand someone messing with my eyes."

She eased a drop into the corner of each eye, recapped the bottle and started to rise. He grabbed her arm. "You could have told me you and Nguyen were lovers. You didn't have to go on letting me think we could—"

She wrenched loose and sprang to her feet. "Lovers! We're not lovers. He's a friend. A good friend. So is his wife."

Simon jerked himself upright. "Don't lie to me. I saw the two of you together."

She backed away from his anger. "You'd like that wouldn't you? Then you'd have an excuse. That's what you're really looking for, isn't it? Some reason to convince yourself I'm not worth the bother." She started out of the room, then turned on her heel and came back. "You don't know what you want, do you?"

"Not know!" He bounded out of bed.

The air whooshed out of her lungs. He wore only a bikini brief. She couldn't help but notice how brief it was.

He grabbed her shoulders. "I can't eat, I can't sleep, I can't work." He shook her. "I can't do one single damned thing except think of you." His mouth came down on hers in a hard kiss.

When he drew away, she lay her palm against his cheek. "I didn't mean to cause you pain." She stroked the back of his neck until he took a great gulping breath that shook his whole body.

He put his arms around her and pressed his cheek to

259

her hair. "You're sweet and patient and . . . and wonderful. How could you possibly care about me?"

She smiled up at him. "Male porcupines attract female porcupines."

"Oh, Amy." He kissed her eyes, cheeks, throat, and finally her lips. His passionate caresses melted her constraint and soon neither of them could bear for their lips to be separated for even an instant.

He got her blouse and skirt off without too much difficulty. But when he started on her panty hose, he and Amy became entangled and tumbled onto the carpet. Struck by their ludicrous position, she began to giggle.

His laughter joined hers and each time they looked at each other, the volume grew. He rolled over on his stomach and gazed down at her. "I love you, Amy."

She waited for a sense of joy to engulf her. She'd wanted him to love her, only now that he'd declared himself, something still seemed to be lacking.

Could Simon fill the dark, unexplainable void that had lain inside her chest for years? He had so many problems of his own, how could he make room for hers? A cold lump of loneliness gathered in her chest. Tears stung her eyes and she blinked them back. What was she searching for? Would she recognize it if it did come along?

She'd been silent too long. His announcement deserved some sort of response, only in her confused state of mind she couldn't be sure what hers was. To make matters worse, she didn't know whether she wanted to continue playing the lover's game they'd begun.

Simon raised himself on one elbow, kissed the corner of her mouth, and stared down at her. "Do you need me, Amy? Really need me, like I need you?"

Did she? There had to be more to love than mere need?

When she didn't answer immediately, a hurt expression tugged at his lips. She couldn't have that. Silencing the cautioning voice inside her head, she lifted her chin. Simon's emotions were fragile—too fragile—she couldn't turn him away.

She hugged him to her and kissed his cheek. "I need you too, Simon." Stifling a sigh, she stood up and began to remove her stockings.

With a beaming smile wreathing his face, Simon settled himself in the middle of the bed and watched her every move. Perspiration gathered on her forehead. She wasn't good at seduction, never had been, never would be.

She took a deep breath and hooked a finger under one bra strap. It slid off her shoulder. She followed with the other one, unfastened the hooks in back and let the scrap of black lace fall. A quick movement of hands and hips and the matching panties lay beside the bra. She turned slowly and tossed him a shy glance. Did he approve of what he saw?

He swallowed and his Adam's apple bobbed. "You're lovely." His features took on a look of tenderness that turned her knees to jelly.

Feeling self-conscious of her nakedness, she moved uncertainly toward the bed. "As a doctor, I have to advise you that"—she gulped in air—"that you shouldn't be d-doing this sort of thing so soon."

His crooked smile clutched at her heart. "It's a perilous world, love. This little bit of time may be all we'll have." He stretched out his hand and she went to him.

Twenty

They made love, slept, awoke, made love, and slept again. The next time they awakened, darkness had fallen. Amy put on her underclothes and padded into the front room. She took a shirt, jeans and sneakers from the overnight bag she'd brought.

After she finished dressing, she took an inventory of the food situation and found Simon's cupboards practically bare. She made a list, donned her holster and jacket, and went to the bedroom doorway. Simon sat in a chair easing the slit leg of his jeans over his cast.

"We'll need some groceries," she said.

"I figured we would." He came over and nuzzled her neck. "Thank you."

"For what?"

"For being loving and forgiving and for making this a wonderful day."

She touched his cheek. "You're pretty terrific yourself." She turned toward the door. "I'll make a quick trip to the store up the street. I shouldn't be long."

"Whoa, there, lady. You aren't going anywhere without me." He grinned. "I agreed to this arrangement so I could look after you."

She frowned. "You need to rest and build up your

strength. All of this"—she waved her arm toward the bed—"messing around saps your energy."

"I've got more energy than I've had in weeks." He scooped her up. "Want to see?"

She laughed and shook her head. "If you're coming, you'd better put on a coat and hat. It's cold out there."

Simon put her down and cocked a green plaid driving cap on his head. "Will this do, Mother?"

"On you it looks good. Got a heavy sock to protect the bare toes sticking out of your cast?"

He looked at the ceiling. "Forgive her. The poor woman thinks I'm ten years old."

She bristled and jutted her chin. "I worry about you. Something wrong with that?"

He kissed her on the tip of her nose. "Nope. I'm just not used to a woman who fusses over me." He smiled. "Who knows? I may learn to like it."

"Since you're a fuss-budget yourself, you'd better." She caught hold of his sleeve. "Let's get going."

When they reached the sidewalk in front of the condo, she glanced up and down the windswept street. "Wow, the place is deserted."

"That's the nice thing about winter," he said. "The shops close early. In the summer, many of them stay open until nine."

As they came alongside her station wagon, a sharp "bang" split the silence. The car's windshield shattered. Simon swept her against him, fell to the sidewalk, and rolled into the shelter of the car. She lay next to him, her heart hammering in unison with his.

"Now what?" he breathed.

She wriggled free and drew her gun. Simon stared at it. "What the hell—"

"Stay put."

"No, Amy—"

She crept forward until she could get a better view and searched the shadowy area for the sniper. Nothing. She took a risk and straightened a little. A faint sound caused her to glance upward at the sky bridge spanning Western Avenue. A form separated itself from the murk and rays from a street light glinted on a rifle barrel.

She sited over the car hood and fired. Before she could duck down, a bullet ricocheted off the car's roof.

Simon yanked on her jacket. "Get the hell out of the line of fire."

"He's not much of a shot."

"He can always get lucky."

When she eased up level with the hood for a quick peek, she found the sniper had ventured to the sky bridge railing. She took careful aim and pulled the trigger. A cry echoed through the night and the rifle clattered onto the pavement below.

Simon leaped to his feet. "I think you got him. I'll get his gun." He dodged into the street.

Keeping a wary eye above them, she followed. The guy might have another weapon. She caught a movement off to her left. "He's headed down the Hillclimb," she shouted. "I'm going after him."

She dashed up the steps to level three. The sniper was tearing down the stairs and had nearly gained the second level. With a surge of satisfaction, she noticed he clutched his right shoulder. She *had* wounded him, and a good thing too. On the Hillclimb trees, shrubs, and massive planters made a clear shot impossible. She rushed down the series of cement steps, hardly noticing the darkened restaurants and specialty shops scattered along the way.

"Wait up," Simon called.

She paused, but only for a second. Her quarry had reached the paved slope beneath the Alaskan Way viaduct.

"Stop, or I'll shoot," she yelled. He broke into a run and her bullet went wild. She took off after him.

Once free of the stairs, she made better time. Just ahead lay Alaskan Way and the brightly lighted aquarium. She couldn't keep this pace much longer. A stitch in her side hunched her over. Each breath seared her lungs.

The man veered off to the right and made for a blue sports car in an empty lot. *The hit-and-run driver's car*—she'd bet money on it. She went down on one knee, snapped off a shot, and heard the satisfying hiss of air.

The man let out an angry howl and scuttled across the thoroughfare to a vacant warehouse on the pier.

She ached to stop and rest, but couldn't—needed to re-load her pistol, but couldn't do that either. She'd forgotten to bring extra ammunition. Her first pursuit and she'd flunked the test.

Behind her, she could hear Simon thumping down the slope. Although light weight, his fiberglass cast slowed him down and made him clumsy. He'd be an easy mark if the sniper had a weapon in reserve. She hurried across the street.

The gray sheetrock covered warehouse extended three-fourths the length of the wharf and looked big enough to house a small plane. Oblong, ship-sized stretches of water separated the pier from adjacent ones.

At the warehouse door, she fingered a broken chain and padlock dangling from the handle. Should she take it with her? No, too heavy. The thing would only be in the way.

She swallowed to ease the burning in her throat. Only one bullet left, she'd have to make it count. She darted around the door and stood still, breathing in the rank aroma of long dead fish. She listened, but heard only timbers creaking in the wind.

She moved forward cautiously, feeling loose planks

joggle under her weight. Desperation gripped her. Unless she wrapped this up in a hurry, Simon would soon be stumbling around in here.

A sound off to the right. She crouched and crept forward, her pistol ready. A swish of cloth and a board smashed across her outstretched arms. Her gun flew out of her hands and clattered off in the darkness. Colored disks spun behind her lids, and she bent half over, grinding torment pulsating from wrist to elbow.

"Gotcha now, bitch."

His words sent shivers along her spine. His voice was muffled, making it impossible for her to tell whether she'd heard it before.

She peered around for something to use as a weapon. "It isn't over yet."

Shrill laughter greeted her challenge. "For you it is." He leaped at her from the shadows. A ski mask covered his face and he wielded a sharp pointed pole.

Step by step, he drove her farther into the building's dim recesses where thin slats of light wriggled through roof and wall crevices. She glanced behind her, searching for an escape route and glimpsed open water between sections of missing planks. She tripped, and flung herself to one side barely escaping the wicked tip of the sniper's pike.

"That's it, crawl, you filthy bitch. I'll teach you. I'll teach you good." His right arm hung at his side, but he thrust the pole repeatedly with his left.

A few more yards and she'd reach a two foot wide gap in the flooring. Beneath her feet, she felt the smash of waves on the pilings and smelled the salt brine. She shivered. Where was Simon? He should have gotten to the warehouse by now.

The man came at her again, forced her back until she teetered on a plank edging the span of open water. "Bye

266

bye, A-a-a—meee." He drew back the pike as if it were a javelin.

"Simon," she shouted in a joyous tone as if he were really there. "I thought you'd never get here."

The man spun around. The instant he took his attention off her, she turned and jumped with all her strength. On the far side of the open water, she righted herself in time to see her attacker go head first into the bay.

Simon stood opposite her, gripping the barrel of the rifle as if it were a baseball bat. "You okay?"

"I'll survive."

He yanked off his clothes and his one shoe. Following his lead, she shed her jacket, jeans, and sneakers. Pain shot up her arms when she tried to unbutton her shirt, so she left it on.

"Stay here," he said. "I'll go after him."

"No." She poised on the splintery brink. "We'll get only one chance. If we don't find him, he's a goner."

She took several fast breaths and plunged into the inky depths at the same instant as Simon. Raw, frigid water enveloped her like an ice sheath. Blessedly it deadened the ache in her forearms so she could swim.

Shafts of light slanted along the water, glimmering on swells that humped and heaved like ravaging killer whales. No sign of the man. She dove and cast about with hands and feet, shuddering when slimy ribbons of kelp wrapped around her legs. She hastened up for a quick gulp of air and heard Simon calling her name.

When she answered, he said, "One more time, and that's it. Okay?"

She heard a splash. "He's over here, Simon." She headed for the struggling man who clung to a loose board. As soon as she got near him, he let go and grabbed for her. She back peddled, but he caught a handful of her shirt and the weight of him pulled her under.

Down, down, down they sank in the pitch black darkness. Striking out at him with her feet, she frantically tugged at her shirt to get it off. Air. She had to have air. With a last wrench she tore free of the cloth and fought her way to the surface.

"Simon," she gasped. "Help me." Her attacker seized her foot and pulled her under again. She beat on him, but couldn't loosen his grip. Her strength ebbed and an overwhelming lethargy took its place. *No use. No use.*

Suddenly, Simon was at her side. He grabbed the man, and shoved her topside. She struggled upward, burst into the open, and gulped in air. A large piece of debris smacked her in the head. She snatched it and held on with half-frozen fingers.

Simon broke the surface a few feet away and towed the man's limp body toward her "Work your way to the side of the pier. Should be a ladder somewhere."

One of her hands slipped off the knobby chunk of styrofoam. "I can't make it."

He treaded water next to her. "Yes, you can. You've got a job to finish. Now go." She didn't move. "Damn you, Amy. Get your ass in gear." He prodded her in the ribs. "Now!"

In her befogged mind, she knew he'd sacrifice the sniper if she had to have his help. She moved her feet to propel herself forward, but the pier's edge seemed so far away. She couldn't go on—she must rest—only Simon wouldn't let her. Shouting and cursing, he drove her ahead of him until they reached a wooden ladder.

He yanked off the sniper's tie, fastened one end to the man's wrist, and the other to the top rung of the ladder. "That'll hold his head above water." He put his arm around Amy's waist. "Just a little farther, love."

He urged her upward. When they stood on the wharf,

he hugged her fiercely before he lay her down on the deck. "I'll get our clothes," he said, and rushed away.

The harsh phenolic odor of the creosoted planks cleared her head and made her conscious of splinters pricking her skin. She sat up and hugged her knees to her chest. Chills shook her body so violently they wrenched her bones.

A few minutes later, Simon returned. He helped her into her clothes, zipped up her jacket, and draped his coat around her shoulders. "Feel up to helping me land our fish?"

"I'll do my best," she said through chattering teeth.

Simon climbed back into the water. With him lifting from one end and her helping from the other, they got the man onto the wharf.

Simon yanked off the man's ski mask. "Damn, it's too dark to see the bastard's face." He swore again and started pulling on his clothes.

While she waited for him to get dressed, Amy felt for the sniper's pulse. To her surprise, it proved to be fairly steady.

Simon tucked his shirt into his jeans and took hold of the man's shoulders. "Think you can handle his feet?"

"I'll try." If her arms stayed numb a little bit longer, she'd be able to make it. She grabbed the man's ankles. "Ok, let's roll."

When they finally lowered him to the sidewalk in front of the warehouse, she squatted beside him. "It's Darryl, the pet shop clerk!" She remembered the sports car. "Holy mackerel, Simon, this could be Roger Norman."

"Rotten bastard! He could have drowned you." He glanced around him. "Soon as I find something to tie him with, I'll call 911. Where's your pistol?"

"Somewhere inside the warehouse. He knocked it out of my hands."

"Damn, we could use it right now."

"Sorry, I goofed up."

He brushed his fingers along her cheek. "Can you watch him while I look for some rope?"

She took his coat from around her shoulders and handed it to him. "Sure. With a wounded right shoulder, and possible hypothermia, he's not apt to be too frisky."

Simon unwound the broken chain from the warehouse door handle and lay it beside her. "If he tries to get away, hit him." Before entering the building, he looked back over his shoulder. "Don't take any chances."

"Don't worry." She bent to check Darryl's pulse again. It seemed a bit fainter, but with her cold fingers, she couldn't be certain.

An icy gust tumbled paper cups along the curb and spurred her to action. The wind and the man's sodden clothing increased his chances of hypothermia. If she wanted to keep him alive, she'd have to get his wet things off. Maybe Simon would be able to find some sort of dry covering.

She forced a leather button on his sports jacket through a button hole and pain shot up her left arm. She gritted her teeth and continued until the buttons were free.

She pulled the sides of the sports jacket away from him. The unusual weight of the fabric puzzled her, but she didn't take time to dwell on it. She'd worked his arms free and started on his shirt when Simon returned.

"I found a piece of fish line. It isn't much, but it'll have to do."

"Give me another few minutes. I want to check his wound and get some of this wet stuff off him before he—" Suddenly, Darryl reared up, grabbed a handful of her hair and scrambled to his feet, pulling her flailing and kicking with him.

Simon snatched up the piece of chain and started toward them. "Let go of her."

"Drop it!" Darryl whipped a knife from his clothing and held it to her throat. "One wrong move and she dies right here."

Simon opened his hand and the chain clanked on the sidewalk. "You hurt her, you sonuvabitch, and I'll kill you."

A wild laugh bubbled out of Darryl's mouth. He thrust the knife up under her chin, piercing the skin. She cried out and felt a warm trickle of blood run down her neck. She held herself stock-still. Of all the stupid amateurish stunts, she hadn't even searched the man for a weapon.

Simon's features went taut. "Leave her be, damn you. I'm the one you want."

Another weird scale-climbing laugh gushed from Darryl's throat. "A lot you know." A spasm went through him and the pressure of the knife he held in his right hand lessened.

Nerves and adrenalin speeded Amy's heart. Soon, the cold water's temporary anesthetic effect would leave his wounded arm. A slim chance, but enough of one to give her hope.

He drew in a labored breath, groaned, and shoved her forward. "We're gonna use your car." He jerked his head at Simon. "Pick up my coat and walk ahead of us. Get cute and"—he took another ragged breath—"and she's had it. Got that?"

"Yeah, I got it." Simon's gaze met Amy's and he made an almost imperceptible nod, she answered the silent signal in kind. He lifted the clerk's sport jacket. "Good Lord, no wonder you damn near drowned."

"Move it, or I'll cut her again."

Simon uttered a guttural sound, strode across Alaskan Way and up the paved slope toward the Hillclimb. Amy and Darryl followed close behind him. As they started up the steps, the clerk let out a snuffling moan interspersed with the foulest expletives Amy had ever heard.

On the first level, Amy thought she saw a movement among the shrubbery, but didn't dare interrupt her concentration. If her captor weakened or made a mistake, she must be ready—her life and Simon's depended on it.

They moved past the office of Olson/Walker Architects and began the next ascent. "You okay, Amy?" Simon asked, stressing "okay."

"Just call me superwoman." She tensed and estimated the distance between herself and Darryl.

"Don't move or I'll shoot!" The command came from above and below them at almost the same instant.

Amy stood stock still for a millisecond, then both she and Simon went into action. She rammed her elbow into Darryl's midriff at the same moment Simon swung the coat. It smacked Darryl's wounded shoulder. He howled, dropped his knife, and fell to his knees.

Simon grasped him around the neck and yanked him to his feet. "You've had a field day, haven't you?" He twisted the man's arm behind his back. "Now, let's see how *you* like it."

"Freeze mister, or I'll blow your head off." A cop who looked to be at least six foot five, motioned Amy over to Simon's side with his gun barrel. "Who are you people and what the hell are you up to?"

"Dr. Amy Prescott," she said and showed him her I.D. "I'm working on a case."

"And you?" he asked, indicating Simon.

Simon tightened his hold on his captive's arm and the man let out an earsplitting yowl. "Pipe down," he said and turned to the police officer. "I'm Simon Kittredge, investigative reporter for *Global News.*"

"Shee-it." The big cop hunched his shoulders—a maneuver that made him look even bigger. "A couple of lone rangers. That's all we need. Pat 'em down, Valdez."

A round-faced, stockily built young man stepped out of the shadows, went over their clothing and extracted Simon's wallet.

"Checks out, Ballantine," Officer Valdez said. "She's packing a holster, but her weapon's missing."

"You the one doing all the shooting people are complaining about?" Officer Ballantine asked.

"Some of it," Amy said. She pointed to Darryl. "He ambushed us and—" She peered at the man and moved in for a closer look. "Good grief, Simon, he's wearing colored contacts. One of his eyes is blue, the other is brown."

"What?" Simon swung Darryl around and bent to get a better look.

"You dirty, whore-hopping bastard," the man screamed. He spit at Simon. "It would a worked." The timbre of his voice rose higher with each word. "I'd a got him. I'd a got him good, if you and that smart-assed bitch had a kept your noses out."

Simon stared open mouthed. "Oh . . . my . . . God!"

Officer Ballantine planted himself in front of Simon and his blubbering prisoner. "Who's the guy and what's his beef?"

"Correction, Officer Ballantine," Simon said. "People aren't always what they appear to be." He leaned over and peeled off the clerk's beard and mustache. "See?"

"Kee—rist," Officer Valdez breathed. "He's a woman."

Ignoring the clerk's sputtering stream of obscenities, Simon continued. "This gutter-mouthed lady is Mona

Sanders, alias Elise Dorset, alias Roger Norman. She's a suspect in a homicide, an attempted homicide and a hit-and-run. She's also an escaped mental patient from Marchmont Hospital for the criminally insane."

Twenty-one

Amy stood as if stunned. The woman they'd known as Elise hadn't been killed by anyone. The whole thing had been a hoax to trap Oren. "Why did you do it?" she cried. "What did Oren do to make you despise him so?"

"He was a two-timing, double-dealing hypocrite just like every other man." Bits of saliva spewed from Mona's mouth. "The fool thought he could run out on me. Well, I showed him." Her eyes went wild. "Nobody—you got that? Nobody is going to mess me over and get away with it."

"But he loved you," Simon said in a quiet voice. "Really loved you."

Mona stomped on Simon's toes, jerked her arm free and sprang at him. "Damn you. Why'd you have to come back?" She raked his face with her nails and leaped away. "I knew you'd set them on me." She crouched like a hissing panther. "I'll get you. I'll get all of you. You'll never lock me up. Never. You hear. I'm too smart for you. I know things." A sly expression crept over her face. "Things nobody knows I know. I got out once, I'll get out again." Her laughter spiraled upward.

"Francine's out of Marchmont," Amy said. "She's told

the Attorney General everything, Mona." She paused so Mona would get the full effect. "Everything."

Mona's laughter ceased abruptly. "They won't find Roger." Her lips twisted into a sneer. "I took care of that. Cringing coward thought I was going to share the money with him." She laughed—a primitive, beastlike sound. "I don't share with anybody." She turned her head right and left, her gaze shifting as though searching for a way out.

"Don't try it, lady." Speaking in a soft, easy tone, Officer Valdez slowly moved toward her. "Just be cool and you won't get hurt." Guns ready the two policemen backed her into a cemented corner and cuffed her.

"Watch her," Officer Ballantine said, and walked over to Simon and Amy. "Any other little tidbits you want to get off your chest?"

"She has a bullet wound in her right shoulder," Amy said.

"You do it?"

Amy nodded. "You'll find my pistol and her rifle in the vacant warehouse at the bottom of the hill. And you'd better notify Lt. Salgado." She winced at the thought of what he'd say. "He's in charge of this case."

"Mona's blue Mazda is parked in a lot at the foot of the Hillclimb," Simon added. "Amy flattened one of the tires."

Ballantine regarded him with a raised eyebrow. "Seems to me you're uncommonly well-informed about this chick. What gives?"

Simon ran a hand over his face and let out a long sigh. "We lived together a while back."

The tall cop whistled. "That's cold, man. Real cold."

Simon gathered up Mona's coat. "Take this with you. I suspect the lieutenant will be interested in its contents."

"You two will have to come down to the station. We'll

need to check your story and make a report. Ready to move out, Valdez?"

"Any time, Bill."

Ballantine gestured to Simon and Amy. "Let's go."

Monday, November 7

The next afternoon, Amy and Simon entered the police conference room and sat down beside Lt. Salgado. He gave a long drawn out sigh. "What a night!" He rubbed a bloodshot eye. "Everyone should be here soon."

"How's Mona?" Simon asked.

"She's still at Harborview. Amy's bullet nicked the bone, and the woman also has some infected scratches on her back and left arm."

"Probably souvenirs from our Manx cat," Amy said. "Did she tell you what happened to Roger Norman?"

Salgado nodded. "Two days after she escaped from Marchmont Hospital, she bashed in his head, weighted his body, and dumped him in the river."

"God, I never once suspected she had mental problems." Simon pressed his fingers against his temples and closed his eyes for a moment. When he opened them, he said, "That's a lie. Both Oren and I sensed an undercurrent of violence. She got the idea I was having an affair with my female photographer and sent her dead pigeons in the mail. Each one had a wire tied around its neck. The same thing happened to Oren's assistant."

Amy swung to face him. "Why didn't either of you tell me?"

He shrugged. "What difference would it have made?"

"A lot," she said through tight lips. "That's the way Cleo died."

He regarded her with a stern expression. "A fact you didn't share with your father or me. Remember?"

The arrival of her father cut off any retort she might have made. B.J. smiled and waved before propping himself against the side wall.

Grim-faced, Sheriff Calder clumped past her without speaking and chose a chair at the back of the room. Lomitas Island's prosecuting attorney joined him a few minutes later. Next came Dr. Bob Takita, a forensic specialist from the Crime Lab. Last to arrive was a tall scholarly looking man she assumed to be Dr. Laroche, the medical examiner who'd agreed to fill in for her father.

Lt. Salgado ambled to the front of the room. "I appreciate all of you coming on such short notice. I thought we'd keep this meeting informal so feel free to speak up whenever you like." He repeated the information about Mona's condition.

Tom Calder leaped to his feet. "This is all a political cover-up. The senator needs his pretty boy back on the team. So he's dug up this poor demented woman to take the rap." His gaze darted from one to the other, looking for agreement. He flung out his arms. "Can't any of you see that?"

"Sit down, Tom," B.J. said quietly. "You're out of line."

"You . . ." Calder pointed a bony finger. "You and that know-it-all daughter of yours, you're at the bottom of all this."

The prosecuting attorney scowled, grabbed Tom's arm, and yanked him onto his chair.

Salgado ran a hand over his face. "Sheriff Calder, we're here to gather facts, not make unfounded accusations."

"No wonder Mona messed up her life like she did," B.J. said, as if hoping to get back on track. "I understand she grew up in a foundling home. People in the commu-

278

nity called it Bessie's pig farm. According to reports, the woman treated her pigs better than she did the kids."

Simon sighed. "That'd account for a lot of her personality quirks."

"And her cunning," Amy said. "She didn't leave her fingerprints anywhere."

"Not intentionally anyway," Salgado said and changed the subject. "Evidently, Dr. Tambor was obsessed with her. According to Mona, he gave her the ten thousand she asked for without a whimper."

"Only she didn't trust him to keep his mouth shut," Simon said.

Salgado's tired-eyed gaze met Amy's for a moment and a faint flush tinged his cheeks. "You're right. She hit him with a brass statuette he kept on his desk, wiped it clean, and left the baseball bat with Oren's fingerprints on it for us to find. Unfortunately for her, one of the rubber gloves she'd worn came off and fell down the elevator shaft when she pushed in the doctor's body. The prints inside that glove matches hers."

He blew out his breath. "Any other questions?"

"Did you recover the doctor's ten thousand and Mona's jewelry?" Simon asked.

The lieutenant smiled. "You guessed right about her sport coat. The money and her jewelry was sewed into a series of pockets. A smart move on her part. The bulk changed her appearance and she knew it was safe."

Amy frowned. "Why didn't she just leave town?"

"For the same reason she did everything else," B.J. said. "In her paranoid brain, revenge overshadowed caution and all other considerations. Once her charade began, she felt she had to get rid of anyone who tried to upset her scheme to make Oren pay for betraying her."

"But he didn't betray her."

Simon lifted his shoulders and let them sag. "Mona

imagined he did, Amy. She distrusted all women and all men. There's no way Oren could have convinced her of his faithfulness. God knows I tried enough times when she threw her jealous tantrums."

Lt. Salgado focused his penetrating gaze on Amy. "You've been in this from the beginning. Any ideas about how Mona managed to pull off the hoax."

Amy sat up straight and stopped fiddling with the velcro strips securing the wrist splint on her injured right arm. "Mona's plan hinged on convincing us her body had been dumped in the sea. She and Oren had been to Otter Inlet and had gone sailing on our ketch." Amy glanced at B.J. "Right, Dad?" He nodded and she continued. "She knew where we kept things and that Dad was seldom home in the daytime."

Amy contemplated her father for a moment. This was the first time she'd taken the limelight off him in public—it made her uncomfortable. "I think she went to Prescott's Byway sometime in the afternoon of the Friday she disappeared. She wore Oren's shoes and deliberately made tracks in mud where they'd dry and be found."

"A cunning move," B.J. said. "Only she didn't realize how revealing footprints can be." He smiled at Amy. "Carry on, you're doing great."

Amy relaxed a trifle. "In her role as Dr. Tambor's nurse, Mona would have had to do the venipunctures. I suspect she found someone with the same blood type as hers and stockpiled a number of vials." Amy's gaze swept the group. "As most of you know, a small amount of blood will go a long way if you use a syringe to disperse it. So . . . when Mona reached the inlet, she strewed some inside the dinghy, then fastened a long rope to the dinghy's painter."

"Hey, that's it. That's where the spindle roll of rope went." Simon smiled at her and looked around at the others as if expecting them to show an equal amount of respect for her investigative technique.

When no one responded, he put his arm around her shoulders in a protective gesture. "It's plain as day to me. Mona walked along the cliff and led the dinghy into Orca Narrows. And that's not just supposition, Amy found mashed vegetation and rope fibers on the cliff." He grinned. "Anyway, in my opinion it was a piece of cake for Mona to put the dinghy right where she wanted it."

"For a man, Simon," Amy said gently. "A woman would have to have been driven by powerful emotion. She had to drag the dinghy high enough on shore so it wouldn't get washed away, turn it over so the blood stains would remain clear, and secure it in a manner that'd look natural."

"Yet, she even remembered to brush out her footprints with a branch of Scotch Broom. Amy has a cast to prove it," B.J. added.

"Right. You take it from there, Dad."

B.J. beamed as he assumed his usual role. "I figure she planned that evening right down to the last detail. She stashed a car somewhere in the vicinity of our byway earlier in the day. When Oren arrived home, she staged the confrontation, knowing he would rush out and try to walk off his anger."

B.J. shifted on his crutches and adjusted his body to a more comfortable angle. "She splashed blood on the kitchen floor, and mopped so it'd appear as if Oren had tried to clean it up."

"Nice touch," Lt. Salgado said. "And from your report, she cinched it by dumping blood down the kitchen and bathroom drains."

"You got it," B.J. said. "Evidently, she'd bought a gray wig and beard to disguise herself." His gaze sought Amy's and she nodded confirmation. "We found gray modacrylic fibers at the crime scene."

Simon let out a long breath. "Then all she had to do was roll up the bloody sheet and knife in the rug, go down the back way to Oren's van and set the rest of the scene at the byway."

No one spoke for a full minute. Finally, Simon gave another long sigh. "Poor Oren, his career is ruined and for no reason, no reason at all."

"Perhaps not," B.J. said. "He's been dissatisfied with the phony hoopla of politics for sometime. He's going into the Peace Corps and try to get his priorities straight."

"Very touching," Tom Calder said. "But I didn't travel all the way to Seattle to listen to some screw-loose story the Prescotts concocted. They haven't got a shred of hard evidence to back 'em up."

"You're wrong, Sheriff," Dr. Bob Takita levered his hefty body out of his chair and lumbered to his feet. "Dr. Laroche and I spent the morning going over the Prescotts' work. They made detailed records to document every step of their investigation and the two of us concur with their findings."

"Dr. Takita is absolutely correct." Dr. Laroche stood, removed rimless glasses and fitted them into a case. "Miss Sanders was clever, but not clever enough. Her blood is type B, Rh positive. The blood stains are all type B, Rh negative."

Dr. Takita nodded. "And of course we found traces of sodium citrate."

Lt. Salgado raised his eyebrows. "Which is?"

The corners of the doctor's mouth quirked. "Sorry, lieutenant, I didn't mean to be unclear. It's a substance used by labs to prevent the coagulation of collected blood."

Dr. Laroche's steely gaze flicked toward Lomitas Island's sheriff and prosecuting attorney. "I'd like this statement to go on record. A great deal of time and false charges could have been avoided if Dr. Prescott had been allowed to test the blood-stained articles at the outset of this case."

"Lies." Tom Calder's feet tangled in his chair as he jumped up. He gave it a vicious kick. "This whole meeting is a farce. A trumped-up pack of lies." He thrust out his beak of a nose, glowered at the assemblage and honed in on B.J. "You're gonna lose your job over this. I'll see to that." He pointed at Amy. "And I'm not through with you either." Pulling himself up to his full height, he marched out and slammed the door.

Lt. Salgado got to his feet. "Well, I guess that about wraps it up." He shook hands with each of them as they left the room.

He smiled at B.J. "Glad you could come. It's not often I get to meet a legend."

"Nice to hear you feel that way, Lieutenant." B.J. laughed. "Amy and I may set up shop in your neighborhood before too long."

Salgado looked at the ceiling. "Oh, God, not another Prescott to heckle me."

When Amy and Simon got back to his condominium, Simon slipped a Glen Miller tape into the stereo and they settled themselves on the couch.

After a few minutes, he reached over and took her hand. "We're both stubborn as a couple of mules. And we've certainly got a helluva lot to learn about team play." He turned to look at her with a fierce intensity. "Do you think we could make a go of it?"

"Maybe . . ." She burrowed her back into the couch cushions. Was she ready to commit to a serious relationship? She chewed the edge of her lip. She had hoped going to bed with him might unscramble her feelings. Foolish of her, when had sex ever cleared up anything?

"Amy?" His voice had a slight edge.

She lifted his hand and pressed her lips against his palm. "Let's learn to be friends, Simon. True friends who understand and trust one another."

He searched her face. After a long moment, the lines at the corners of his mouth relaxed. "You're probably right, considering our dismal track record." With a mischievous grin, he hoisted her onto his lap and nuzzled her neck. "When do we begin?" She laughed and disentangled herself. "I think we'd better consult the dictionary first."

Please turn the page for an exciting sneak preview of Louise Hendricksen's next Dr. Amy Prescott mystery to be published by Zebra Books in November 1994.

One

A metallic click jolted Simon Kittredge awake. Dazed, he groped for the pistol at his side. A rifle barrel jammed into his gut.

"Make a move flatlander and I'll blast your innards."

A chill clutched Simon's bowels. *I can't die yet, I have to prove* . . . His fingers closed around the butt of his .38.

"Watch him, Bear. He's gotta gun."

"Don't worry." Moving shadows became men beneath a pale night sky. "Sonuvabitch'll never use it." A big man loomed over Simon and rammed down his boot heel with pile driver force.

Simon heard a bone in his right arm snap and a scream. His own scream.

A kick jolted his spine. "On your feet, wise guy. Let's see who the hell you are." Ham-sized hands dragged Simon from his sleeping bag.

"What do you want?" Simon tottered and fell against the man's bulky body. "Why—" An open-handed cuff silenced him.

"Them's his pants beside ya, Bear. Git his wallet."

A flashlight gleam pierced the darkness. Simon registered masked faces.

"Says here, he's Simon Kittredge."

"He with the other one?"

Simon swayed. *The other one! What other one?*

"Christ almighty, he's a goddamned reporter. Works for *Global News Magazine* out in Seattle."

"Holy shit! That's all we need."

Supporting his throbbing arm, Simon faced the one with the Tennessee mountain drawl. "You guys have the wrong man. I'm just a fisherman who happens to be a writer."

"Cut the jawin', Kittredge." The Tennessee man took cord from his pocket and jerked Simon's hands down in front of him.

Simon choked on his scream and dropped to his knees. "No!"

"Shesh your trap." He clamped Simon's wrists together and bound them.

The one called Bear hung the strap of Simon's camera around his thick neck, tossed Simon's gear into the middle of the sleeping bag, and flung the improvised sack over his shoulder.

The tall, skinny one gouged Simon in the ribs. "Move it, we gotta fur piece to go."

With only brief stabs of torch light to guide him, Simon stumbled into the darkness. Thorns and jagged rocks ripping the soles of his bare feet, he scrambled up hills, slithered into brush-filled ravines and slogged waist deep in a foul slimy swamp.

Blood pounded in his head. Cold air stung his lungs. His captors heckled him, urged him to a swifter pace. A swinging branch smashed into his arm. He reeled, staggered and fell. The rifle barrel caught him and jabbed into the pain. He gagged on his vomit. "Stop!"

The man prodded him again. "Hike your ass. We ain't got all night."

With tears running down his face, Simon staggered on. *How long? How long?*

Simon squinted and saw a faint glow ahead before a sack was drawn over his head. He'd gone only a few steps when a low growl sounded.

"Christ almighty, some pea-brain let the dogs out," Bear said. The growling rose to a snarl. "Get back, damn you!" Something hard thudded against flesh and a dog's high-pitched yelp followed. "That'll teach him."

A short way farther on Bear let out a curse. "Stupid camera got hung up in the brush."

"Shuck the no-good thing."

"Can't. He coulda taken pictures."

Simon shuffled forward. He couldn't see through the gunny sack, but with each step he could tell the light got brighter. From all sides came the steady chunka-chunka-chunk of countless large engines. The men stopped. Chains rattled, metal clinked against metal, gate hinges creaked. Off to the right, he imagined he heard the murmur of voices.

Simon felt the wires of a Cyclone fence press against his shoulder and the side of his head. Now he knew where they'd brought him. He'd found the place that morning. Watched it from the woods most of the day.

One of the men poked him. He trudged a few feet and heard the gate clang shut behind him. The light became much brighter. A door opened, they thrust him through and he plodded down what seemed like a hall.

"What'll we do with him?" Bear asked.

"What about the time keeper's office? Nobody's used it since they closed the place down."

Rusty hinges creaked and Bear said, "Yeah, this'll do. Those white-shirted bastards ain't paying us to think. Just deliver."

They wrenched Simon sideways, backed him onto a

chair and began to bind him. He drew a ragged breath. "Take it easy, dammit. I'm not going anywhere."

Bear gave a wheezing laugh. "Ya got that right." He cinched the rope a notch tighter around his legs. "That's it, pard. We're out of here."

The door slammed. Simon listened to an instant of silence. Biting the pain, he worked the sack off his head with his teeth, nose and chin. On his right, drawers of a file cabinet hung open, their contents spilling onto a floor littered with papers, file folders, and grimy supply books. To his left, sat a dented metal desk. Dust covered scratch pads, a jumble of pencils with broken leads and a two-year-old calendar.

His shoulders sagged. *Thought you were going to show your old man how great you were, didn't you, Kittredge? Going to nab the con men who skunked him, get his money back, be your daddy's fair-haired son for the first time in your whole damn thirty-four years.*

He scanned the plywood-lined room. Near the baseboard of a wall, half hidden by the desk, he spied the edge of a small ivory-colored box.

Adrenaline speeded his pulse. *Keep calm. Think it through.* He clamped his lip between his teeth and tipped the chair back and forth. Gradually he managed to work himself closer to the desk. *Good.* He twisted the chair back from side to side. The rope bindings set up a see-sawing motion against his bare chest. His teeth sank into his lip until he tasted blood.

Bracing, he lunged right, then left, and heard a creak. More precious minutes dragged by before the round, wooden, spindles pulled out of their sockets and his ropes slackened enough for him to get his arms loose.

Without pausing to free his hands and feet, he fell forward, taking the chair with him, and landed on his injured arm. Flashes of color pierced his brain. He fought to keep from blacking out. "Jesus, not now . . . not now."

He blinked to clear his vision, and peered into the narrow crack between the desk and wall. God, a break at last. The box he'd spotted was a phone jack.

His heart pounded in his ears as he traced the cord until it disappeared into the shadowy recesses under the desk. He plotted his next move, clenched his jaw tight shut and put his hands under the desk. Working blind, he felt along the floor. Nothing. He inched closer, reached out, and strained until a moan wrenched from his throat.

He rested his cheek on the splintery floor boards, turned until he lay parallel with the desk and tried again. He had it! Relief made his fingers weaker. He had difficulty closing them on the flat plastic line.

Slowly, ever so slowly, he tugged the line toward him until coils of it began to gather near his midriff. Sweat stung his eyes. He gritted his teeth so hard his head hurt. A frantic pull, a noisy clatter, and a phone detached itself from under a pile of trash behind the desk.

He drew it to him, sent up a quick prayer and maneuvered the receiver to his ear. A dial tone! Tears sprang into his eyes and he didn't give a damn.

No sense in calling Rock Springs' police chief or his deputy, he'd asked them for help when he first arrived and gotten nowhere.

He felt the room slowly turning gray at the edges and lay back to gather his strength. He'd call Amy, she'd know what to do. He closed his eyes and his mind began to float. *Forgive me, Amy. I truly thought I loved you—until I met Erika. Meant to tell you, when you met my plane in Seattle.* His bitter laugh made a harsh sound in the silent room. *Meant to—until I looked into your trusting brown eyes—then I didn't have the guts.* He snorted in disgust. *That makes me as big a bastard as your ex-husband, doesn't it?*

He groaned and pressed his head on the desk's cold steel until his mind responded. By contorting his body, he got the receiver into place and held it steady with his knees.

Perspiration slicking his hands, he punched in the 800 number of the Prescotts' forensic investigator's office.

Just as Amy's taped message began, his thoughts blurred and he failed to make out her words. *Stay alert. This is for keeps.* He began a halting report and was interrupted by a beep—he hadn't waited long enough. A terrible tiredness came over him.

He took a shaky breath, then another. "Screwed-up again, Doc. Need . . . help." Darkness closed over him. "Sun . . . rise," he mumbled. "Ruby-eyed . . . ra-a—ven . . ."

Two

Dr. Amy Prescott rushed to Carson Flight Service's counter and pulled her ticket from her purse. "I'm Dr. Amy Prescott and I'm late," she said. "Fog socked in Seattle-Tacoma Airport. We couldn't get off the ground."

The clerk snatched up a phone, punched some buttons, and snapped, "Dr. Prescott's here."

Beside Amy, a young man fastened tags to her suitcase and forensic satchel. "Let's go lady, the pilot's about to take off." He triggered the automatic glass doors and vaulted through the opening. Out on the apron, a tall, broad-shouldered man ambled unsteadily toward a two-engine commuter plane. The baggage clerk dashed off in the same direction.

Amy hitched up her skirt and sprinted after him, her high heels clicking a rapid tattoo on the pavement. She'd only known Simon Kittredge a year but she learned early on that he couldn't resist a meaty story regardless of the danger involved. The sound of his garbled words on her answering machine this morning had started her imagining terrible things.

Soon now, she'd be in Rock Springs. Once on the scene, she'd find him and send him off to Erika, his new love. As she ran, she gloried in the exertion, the rush of wind against her cheeks. Each stride she took brought her closer to Simon. The thought eased the harried sensation she'd carried in her stomach since her journey began.

In her haste, she failed to notice the crack in the pavement. She tripped, pitched forward and landed on all fours. Cinders, gravel, and bits of concrete ground into her palms, cut her knees, shredded her stockings.

"Damn," she muttered. "Damn, damn, damn." She clamped her teeth on her lip and pried herself off the pavement. Her battered and bleeding knees made it difficult to stand, a minor detail compared to her acute embarrassment.

She averted her eyes from passengers who might be watching, picked up her purse and hobbled up the steps at the rear of the plane. Inside, a single row of four seats extended down each side. Men filled seven of them. She walked up the aisle and apologized to the pilot for detaining him.

He shrugged. "Won't be the first time—or the last."

Quailing inside, she faced her fellow travelers, took a breath and smiled. All returned it, except one man. He sat with his head braced against the wall, his eyes half closed. From force of habit, her mind registered his description: male, Native American, at least six feet in height, 170 pounds, medium build, jet black hair and eyes—the type of man her women friends called, "a hunk."

As if in answer to her appraisal, he let his gaze travel up her slender 5'7" frame to her short brown hair. When his eyes shifted to meet hers, he lifted one shoulder in a gesture of casual indifference. Thus, having put her in her place, he slumped down in his seat and tilted a battered, low-crowned, Stetson over his face.

Heat flooded her cheeks. *Same to you, mister.* The

smugness of good-looking men irked her. Throughout their four-year marriage her ex-husband, Mitch Jamison, had used his handsome face and body to attract a steady stream of sex partners. If she ever married again, the man would be homely as a basset hound.

She raised her chin and marched down the aisle. With the kind of luck she'd had today, it came as no surprise the only vacant seat lay across the aisle and one row back from the dark-eyed man.

As she passed him, she got a strong whiff of bourbon and pressed her lips together. Alcohol and drugs had been another of Mitch's weaknesses. She slid into her seat and fastened the belt across her lap.

After the plane took off and settled into its flight pattern, the gray-haired man in front of her turned around. "I'm Dr. Miles Leibow." Wet, pointy lips separated his mustache from a skimpy beard that failed to conceal his double chin. "This your first visit to Silver Valley?" His bellow overrode the rumble of the plane's engine.

She stopped pawing through her cavernous purse in search of the extra nylons she always carried and forced a smile. "Yes, it is."

"Ah!" He straightened his tie with fleshy fingers. "In that case, I must ask you not to judge our area by the landscape around the airport when we land." His small, watchful eyes peered from behind thick rimless glasses. "Noxious emissions." He nodded knowingly. "The smelter disrupted the intrinsically balanced ecosystems."

Intrinsically balanced ecosystem? The pompous buzz words grated on her already frayed nerves. "Really?" She extracted a pen and a small black notebook from her bag, hoping the doctor would take the hint and discontinue his shouted conversation.

"Oh absolutely. Since it's September, you can't tell as

295

easily, but believe me the topography has improved remarkably."

"Hm-m-m, that's nice."

"Isn't it though?" He cleared his throat noisily. "Takes know how." He tapped his forehead with a well-manicured fingertip. "Pressure in the right places pays off. Regrettable, but necessary, if you expect progress."

"So politics fuels fires even in Idaho. Amazing!" Amy opened her notebook.

"Oh, they acted as if the whole project was their idea." He thumped his chest with his fist. "But my committee and I know who really lit the fire."

"I see." She dated a blank page in her notebook.

"How far are you going?"

She hesitated, unsure whether she wanted her fellow passengers to know her plans. Finally, she decided anyone who really wanted to find out would do so anyway. "Rock Springs."

The dark-eyed man jerked and his knees dislodged from the seat in front of him. The heels of his scuffed western boots came down hard on the floor.

Dr. Leibow swiveled his head in the man's direction and without lowering his voice an iota said, "Looks like the redskin's got a snootful. You'd think they'd at least have brains enough to know they can't handle the stuff."

She scowled at the doctor and waited for the Indian to tell him what he could do with his opinion. Instead, he acted as if he hadn't heard. She stared at his back. *Do something!* When he didn't, she cringed with shame, not for him, but for mankind. His placid acceptance had to have come from a lifetime of slurs.

She leaned toward the doctor. "Why should they? Us Anglos haven't learned, and we've been at it a hell of a lot longer." She held his squint-eyed glare until he flushed and dropped his gaze.

"Watch your mouth, girl. Talk like that'll get you in trouble around here." Holding himself ramrod straight, he turned his back to her.

Narrow-minded bigot! She tried to put the incident out of her mind, but each time her glance wandered to the Native American, she got a knot in her stomach.

America, land of freedom and equality. What a laugh.

A man up front turned his head. He had a long, sharp-planed face that looked as if it would break into ice shards if he smiled. His half-hooded eyes flicked over her and she felt her flesh creep.

She ignored him, forced herself to relax and began to mull over the profound changes that had taken place in her life. In a short span of time, she'd acquired a divorce, a degree in medicine, and a degree in forensic pathology. A week after getting her pathology degree, she'd started work at the Washington State Crime Laboratory in Seattle. For the next two years, she labored to pay off her ex-husband's old debts.

Four months ago, she and her father, a former medical examiner, had gone looking for an office. They found what they wanted in Ursa Bay, a town thirty miles north of Seattle.

She smiled as she remembered the two of them admiring the gold-edged sign in their front window. Dr. B.J. Prescott and Dr. Amy Prescott, Forensic Investigators—that moment had been the fulfillment of their dreams.

The plane bucked, bringing her back to the present. She sighed, gazed down at her notebook and wrote Simon's name beside the date. Below, she started her usual who, what, where, when, how, and why questions.

Who had a motive to harm Simon? Three weeks ago, Simon's father had summoned him home from Central America where he had been on assignment. Simon detoured through Seattle in order to apply for his vacation at *Global News*. He'd asked her to dinner and they'd talked non-stop for three hours.

Last October, before he left the States, she and Simon had started a relationship. Both of them hoped their feelings were based on love and not just their intense physical and emotional needs. In the past ten months, his trips to Seattle had been at wider and wider intervals. Recently his letters had dwindled to a trickle and in them he made frequent references to another journalist named Erika Washburn.

She had felt him slipping away and wondered what qualities she lacked. She must have a major flaw of some kind. Why else would she be incapable of holding a man's interest and affection?

Amy frowned at the few words she'd written and re-traced Simon's name. Although a talented writer, he considered himself a literary failure—a feeling fostered by a domineering father who'd totally ignored his youngest son's achievements. It had been a bittersweet experience to witness Simon's exhilaration over his father's call for help.

During dinner and while they talked later in the lounge, she had noticed a short, nondescript man watching them. When she brought him to Simon's attention, he'd sluffed it off.

"I think he's a government agent," he said. "They often put a tail on you when you enter a sensitive country. He's been following Erika and me for weeks."

"How can you be so casual about it," she asked. "What if he's following you for some other reason?"

"Erika reported it to the American Embassy, but nothing changed. After a while, we ignored him and concentrated on getting the story we'd come after."

"I don't like it. I don't like it one bit. For all you know, a drug baron in one of those Central American countries could think you're getting too nosy. Maybe the guy following you is just waiting for the right time and place. Did you ever think of that?"

"Well, yes, I did."

"So?"

He grinned at her. "I talked to some friends. They're going to check with a couple of sources and let me know if they learn anything."

After leaving Seattle, Simon had contacted her twice. His first call came from his boyhood home in Coeur d'Alene, Idaho. He'd been shocked to learn swindlers had conned his father into buying phony stock in a silver mine.

Simon's next call came from Rock Springs, a small town in Northern Idaho, where the trail of one of the swindlers had led him. Simon had told her he was staying at the Riverside Motel. He didn't mention the man tailing him either time he phoned and she'd forgotten to ask him.

Under the "WHO" heading, Amy wrote, "Man Shadowing Simon" and "Swindlers." She turned to a new page and labeled it "WHAT?" What had happened? Had Simon gotten too close to the swindlers? She shivered—or had the man stalking him found Rock Springs an ideal place to carry out his orders?

About the Author

Before devoting herself to full-time writing, Louise Hendricksen worked in the medical field. During those years she developed an interest in forensic science and its relationship to crime detection. As a result, she sets her mystery novels in a world she knows best.

Mother of two grown children, she lives in Northwest Washington with her husband, Gene, and is currently at work on her next Dr. Amy Prescott mystery.

WHO DUNNIT? JUST TRY AND FIGURE IT OUT!

THE MYSTERIES OF MARY ROBERTS RINEHART

THE AFTER HOUSE	(2821-0, $3.50/$4.50)
THE ALBUM	(2334-0, $3.50/$4.50)
ALIBI FOR ISRAEL AND OTHER STORIES	(2764-8, $3.50/$4.50)
THE BAT	(2627-7, $3.50/$4.50)
THE CASE OF JENNIE BRICE	(2193-3, $2.95/$3.95)
THE CIRCULAR STAIRCASE	(3528-4, $3.95/$4.95)
THE CONFESSION AND SIGHT UNSEEN	(2707-9, $3.50/$4.50)
THE DOOR	(1895-5, $3.50/$4.50)
EPISODE OF THE WANDERING KNIFE	(2874-1, $3.50/$4.50)
THE FRIGHTENED WIFE	(3494-6, $3.95/$4.95)
THE GREAT MISTAKE	(2122-4, $3.50/$4.50)
THE HAUNTED LADY	(3680-9, $3.95/$4.95)
A LIGHT IN THE WINDOW	(1952-1, $3.50/$4.50)
LOST ECSTASY	(1791-X, $3.50/$4.50)
THE MAN IN LOWER TEN	(3104-1, $3.50/$4.50)
MISS PINKERTON	(1847-9, $3.50/$4.50)
THE RED LAMP	(2017-1, $3.50/$4.95)
THE STATE V. ELINOR NORTON	(2412-6, $3.50/$4.50)
THE SWIMMING POOL	(3679-5, $3.95/$4.95)
THE WALL	(2560-2, $3.50/$4.50)
THE YELLOW ROOM	(3493-8, $3.95/$4.95)